**Willian**



# Notes on Brazilian Questions

SALZWASSER
VERLAG

**William D. Christie**

# Notes on Brazilian Questions

Reprint of the original, first published in 1865.

1st Edition 2022 | ISBN: 978-3-75258-918-4

Verlag (Publisher): Salzwasser Verlag GmbH, Zeilweg 44, 60439 Frankfurt, Deutschland
Vertretungsberechtigt (Authorized to represent): E. Roepke, Zeilweg 44, 60439 Frankfurt, Deutschland
Druck (Print): Books on Demand GmbH, In de Tarpen 42, 22848 Norderstedt, Deutschland

# NOTES

ON

# BRAZILIAN QUESTIONS.

# NOTES

ON

# BRAZILIAN QUESTIONS.

BY

W. D. CHRISTIE,

LATE HER MAJESTY'S ENVOY EXTRAORDINARY AND
MINISTER PLENIPOTENTIARY IN BRAZIL.

"Longa est injuria, longæ
Ambages, sed summa sequar fastigia rerum."

London and Cambridge

1865.

# CONTENTS.

## NOTE.



## INTRODUCTION
## ADDRESSED TO VISCOUNT PALMERSTON.

## CHAPTER I.

### THE STORY OF THE FREE AFRICANS.



## CHAPTER II.

### THE STORY OF THE FREE AFRICANS.



## CHAPTER III.

### THE STORY OF THE FREE AFRICANS.



## CHAPTER IV.

### THE STORY OF THE FREE AFRICANS.

## CHAPTER V.

### THE ABERDEEN ACT AND ITS PROPOSED REPEAL.



## CHAPTER VI.

### SLAVERY IN BRAZIL.



## CHAPTER VII.

### SLAVERY IN BRAZIL.

## CHAPTER VIII.

### SLAVERY IN BRAZIL.



## CHAPTER IX.

### COMMERCIAL RELATIONS WITH BRAZIL.

## CHAPTER X.

### COMMERCIAL RELATIONS WITH BRAZIL.



## CHAPTER XI.

### COMMERCIAL RELATIONS WITH BRAZIL.



## CHAPTER XII.

### BRITISH CLAIMS ON BRAZIL.

## APPENDIX.

### I.

Extracts from "Correspondence with British Ministers and Agents in Foreign Countries and with Foreign Ministers in England, relating to the Slave-trade. Class B." Presented to Parliament.

## NOTE.

*"Cartas do Solitario" of Dr. A. C. Tavares Bastos.*

THE publication of this volume has been unexpectedly delayed till the beginning of 1865.

Since all that follows this note was in type, I have received from Rio de Janeiro the second and enlarged edition of the "Cartas do Solitario," of Dr. A. C. Tavares Bastos, published in December, 1863. The author of these "Hermit's Letters" was formerly an official in the Ministry of Marine; he has been, and perhaps still is, a Deputy; he has been lately, in 1864, since the publication of the work from which I am about to quote, appointed Secretary of Legation to the special mission to the River Plate.

Dr. Tavares Bastos quotes in his work, from the *Diario do Rio,* the same account of the difficulties in the way of freedom for the *emancipados* which, some months later, was used in the House of Commons by Lord Palmerston. He introduces his quotation with these words :—

"In addition to what I have written on the delays in giving letters of freedom to the Africans who have completed the term of service, I will transcribe an article from the *Diario do Rio de Janeiro,* showing that it is not without innumerable formalities, without vexatious conditions, and without running the gauntlet of many departments, that the 'free African' succeeds in obtaining his emancipation."

And having transcribed the passage at length, the author observes :—

"The accusations of the philanthropic writer are unanswerable. The central government is the first to give the evil example of scandal. It is not scrupulous. It does not keep decency with the free Africans in the House of Correction, and banishes them to Itapura, to the Upper-Amazon, or to the famous iron-foundry of Matto Grosso. Its false position with reference to the English government inspires more and more serious apprehensions."

This was published by the Brazilian official writer in December, 1863, seven months before the speech of Lord Palmerston, of July 12, 1864, in which he produced the same account from the *Diario do Rio ;* whereupon, six days after, on July 18, Mr. Osborne was instructed to speak as follows :—

"I now come to the most extraordinary statement that ever issued from the Treasury bench. It was said that there were twenty requirements, without satisfying which no negro could obtain his freedom. I was puzzled to find where the document containing those requirements came from. It is well known that our agents and consuls abroad all know what the Foreign Office wishes, and they know the spite of the noble lord at the head of the government against Brazil, and these twenty requirements were forwarded in a despatch from Mr. Christie. But where did he get them from? From any official document? By no means. They are contained in an Opposition newspaper, which is a sort of half-*Owl* and half-*Punch*, and the object of publishing them was to ridicule the law's delays in Brazil. However, Mr. Christie was only too happy to see them in the newspaper, cuts them out and sends them to this country, and the noble lord, the Prime Minister, seriously produces them in this House as official (Hear, hear, and laughter). What would the noble lord say if he saw quoted in the Brazilian Chambers *Punch's* 'Essence of Parliament' as authentic? and yet that would be just an analogous proceeding (Hear)."

And Mr. Seymour Fitzgerald, following Mr. Osborne, also censured Lord Palmerston for having quoted what he described as a "squib in an Opposition newspaper cut out by the Chargé d'Affaires."

I have referred at page 86 of the following work to a published statement of Dr. Octaviano, a Brazilian Deputy, of the Liberal party, praising the tone of my notes to the Brazilian government on the subject of the *emancipados.* Dr. Tavares Bastos, in his work, quotes at length the testimony of Dr. Octaviano, published in July, 1862, and containing the following passage :—

"It is right to say that the notes of the English Legation to our government and its despatches addressed to Lord Russell breathe always the greatest cordiality and the desire of arriving at solutions favourable to the Africans, without, however, creating embarrassments for Brazil. This amicable mode of proceeding, which was, indeed, spontaneously initiated by Mr. Christie, was afterwards expressly recommended by Lord Russell."

Dr. Tavares Bastos speaks also of the coasting traffic in slaves, which is treated of in Chapter VIII. of the following work, and which has been defended by the "Brazilian agent" in his character of "Friend to both Countries." The Brazilian author of the "Cartas do Solitario" speaks of it as an abomination. "It is," he says, "in any case undeniable that there is nothing more barbarous than this traffic, which tramples under foot all the respect due to the ties of family and the requirements of decency."

These are statements of a Brazilian Deputy and official, which cannot be disposed of by charging Lord Palmerston or myself with spite and hostility to Brazil.

W. D. C.

*January* 1, 1865.

# INTRODUCTION.

## ADDRESSED TO VISCOUNT PALMERSTON.

ORIGIN OF THE WORK—THE BRAZILIAN AGENT—MISREPRESENTATIONS IN "DAILY NEWS" ABOUT REPRISALS—THE RIO CORRESPONDENT OF THE "DAILY NEWS"—HONOURABLE CONDUCT OF THE EDITOR OF THE "DAILY NEWS"—EMANCIPADOS—RECENT PROCEEDINGS OF THE BRAZILIAN GOVERNMENT FOR THEIR BENEFIT—GOOD EFFECT OF REPRISALS AND LORD PALMERSTON'S SPEECH OF JULY 12—FORMER INATTENTION TO SIR JAMES HUDSON'S AND MY REPRESENTATIONS—LORD PALMERSTON'S AND SIR JAMES HUDSON'S FORMER ADVICE TO BRAZIL ON NATIONAL DIGNITY—SIR JAMES HUDSON'S LANGUAGE TO AND OF BRAZILIAN GOVERNMENT—SLAVERY IN BRAZIL AND ITS INEVITABLE EFFECTS—SIR WILLIAM OUSELEY AND MR. CONSUL VREDENBURG—SALE OF INFANTS BY NURSES OF RIO FOUNDLING-HOSPITAL FOR SLAVERY—MR. COBDEN AND MR. BRIGHT ON BRAZIL—MR. MILNER GIBSON AND MR. HUTT FORMERLY MISINFORMED ABOUT THE BRAZILIAN GOVERNMENT AND SLAVE-TRADE—MR. ROEBUCK'S MOTION OF MAY, 1857—ARTS OF BRAZILIAN AGENTS—MISREPRESENTATIONS, CONTRADICTIONS, AND CALUMNIES—DELUSIONS ABOUT BRAZIL IN ENGLAND FROM SYSTEMATIC MISREPRESENTATION—INFLUENCE OF GREAT CAPITALISTS—"EDINBURGH REVIEW"—LORD RUSSELL AND LORD PALMERSTON ON REPEAL OF THE "ABERDEEN ACT."

MY DEAR LORD PALMERSTON,

I venture to preface this publication with some introductory remarks addressed to you. I do so without asking your permission, and you will not see or know of what I write till it is published. Your lordship, therefore, is entirely free from responsibility for this publication.

Otherwise, I hope your lordship will not object to the association of your name with this publication, made by one whom you introduced into the diplomatic service, and have constantly honoured with your kindness and friendship; and I am anxious to have the aid of your name for engaging public attention to a subject in which I know that you feel a deep interest, and about which unfortunately great ignorance, indifference, and prejudice prevail in this country.

The following chapters are in the main letters which appeared in the *Daily News* from July 2 to October 5, with the signature "C." This newspaper had for a long time systematically attacked and misrepresented the policy and acts of Her Majesty's government as to Brazil, and been the vehicle of incorrect accounts of that Empire. It led the way in attacking Her Majesty's government and myself, their agent, for the reprisals of January, 1863, and the elaborate misrepresentations which appeared in its columns greatly contributed to the general misleading of opinion. It was well known to me, indeed it is notorious to every one connected with Brazil, that the misleader of the *Daily News*, whose operations and misleading influence were, however, by no means confined to that newspaper, was a virtual agent of the Brazilian Legation. Your Lordship, in alluding in the House of Commons to this "Brazilian agent," declined to mention his name; and I shall follow your example. But his name is no secret at Rio de Janeiro or among London merchants connected with Brazil. It is enough to say that he is a member of the Reform Club, who has been for many years in the closest relations with the Brazilian Legation in London and London Brazilian Companies, and is the paid correspondent of the chief journal of Rio de Janeiro, the *Jornal do Commercio*, the Editor of which has lately declared in its columns that its London correspondent had inspired all the speeches in both Houses of Parliament, and all the chief articles of the English journals, in favour of Brazil in connexion with the question of the reprisals. I take the opportunity of mentioning and exposing a few of the studied misrepresentations which appeared in the *Daily News* as to my own conduct about the reprisals.

"The correspondence shows that Earl Russell, in issuing instructions to Mr. Christie, expressly gave him authority to make another reference to Her Majesty's government concerning the response that might be made to his ultimatum before resorting to reprisals, and that Mr. Christie, concealing that authority from the Marquis of Abrantes, preferred the abuse to the use of those instructions." (*Daily News*, February 23, 1863.)

Lord Russell instructed me as follows, November 4th, 1862: "Her Majesty's government are very reluctant to proceed to extreme measures against Brazil but as a last resource, and any proposal on her part for arbitration on the questions at issue may be referred to Her Majesty's government." That is, I was told that I might, not must, refer to Her Majesty's government any proposal made by the Brazilian Ministry for arbitration. They made none. I was not told to refer any and every answer to Her Majesty's government, and I was not told to communicate to the Marquis of Abrantes the readiness of Her Majesty's government to consider a proposal of arbitration. That would have been equivalent to telling me to propose arbitration myself. Mr. Layard observed in his speech, March 6th, 1863: "It was not for the party who demanded redress, but for the party of whom it was asked, to offer arbitration." Lord Russell also said in the House of Lords, June 19, 1863: "Mr. Christie was not told to make an offer of arbitration, because I did not think that it lay with Her Majesty's government to make it. If we had made such an offer, the Brazilian government might have said in its evasive way, 'This shows that you are not confident of your case,' and they would have tried some further delays." I need not say that, if arbitration had been proposed to me, I should have acted on Lord Russell's permission to forward the proposal to him, treating it indeed as an order; but it escaped the interested critic that, in the absence of any such proposal from the Brazilian government, I might have believed that they were going to yield, and should, in that case, by suggesting arbitration have prevented their doing so. It is fully explained in my published despatches to Lord Russell that I had made known to the Brazilian Minister that the great heat of the season, and the beginning of illness in the crews of Her Majesty's ships detained at Rio for this business, made it my duty to do everything in my power to prevent unnecessary delay. (See my despatches to Lord Russell, December 8 and 24, 1862, and my note to the Marquis of Abrantes of December 30.)

"Brazil has submitted to pay under protest such damages as the Foreign Office may assess, and that submission under duresse Mr. Christie, with a perversion of all sense of justice and moral sense, warned the Brazilian government might aggravate the amount of the assessment. Lord Russell, however, gave no sanction to this monstrous doctrine of Mr. Christie, but, practically rebuking his extravagance and spite, tells him, 'the sum to be fixed as indemnity will be based upon the most accurate estimate that Her Majesty's government can form.'" (*Daily News*, February 23, 1863.)

It is quite clear from the correspondence that I never said anything of the sort to the Brazilian government, and that Lord Russell did only what I left it to his Lordship to do. Having urged the Brazilian government to refer the questions of their responsibility and of the amount of indemnity in the "Prince of Wales" case to arbitration, and the Brazilian government declining to do so, and preferring to pay under protest, I wrote to the Marquis of Abrantes:—

"The force of a protest against responsibility cannot, I think, but be weakened by a refusal to submit the point to arbitration; but at any rate Her Majesty's government cannot be open to any imputation of indelicacy in taking on themselves to fix, as they are requested to do, the amount of compensation." (January 5, 1863.)

I thus explained to Lord Russell that I proposed to leave it to his Lordship to fix the sum:—

The Brazilian government had declared their readiness to pay immediately under protest whatever sum I or Her Majesty's government might demand in the affair of the "Prince of Wales." I voluntarily proposed that they should oblige themselves to pay whatever Her Majesty's government might demand. I was not able myself to fix the sum, and could only have named a sum large enough to cover all contingencies, which would have been invidious, and I wished to show perfect confidence in the honour of the Brazilian government on this point." (January 8, 1863.)

I think that none but a "Brazilian agent" could pretend to see any extravagance or spite in the above.

"A deep censure on Mr. Christie's note as to the "Forte" is involved in this reference to the King of the Belgians. For so confident in the justice of its case in that matter did the Brazilian government feel, that it proposed to constitute the British government itself the arbitrator to judge and decide on the whole case. But that did not suit Mr. Christie, he rejected the proposed reference to his own government. He resorted to reprisals, and then, when effectually frightened by the storm his conduct had raised, he accepted the arbitration of another government on a single point of the case." (*Daily News*, February 23, 1863.)

The Brazilian government did not propose to make the English government arbitrator; they proposed to instruct their Minister in London to treat the question with the English Cabinet. If the Brazilian government had said that their Minister would be instructed to agree to whatever the English government demanded, the question would have been at once settled, but this of course they did not say. The Brazilian government was not likely to propose to make its own adversary "arbitrator"; malice only could have so far blinded the critic that he should emit so ridiculous an idea. The Brazilian government not having proposed arbitration before the reprisals, I took on myself the responsibility of suggesting it soon after they had been begun. Your lordship and Lord Russell regarded this step of mine as a proof of conciliatory conduct; the "Brazilian agent" asserts that I was frightened. My suggestion, however, led to proposals from the Brazilian government of payment in the case of the "Prince of Wales," and arbitration in the case of the "Forte," which, I felt, justified me in stopping reprisals and restoring the vessels which had been captured, while I referred the proposals to Her Majesty's government; and if the Brazilian government had adhered to their agreement with me, which Her Majesty's government accepted, the whole question would have been long since settled. The subsequent demand of satisfaction and pecuniary indemnity, ending in the withdrawal of the Brazilian Minister from London, was a departure from the agreement made with me by the Marquis of Abrantes, under which I stopped reprisals and restored the captured vessels.

The *Daily News* has also had a "correspondent" at Rio de Janeiro, of whom I will say a word. The tone of his letters sufficiently reveals to those acquainted with Brazilian matters Brazilian influences; and he is known to be a person, closely connected with the bank of Viscount Souto, which has lately failed. This person last year was in England, and wrote some letters in the newspapers signed with his name. The accuracy of his anonymous letters in the *Daily News* may be judged by his misstatements when he puts his name to an epistle. On June 22d, 1863, he addressed a letter to the Editor of the *Morning Herald*, which appeared in that journal on the 23d, and which was written in consequence of Lord Russell's speech in the House of Lords of June 19th, warning Lord Russell against the danger to lives and properties of Englishmen in Brazil from a persistence in his policy, and recounting the perils, which, he said, had been dreaded, but which were not realized, when the reprisals were made in January, 1863. "Mr. Christie can himself inform Lord Russell," said this accurate gentleman, "that he judged it necessary to have an armed cutter belonging to the 'Forte' at his orders, stationed at the back of the *Hotel dos Estrangeiros* where he resided, and to ask the Brazilian government for a detachment of infantry for his own protection, which was granted." Both these statements about me are absolutely untrue. The origin of the story of the "armed cutter" I cannot conceive; it is entirely without foundation. It is equally untrue that I asked for a detachment of infantry. It is true that the Brazilian government placed a guard near my residence; I stated this to Lord Russell in my published despatch of January 8th, 1863, but I also stated that the Brazilian government did this "without any application direct or indirect from me, and without any communication with me." I am by no means satisfied that there was any danger. Great attempts were made to terrify me. I had so little fear, though I was receiving anonymous letters threatening assassination, and though the official journal was directing indignation against me personally and fixing on me personal responsibility, that I walked out every evening either alone or with a single companion, and without arms. It has since been the game of the Brazilian agents to accuse me of grave indiscretion, and to support this accusation by asserting the immense danger to which I exposed the lives and properties of Her Majesty's subjects. I thought I knew Brazil well enough to feel satisfied that there was no danger for them; and the result was that, with a great deal of spurious agitation, and many vain attempts to frighten me by magnified representations of danger, no harm whatever was done to Englishmen.*

It was always with sorrow that I saw a paper of the character and antecedents of the *Daily News* so misled by its philo-Brazilian informants, and I always clung to the hope that its Editor was unaware of the untrustworthiness of those to whom he trusted. It is not improbable that an unavowed agent of Brazil would represent himself to acquaintances, knowing nothing of the affairs of that country, as a disinterested friend to both nations; and while it is notorious in Rio, who is the paid London correspondent of the *Jornal do Commercio*, this would possibly not be known in the Reform Club, or to the Editor of a London journal. When I saw frequent positive misstatements of Brazilian matters, I felt, indeed, sure that the Editor of the *Daily News* neither knew nor suspected what he was publishing. At last, counselled by some of my friends, when, in July of this year, after a long suspension, I saw a renewal of misinformation in an article

* The "Brazilian agent" who has been writing letters in the *Daily News* under the name of "A Friend to both Countries," reproduced the false statement that I had applied to the Brazilian government for a guard. I denied it. The "Brazilian agent" then asserted that "the Marquis of Abrantes received a visit at his own house, not at the Foreign Office, *from a messenger who professed to come from Mr. Christie*, begging that some measures might be taken for, *it was to be presumed, the safety of the English Minister.*" A few sentences further on, he puts it more strongly, "That the Marquis did receive a communication *from a member of the English Legation* is a fact." I know nothing of this fact. The writer proceeds—"That Mr. Christie was alarmed, is, I think, clear from his own despatch to Lord Russell; that he was protected by the Brazilian government he himself informed Lord Russell." I was not alarmed, but I did not choose to go to the house of the Brazilian Minister for Foreign Affairs for a conference, while the official journal, exclusively under the control of the Brazilian government, was, unchecked and uncensured, directing excitement against me personally.

in the *Daily News* on your lordship's speech about the "free Africans" consigned to the care of the Brazilian government by the English and Brazilian Mixed Commission of Rio, I determined to address a letter to the Editor, and try if he would admit a counter-statement of facts from me. The letter was signed "C.," but I privately communicated to him my name, telling him that he might make it known to any one who cared to inquire about the authorship of the letter. The Editor honourably inserted my letter. It was immediately replied to by the "Brazilian agent" under the signature of "A Friend to both Countries." Thus began a long correspondence. The "Friend to both Countries" announced in his second letter that he had "no inclination for a profitless polemic with 'C.,'" and proceeded to say:—

"The question of Brazil will be discussed on equal terms in Parliament next session, when public opinion, correctly informed, will decide whether that Empire has been fairly or justly treated by the English government and English Ministers. To wrangle meantime with an uncandid adversary is merely to waste powder and shot."

A day or two after he "took leave of the subject." But, notwithstanding, he returned to it, and returned to it, and writing for a time even, as by way of supererogation he informed us, from Germany ("It will, I presume, be obvious that my letters have been written at a great distance from London,—in fact, from the centre of Germany,") he continued to inundate the columns of the *Daily News* with voluminous replies, and has had the satisfaction of having the last word in a letter of a column's length published on October 13th. It is the more surprising that he has pursued so long and so laboriously what he pronounced, at starting, a "profitless polemic," as in one of his latest letters he has further declared that what I wrote was of no importance, "as there are probably not a dozen persons who read so tedious a controversy." In this same later letter he defends himself against an accusation which had not been made by me, but which, under the circumstances, is a not unnatural accusation, that he is "a degenerate Englishman," by giving his own account of his interest in Brazilian affairs;

"And I am a 'degenerate Englishman' because, having for twenty years studied and made myself acquainted, by every means in my power, with the course and tenour of English diplomacy in these countries, I insist that such diplomacy is unworthy of my country, tends to defeat every legitimate end and object which England pursues in Brazil, persuades the Brazilians that the English government detests and abominates their country, and acts towards that empire as it conducts itself to no other country on the face of the earth."

During the last twenty years Lord Aberdeen, your Lordship, Lord Granville, Lord Malmesbury, Lord Clarendon, and Lord Russell have been the Secretaries of State for Foreign Affairs, and Mr. Hamilton Hamilton, Lord Howden, Sir James Hudson, Mr. Southern, Sir Henry Howard, Mr. Scarlett, and myself, have been Her Majesty's Ministers at Rio. He admits in one of his letters one solitary exception to the long course of British folly and injustice as to Brazil, which was one act, he says, of Lord Malmesbury, "who, to say the simple truth, has better understood the Brazilian question than greater Ministers."

This one act, however,—the suspension, by Lord Malmesbury, when he came into office in 1852, of the orders for capture of slavers in Brazilian ports and waters, by which your lordship had stopped the slave-trade,—he has misrepresented.* He appeals to Mr. Seymour Fitzgerald, as being known by him to know what Mr. Fitzgerald could have known only officially or from the Brazilian government. "Brazil, as Mr. Seymour Fitzgerald knows, is not unwilling to conclude a new Slave-trade Convention, if the English government will fulfil the promise made by the Earl of Aberdeen on behalf of Her Majesty's government, and repeal concurrently the Act of 1845." He arrogates to himself much knowledge of the sentiments of Lord Russell, of whom he writes in a patronizing tone of kind-hearted compassion; † and he concludes his correspondence with a declaration, which will probably produce more amusement than conviction, that he is certain that his own opinions as to the mischief and injustice of the policy of Her Majesty's government towards Brazil have "the full assent of many members of the present Cabinet." As I write, I learn that he has informed the Brazilian public,

* See, at p. 88, Lord Malmesbury's instruction to Mr. Southern, June 18, 1852, to tell the Brazilian government that he would, on the first representation from Mr. Southern that the slave-trade was not effectually kept down, "immediately renew the lately suspended orders which were issued by Her Majesty's Government in 1850, authorizing Her Majesty's cruisers to make captures within the Brazilian waters." Mr. Addington also wrote, by order of Lord Malmesbury, to the Secretary of the Admiralty, April 27, 1852, "Those orders must be instantly renewed if the slave-traders should be allowed to resume the scandalous violations of the Treaty of 1826 and of Brazilian law, which obliged Her Majesty's government to issue the orders."

† "It is Earl Russell's personal misfortune, not his fault," says the "Friend to both Countries," "that the seed sown by others has ripened in his time. And perhaps if Lord Russell's own policy were now to predominate in the negotiations, the quarrel would be quickly composed."

through the *Jornal do Commercio*, that Lord Russell is not indisposed to grant a pecuniary reparation for the reprisals, but that his pride will not allow him to make an apology; and that the letters of which I now republish the substance have been victoriously answered by the "Friend to both Countries."

It is highly to the honour of the *Daily News* that its Editor so readily and liberally inserted letters impugning opinions with which it had unfortunately become identified, and exposing misrepresentations of informants to which it had long trusted. The honour of the English press is of national interest and concern; and all must rejoice at this high-minded candour. The beginning of the *Daily News* is not forgotten; it was ushered into the world under the the great name of a living writer,—one of our greatest reputations,—on a mission of truth. Other men, not less remarkable for high honour than for literary ability, have been its Editors after Charles Dickens, of whom I will mention Mr. Eyre Evans Crowe, the able historian of France, and William Weir, whose untimely death has made his virtues known beyond the circle of his personal and literary friends. The *Daily News* has been always the enemy of slavery. It can only have been an unhappy accident that made such a journal the organ of Brazilian agents in aid of slavery and against Her Majesty's government.*

* See pp. 67 and 73 (note) for misrepresentations of the Rio correspondent of the *Daily News* about slavery, and his unfulfilled promise of statistics of manumissions. The precise nature of this gentleman's connexion with Messrs. Sonto's bank has been lately described, I believe correctly, in a Rio correspondence of the *Globe* newspaper. He is coffee-broker to the firm, receiving a commission on all the accounts with the coffee-planters (all slave-owners working their plantations with slaves). Is it in human nature that statements and opinions about slavery, coming from such a source, should be free from bias and beyond suspicion?

My letters began with the subject of the *emancipados* or "free Africans," whose freedom Brazil guaranteed to England by treaty; and they would not have gone beyond that subject, but for the taunting and discursive replies of the "Brazilian agent," whose plan of warfare was always to ignore corrections, shamelessly reproduce refuted statements, and ride off into general vituperation and new misstatements on other subjects:—

> "Mistakes, misstatements, now so oft o'erthrown,
> Rebuild and prop with nonsense of his own,
> Pervert my meaning and misquote my text,
> And furnish me a motto for the next."

The answer which has been made, and may be attempted again, to your lordship's statements about the long neglect of all representations and requests of Her Majesty's government as to the *emancipados,* and the harsh and unjust treatment of these unfortunate creatures, and their retention in slavery contrary to treaty obligations, is that now the Brazilian government is doing wonders. The "Friend to both Countries" stated triumphantly, in one of his first letters, that four hundred had been emancipated during the four years 1859–63, omitting, of course, to mention that these were four hundred out of some ten thousand, and that the fourteen years' apprenticeship prescribed by Brazilian law expired for the last of the "free Africans" of the English and Brazilian Mixed Commission, four years ago, in 1859. We are now in possession of authentic information of more vigorous proceedings. The reprisals of January, 1863, and the subsequent suspension of diplomatic relations had quickened the liberation of *emancipados;* and it has been made known on official authority that while, during eight years and a-half, from January, 1854, to June, 1862, only 728 in all had been set free, and 228 in the eighteen months from June, 1862, to January, 1864, no less than 848 were freed from the beginning of January to the end of July of this year,—seven months. A later statement informs me that in the month of August 132 more were set free; and that during the twelvemonth from September 1st, 1863, to August 31st, 1864, 1115 in all had been freed. Your lordship's speech of July 12th was known in Rio de Janeiro in the middle of August, and the result has been a decree, dated September 28th, for the immediate emancipation of all "free Africans" who have served a fourteen years' apprenticeship. This necessarily includes all who were released through the English and Brazilian Mixed Commission, which ceased to exist in 1845, nineteen years ago.

The course of the Brazilian Government about the *emancipados* has been like that which it pursued about the slave-trade. Left to itself, it did nothing; it treated for a long time with neglect representations of the English Government; it did not answer notes. When obliged to reply, it protested that its dignity did not allow it to act while pressed by a foreign Government; it resented interference, and claimed to be left free to execute its own laws, forgetting that treaty-stipulations gave a right to England to interfere. At last, after force had been used, and the English Government was known to be serious, and there seemed no help for it, it has done what it ought to have done long before; and it is now contended that this has been done spontaneously, and that all past reproaches are unjust.

The first general inquiry about the ill-treated "free Africans" was made by Sir James Hudson, in March, 1847. On the 26th of June, 1848, he addressed, by your lordship's order, more searching inquiries to the Brazilian government, and asked for a list. These inquiries were never answered, and the list was never given. On September 4th, 1848, I find Sir James Hudson writing to the then Minister for Foreign Affairs, Senhor Souza Franco, who is still living, and an active Senator and Councillor of State :—

"Your Excellency is aware, from the recent correspondence of this Legation—a correspondence which yet remains unanswered by your Excellency—that there are, in Brazil, many negroes who were released from on board ships captured by Her Majesty's cruisers, who have been apprenticed in Brazil, and who have not yet received their freedom."

On the 8th of March, 1861, I applied, by Lord Russell's order, for a list of the "free Africans," such as Sir James Hudson had asked for in 1848, and from the previous December to the period of the reprisals I was continually applying in vain for information about some of these "free Africans" in government establishments. On the 24th of November, 1862, six weeks before the reprisals, I thus called Lord Russell's attention to the extraordinary neglect of the Brazilian government in not answering my notes :—

"Though I have been endeavouring, during the last two years, to obtain, for Her Majesty's government, information about the free Africans at Itapura, none has been given me ; and I cannot inform your lordship of their number, or periods of service, or ages, or how they came to Itapura.

"On the 19th of December, 1860, I wrote to Senhor Sinimbú about sixty blacks, including twenty free Africans, who were said to have been sent from Ypanema to Itapura, reminding him that he had already in conversation promised me information about them; and I, at the same time, expressed a hope that he would assure me that no more of the free blacks of Ypanema would be sent to Itapura, a distant and unhealthy place, to be reached only by a most toilsome journey.

"On the 28th of December, 1860, I repeated to Senhor Sinimbú my hope that no more free Africans would be sent to Itapura.

"On the 10th of January, 1861, I called Senhor Sinimbú's attention to statements in the Report of the Minister of Marine of 1860, that fifty free Africans had left Ypanema for a military colony near Itapura, and thirty more for the naval establishment of that place.

"On the 8th of March, 1861, I wrote to Senhor Paranhos, by express instructions from your lordship, asking for 'a list of the free blacks who were handed over by the Mixed Commission to the care of the Brazilian authorities, specifying what has become of them, whether dead, emancipated, or still in service.'

"On the 3rd of June, 1861, I wrote to the Minister for Foreign Affairs, calling attention to a passage in the Report of the Minister of Marine of that year, mentioning the difficulties which attend the naval establishment of Itapura, owing to the unhealthiness of the climate and great distance from peopled districts, and also mentioning the departure of fifty Africans for Itapura; and I requested to be informed whether there were any free Africans among these fifty.

"Lastly, on the 17th of April of this year, seven months ago, I addressed two notes to Senhor Taques, which obtained your lordship's approval, reminding him that none of my previous inquiries had been answered: and I am still, my lord, without any answer at all to these inquiries."

Shortly after the reprisals, on February 26th, 1863, I addressed, by Lord Russell's instruction, another note to the Marquis of Abrantes about the "free Africans" of Itapura, and I then obtained an immediate answer.

There are many passages in the correspondence of your lordship and Sir James Hudson about the Brazilian slave-trade, explaining, in clear and strong terms, what the true "dignity" of Brazil enjoins,—faithful observance of treaty-engagements on its part, not refusal of just demands of Her Majesty's government. Let me reproduce a few of these passages.

Your lordship wrote to Sir James Hudson, December 21st, 1844:—

"Her Majesty's government can, with great sincerity, assure the government of Brazil that, in ordering the British naval officers on the coast of Brazil to continue to take measures which are necessary for the suppression of the slave-trade, it is far from the intention of Her Majesty's government to infringe on the honour and dignity of the Brazilian Crown. Their intention, on the contrary, is to support that dignity and honour by putting an end, if possible, to a state of things which, being a direct and flagrant violation of the solemn engagements of the Crown of Brazil, is highly derogatory to the honour and dignity of the Imperial government."

On the 20th February, 1850, Sir James Hudson thus wrote to your lordship:—

"In the note which I have received from Senhor Paulino, his Excellency persists in considering that the 'national dignity' is wounded by the capture and destruction of such a floating shambles as the 'Santa Cruz.' It is to be lamented that his Excellency's sense of the national honour of his country is not as keen as it is respecting his 'national dignity,'—a dignity which is attempted to be maintained at the expense of her honour, the deterioration of her interests, and the gradual but certain degradation of her people."

Again, your lordship wrote, on April 30th, 1850, to Senhor Amaral, the Brazilian Chargé d'Affaires in London:—

"The Undersigned can assure M. de Amaral that nothing can be further from the wish of Her Majesty's government than to do anything which can justly be considered as derogatory to the honour and dignity of the Brazilian government and nation; but he would beg to observe that the honour and dignity of a nation and of its government are best promoted by a faithful observance of treaties with foreign powers, and by a watchful enforcement of the laws which, in execution of those treaties, may have been enacted for the prevention and punishment of atrocious and debasing crimes."

As regards what is now being done by the Brazilian government for the "free Africans," it is to be borne in mind that the English government have not yet been informed, and have a right to know, what has become of every "free African" handed over to the care of the Brazilian government by the English and Brazilian Mixed Commission of Rio de Janeiro,—have not received any list of the "free Africans," such as by right they have asked for, "specifying what has become of them, whether dead, emancipated, or still in service." The archives of the

Mixed Commission, which are in existence, should contain the name of every "free African" entrusted to the Brazilian government. The registers of the Judge of Orphans and Chief of Police of Rio must contain the name of every "free African" let out to private individuals. There must be entries of payments of their wages to the government. In May, 1861, I offered to the Brazilian Minister for Foreign Affairs "the assistance for the necessary inquiries of a gentleman who has given much attention to the subject, and has the confidence of Her Majesty's Legation," and I renewed the offer in April, 1862. No notice was taken of this offer on either occasion. It is said that upwards of a thousand "free Africans" have been liberated during the twelve months ending August 31st of this year, and nearly two thousand during the ten years and eight months from January, 1854 to August 31st, 1864. But the English government have as yet no means of knowing how many of the "free Africans" so liberated belong to the category of "free Africans" released by the Mixed Commission of Rio de Janeiro; many of them may be, and probably are, "free Africans" of a later date, as to which Brazil is under no special engagement to Great Britain. The number of men, women, and children of those released by the Mixed Commission has been estimated at about ten thousand; and the English government have been favoured with no information as to how many of these remained to be emancipated. A decree has now been made for the immediate emancipation of all. But how is the English government to know that all are emancipated? What security is there for the full and proper execution of this decree, if no information is vouchsafed to the English government? It is also to be observed that no payments are made to any of these poor creatures, when they are freed after more than fourteen years of apprenticeship, though the government has been receiving wages for those let out to private persons, and has given nothing but food and clothing to those worked in government establishments, and though the destination of these wages to the expenses of re-exportation, or in some other way to their benefit, has been often officially proclaimed.

I am unwilling to leave this subject without producing a few passages from the notes and despatches of my distinguished predecessor, Sir James Hudson, to show that the language and tone of recent communications to the Brazilian government, both as to the *emancipados* and as to the questions which occasioned the reprisals, have not been stronger than, if indeed so strong as, the language and tone of one whose prudence and conciliatory qualities have been recognised in a subsequent career at a sympathetic Court in Europe.

In the following passage of a despatch to your lordship, October 17th, 1846, Sir James Hudson exposes the readiness of the Brazilian government to make excuses:—

"Your lordship will perceive from the enclosed copy of the note which the Baron de Cayrú has addressed to me, that his Excellency adopts the defence set up by the public officer at Victoria, whose conduct has been called in question, and that he is satisfied and accepts—and expects Her Majesty's government will be satisfied and will accept—the explanation given by this provincial authority, viz. that 'his good faith is not to be doubted,' and that 'a slip of the pen' caused Brazilians to be entered on the muster-roll of the 'Diana' as Portuguese. It is hard to conceive that so lame an excuse would satisfy the government, but it does."

Here is another passage, February 13th, 1847, in which Sir James Hudson sarcastically compares the acts of the Brazilian government with its professions:—

"With reference to your lordship's despatch of the 18th November, on the subject of the fraudulent abduction which took place in the month of January, 1846, in the port of Maranhâo, of fifty-six negroes from a slave-vessel which had been captured by Her Majesty's sloop 'Alert,' and instructing me again to press the Brazilian government for a reply to the notes on this subject, which had been addressed to them from the Legation, I have the honour to enclose herewith the copy of a note which the Baron de Cayrú has addressed to me in reply to those notes, from which your lordship will perceive that the Brazilian government hold it to be their most sacred duty to punish those subjects of this Empire who dared to place those unfortunate Africans in slavery.

"If the exertions of the Brazilian government are attended with no greater energy in pursuing and in bringing to justice the abductors of the Africans in question, during the present year, than in that which has just passed, these unfortunate negroes have but little hope of being rescued from bondage."

The following is an indignant remonstrance addressed by Sir James Hudson to a Brazilian Minister for Foreign Affairs, Senhor Souza Franco, November 4th, 1848.

"Upon several occasions of late I have had the honour to receive from your Excellency assurances, conveyed to me in a manner so positive, solemn, and impressive, of the determination of the Imperial government to put a stop to the scandalous importation of slaves into Brazil, that I did not hesitate to convey them to my government with entire conviction that Brazil, under the auspices of your Excellency and your colleagues, was about to enter upon a series of measures which had for their object the complete and effectual repression of the traffic in slaves.

"The assurances which I received from your Excellency of the determination of the Imperial Cabinet to put a stop to the traffic in slaves, the recorded declarations of your Excellency and of your colleagues before the world, as given in your speeches from your places as Ministers of this empire in the Legislative Assembly at Brazil, wearing the solemn air of truth, and carrying with them that complete conviction which unsullied justice invariably commands, left no doubt on my mind of the honesty of purpose and singleness of heart which animated and guided the Imperial Councils. I so expressed it to the government of the Queen.

"It was not therefore without surprise that I recognized in the Project of Law No. 133 the same scheme which the late Marquis of Barbacena presented to the Senate in 1837, and which in its thirteenth paragraph contains the deadliest blow ever levelled by a Brazilian statesman at the only remedy which Brazilian law affords to the slave to assert his rights to freedom.

"I am willing to believe that your Excellency and your colleagues do not comprehend the drift and scope of the thirteenth paragraph of this decree.

"Your Excellency and your colleagues cannot intend to offer this specimen of the legislation of Brazil to the world as the great and crowning work which your Excellency vaunted to me, and which I was led by you to laud beforehand to my government." *

I will conclude these extracts with two notes addressed

* More strong language of Sir James Hudson about this conduct of Senhor Souza Franco and his colleagues, in a despatch, may be read in the Appendix, p. 186.

by Sir James Hudson to the Brazilian Minister for Foreign Affairs, condemning a favour granted by the Brazilian government to a notorious slave-dealer, actively engaged at the very moment in importing slaves :—

"Rio de Janeiro, July 9th, 1851.

"The Undersigned, &c. having informed his government that one of the most notorious slave-dealers in Brazil, the Portuguese José Bernardino de Sá, had been raised by the Portuguese government to the dignity of a Baron of Portugal, by the title of Baron de Villa Nova do Minho, and further, that the Emperor of Brazil had granted permission to that slave-dealer to accept and use that title in Brazil, is now instructed by the government of the Queen to observe to his Excellency Senhor Paulino José Soares de Souza, &c. that it will be difficult for mankind to believe in the sincerity of those declarations which the Brazilian government make of their desire to fulfil the obligations of treaties, when they see the Brazilian Crown conferring favours upon such notorious slave-dealers as this José Bernardino de Sá.

"The undersigned, &c.

(Signed) "JAMES HUDSON."

### *Mr. Hudson to Senhor Paulino de Souza.*

"Rio de Janeiro, July 31st, 1851.

"EXCELLENT SIR,

"I have the honour to acknowledge the receipt of your Excellency's note of the 26th instant, asserting the right of the Imperial government to submit the names of whatever persons they think proper for honourable distinction by the Crown of this country, and stating the reasons which induced the Imperial government to propose that a titular distinction should be granted in this empire to the notorious man-stealer José Bernardino de Sá; and I have to assure your Excellency that I will not fail to convey a copy of your Excellency's note to the government of the Queen.

"At the same time, I imagine that your Excellency will coincide with myself in thinking it a remarkable circumstance that, almost at the period when your Excellency, in Rio, was demanding, not rumours, but the legal conviction of the complicity of this Sá in the slave-trade, the Imperial steamer "Urania" should have captured at Itabapoama, a slave-vessel with 400 Africans on board, belonging notoriously to this slave-dealer Sá, whose cashier, one Antonio Sevelino de Avellar, a well-known slave-dealer of the River Zaire, was on the spot, waiting to receive these unhappy victims of this ennobled kidnapper.

"I avail, &c.

(Signed) "JAMES HUDSON."

---

From the ten thousand, more or less, of "free Africans," towards whom your lordship lately complained of the conduct of the Brazilian government, I passed, in my letters, to the general subject of slavery in Brazil, where the number of slaves is estimated to exceed three millions in a population of about seven millions and a half. When a motion for the repeal of Lord Aberdeen's Act of 1845 is loudly threatened, this large number and proportion of slaves, the hold of the "institution" in Brazil, and the absence of effort and disposition in the Brazilian government to prepare for the abolition of slavery, or even to mitigate existing evils, are considerations of the highest importance for those who believe that, where slavery prevails, slave-trade is likely. Such was the opinion, succinctly stated, of Mr. Burke:—"I conceived that the true origin of the trade was not in the place it was begun at, but in the place of its final destination. I am very apprehensive that, so long as slavery continues, some means for its supply will be found."* The "Aberdeen Act" remains on our statute-book, the Brazilian government having refused, both before it was passed and since, to make a new Treaty, such as other nations have made with us, for the suppression of the slave-trade; and an assertion made for another purpose by Lord John Manners, in the discussion in the House of Commons of July 12th, that "the slave-trade treaties with Spain and Portugal are ineffectual,"—an assertion reproduced by the "Friend to both Countries" in his letters in the *Daily News*,—suggests, as a legitimate inference, that the "Aberdeen Act," which has suppressed the slave-trade in Brazil, is the better security.

As to the treatment of slaves in Brazil, there is really very little reliable information in England. In the general indifference and ignorance about that Empire, and with the paucity of English travellers in Brazil and books of travel, the "Brazilian agents" have, I believe, succeeded in establishing a general impression that slaves are very well treated in Brazil. I do not doubt that there, as in other

* "Letter to the Right Hon. Henry Dundas, with the sketch of a Negro Code." In former years, Mr. Milner Gibson pressed Sir Robert Peel much to endeavour to obtain the mitigation of slavery in Brazil. See Hansard, April 29th, 1842, and April 25th, 1843. It is known to have been part of Mr. Ellis's instructions in his unsuccessful mission of 1842 to obtain the assent of the Brazilian government to measures for the amendment of slavery. These instructions were defended, with a clear exposition of the connexion between slavery and slave-trade, by Mr. Gladstone, then President of the Board of Trade, March 7th, 1844.

slave-countries, there are good masters and mistresses. I have known some myself. But I am sure that there, as in all slave-countries, there are bad masters; and that Brazilian nature would not be human nature, if the slavery of three millions out of seven millions and a half of men did not produce a large crop of vice, cruelty, and crime. Brazil is not known in England. The general English public have, for many years past, had little or nothing before them but the flattering pictures of Brazilian agents.

I find the following remarkable statement in a pamphlet published in 1850, by Sir William Gore Ouseley, who had been for some years Chargé d'Affaires at Rio Janeiro, and was afterwards Her Majesty's Minister at Buenos Aires:—

"In Brazil, where the laws have, as in all civilized states, abolished torture in judicial proceedings, the practice is exceptionally continued as regards slaves. Thumbscrews or *anginhos* are often applied to slaves, perhaps at the will and pleasure of some ignorant or possibly culpably cognizant petty authority, for the purpose sometimes of shielding the real criminal, or they are thus cruelly treated at the caprice of some brutal and inhuman *feitor* or overseer; while the masters or others, who may just as likely be the culprits, are not subjected to this mode of extorting from the innocent or guilty a confession. On one occasion I recollect my coachman hastening to my room to inform me that some horrid cruelties were evidently being practised in a barn adjoining my stables. I at once went there, and found several negroes undergoing the torture of the iron thumbscrew, on account, it was alleged, of the loss of a key, which the overseer himself might have probably dropped when intoxicated, as he often was. At all events, seven or eight unfortunate wretches were tortured for the possible though doubtful fault or misfortune of one of them. The energetic, though non-official, intervention that was promptly employed on this occasion to put a stop to the 'wholesome discipline,' as it was doubtless generally considered, was, I will admit, extremely undiplomatic in its character. But the amazement it caused seemed quite as much felt by the sufferers as by the inflictor of this mode of examination. They were astonished, doubtless, that so common an occurrence should cause so much excitement." *

Sir William Ouseley adds some reflections which, in the present state of writing and speaking about Brazil in this country, have not lost their value;

"Unhappily, such is the deadening effect on all our better feelings of the daily presence of facts like this, that Europeans are too apt to end by thinking lightly of such horrors, and speak of them with indifference, as being sanctioned by the usages of the country. After a long stay in slave-states, especially if they have themselves so far forgotten the laws and principles of their own country as to become owners of slaves themselves, they lose the sense of just appreciation, not only of the iniquity of such deeds, but of the often-proved absurdity and illogical nature of a resort to such atrocities as a test of truth. It is a startling and deplorable fact, and one that is calculated to lower our opinion of human nature, to witness the rapid adoption by those Europeans who leave their own country animated with the best and most generous principles respecting their fellow-creatures, of the maxims and practices of hardened slave-holders."

Eight years later, Mr. Vredenburg, the British Consul at Pará, reported to Lord Malmesbury, October 15th, 1858, the trial, at Pará, of a Brazilian lady for the murder of one of her slaves. She was acquitted, the jury being

* "Notes on the Slave-trade," by W. G. Ouseley. London, 1850.

equally divided. Mr. Vredenburg pays a high compliment to the inflexibility of the Acting-President of the Province, and to the conscientiousness of the Judge who presided at the trial and of the public prosecutor. But he implies that all officials would not have acted as uprightly, and that this was not a solitary or unprecedented case of cruelty.

"Donna Maria Magdalena Pia Martinez, a person of position and wealth, and the widow of a Commander of the Imperial Order of Christ, was put on her trial for the murder of one of her female slaves. It was generally reported that the murder had been committed under circumstances of great atrocity; that the unfortunate victim had been kept without any description of nourishment for several days; that she had been repeatedly castigated, and that death had been finally caused by a blow on the temple. It was also currently reported and generally believed, that this woman had previously, by ill-usage, caused the death of one or two children, her slaves; and that her slaves were generally subjected to every description of brutality which the imagination of a violent and ignorant woman could devise. Since her committal for trial, money is believed to have been lavishly distributed, and some parties, it is said, have been unable to withstand its influence. There was, doubtless, some exaggeration in these reports, but I have reason to think that in the main they were correct.

"It was with some interest that I observed the conduct of Senhor Leitão da Cunha, the Vice-President, during the period intervening between the arrest of the prisoner and her trial. That gentleman is Chief of Police; but he is at present, in the absence of the President, administering the affairs of the Province. I had formed the highest opinion of his inflexible justice and determination to punish wrong-doers; but he is a native of the Province, and was, I understand, on terms of intimacy with the late husband of the prisoner; and, although venality in this country is but too general, I was satisfied that no one would attempt to influence him by pecuniary considerations; nevertheless, as I knew that every description of family and other influences would be brought to bear upon him, I feared he might be unable to resist them. I am happy to inform your Lordship that I was right in my appreciation of Senhor Leitão's character. I am informed that he peremptorily refused to interfere, and declared that the law should take its course. I thought it my duty to attend the trial, and have much gratification in being able to report most favourably on the conduct of the authorities. The jury remained in consultation for about three-quarters of an hour, and acquitted the prisoner, there being six votes in her favour, and the same number against her.

The decision in this particular case may be of trifling importance; but the principle has been established that no one, however high in rank, will henceforth be permitted, with impunity, to ill-treat, torture, and murder their slaves; and this prosecution will necessarily tend to protect the slaves against the brutality of some of their owners."

Messrs. Kidder and Fletcher, two North American missionaries, who have written a work on "Brazil and the Brazilians," give an account of the Foundling Hospital of Rio de Janeiro. There is in front of the building a wheel in which infants are placed by those who abandon them; by a turn of the wheel the infants pass into the building, and the depositors go away unobserved. I premise that it will ultimately appear that the dreadful mortality commented on by the worthy missionaries is in great part fictitious:—

"Out of 3,630 infants exposed in Rio during ten years

anterior to 1840, only 1,024 were living at the end of that period. In the year 1838-9, 449 were deposited in the wheel, of whom six were found dead when taken out; many expired the first day after their arrival, and 239 died in a short period. The Report of the Minister of the Empire for the official year 1854-5 gives the following alarming statistics, and the comments of the Minister:—'In 1854, 588 infants were received, in addition to 68 already in the establishment; total 656, died 435, remaining 221. In 1853, the number of foundlings received was 630, and of deaths, 515. Up to the present time it has not been possible to ascertain the exact causes of this lamentable mortality, which with more or less intensity always takes place among such infants, notwithstanding the utmost effort and care that has been used to combat the evil.' Well might one of the physicians of the establishment, in whose company a gentleman of my acquaintance visited several departments of the institution, remark, '*Monsieur, c'est une boucherie.*'"*

But this wholesale murder is only a cloak for slavery. This is the explanation published by M. Dabadie on the authority of the leading journal of Rio, the *Jornal do Commercio*, of August 3rd, 1857:—

"These children, whatever be the colour of their skin, are free by law. Well, what happens? If they belong to the privileged race, the nurses, whose business it is to suckle them, give account of them to the Hospital, the mother of the foundlings; but if, on the contrary, they

* "Brazil and the Brazilians," by Rev. D. P. Kidder, D.D., and Rev. J. C. Fletcher, 1857, p. 113. These gentlemen further state:—"One peculiar circumstance connected with this state of things consists in the alleged fact that many of the foundlings are the offspring of female slaves, whose masters, not wishing the trouble and expense of endeavouring to raise the children, or wishing the services of the mothers as wet-nurses, require the infants to be sent to the *engeitaria* (foundling-hospital,) where, should they survive, they are of course free."

come of the race which is beyond the pale of humanity, the same nurses do not fear to report them as dead, and sell them for their own profit." *

Here is one of the moral developments of slavery. The wet-nurses of the Foundling Hospital sell the children for slaves, and fictitious bills of mortality deceive Brazilian Ministers into official reports describing the Hospital as a slaughter-house of innocents. For another moral development of slavery in Brazil—the mode in which masters and mistresses in the cities extract income from female slaves—I refer to the works of M. Dabadie and M. Expilly for details which I cannot here reprint.†

---

The eager support invariably given to the Brazilian government by what is known as the Manchester school of politicians is in many ways matter of surprise. That eminent politicians and conscientious journalists, whose horror of slavery in the Confederate States of North America has no limit or qualification, should be the ever-sympathising advocates of a South American government, under which exist three millions and more of slaves, and which does nothing to reduce or mitigate slavery, is alone surprising. This is not a question of interference with or against Brazil for abolition of slavery, beyond any existing

* Dabadie, "A Travers l'Amérique du Sud," Paris, 1859, p. 58.

† Expilly, "Le Brésil tel qu'il est." Paris, 1863. (Second edition.) Some further notices of slavery in Brazil will be found among the extracts of official correspondence in the Appendix. See especially Mr. Cowper's despatch to the Earl of Malmesbury, p. 206, and Mr. Howard's to the Earl of Clarendon, p. 218.

treaty-rights; it is a question of sympathy and approval, or the contrary.

"Homo sum, humani nihil a me alienum,"

must apply to nations as well as to individuals; and England, I trust, is not to abandon in South America the privilege, which Mr. Bright freely uses in the North, of "teaching the nations how to live." But it is further surprising that the special friends and promoters of commerce should be eager to upbraid and oppose their own government when measures are taken for the protection of traders with Brazil, which excite resistance and anger of the Brazilian government. English merchants in Brazil need the strong arm of their government to protect them. None know better than the traders of Manchester and Liverpool, or at any rate than their agents and correspondents in Brazil, that fear is the only effectual security for justice, and that the British navy is the right arm of British merchants. The gross amount of commerce will be, in the main, regulated by wants, without treaties, which wants dispense with, and in spite of bad legislation, which wants baffle.* But individuals from time to time need aid and protection; their government protects them with reference to general duty and general interest; other individuals not immediately concerned, being, or fearing to be, inconvenienced by a dispute with Brazil, having acquired sympathies or made ties with that country, misled perhaps by interested accounts which, where the case is not their own, they are prone to believe, raise an outcry

* See p. 129, Chapter xi. for the recent growth of trade with Brazil.

against their own government. Your lordship happily pointed out, in one of the discussions on the late reprisals, that traders with Brazil who make agitation in her behalf gain the double advantage of the favour of the Brazilian government and the benefit of the action of their own. And Mr. Layard not less happily likened the conduct of some Brazilian merchants towards one of their body who goes to the Foreign Office for redress to birds pecking to death another that has got loose from a cage. I have long had the privilege of the acquaintance of Mr. Cobden and Mr. Bright, who know my respect for them, and I am as firmly convinced of their conscientiousness as of their great abilities. But I fear that they yield too readily to short-sighted fears and narrow prejudices of Manchester and Liverpool.* I know that they have had much erroneous information about Brazil. Many years

* Mr. Cobden, in his speech on Mr. Bramley-Moore's motion, March 6th, 1863, seemed to contend that the question with the Brazilian government about the "Prince of Wales" should have been left to be settled, and would then have been well and quickly settled, by the British merchants at Rio. Would he then have allowed the question arising out of the treatment of the officers of the "Forte" to be settled by the British navy? It is very easy for those who do not know Brazil and the Brazilian government to assume that good advice would be easily taken. A wise and dispassionate writer, several years since, exhorted English Ministers to press the Brazilian government to establish a registration of slaves ("Friends in Council," 1849). Such advice was given, under Lord Clarendon's instruction, by Mr. Jerningham, December 7, 1855. No attention was ever given to the advice; Mr. Jerningham's note was not even answered.

Entertaining a sincere respect for Mr. Cobden, I much regret that he never publicly retracted a misstatement made by him in the Brazilian debate of March 6th, 1863, that "the merchants at Rio and in Brazil generally were unanimous in disapproving the course taken by the English government." His subsequent attempt, May 7th, 1863, to represent an address, presented to me by twenty-six of the most respectable residents in Rio, including members of sixteen commercial houses, as a compliment to my manner of execution at the expense of Her Majesty's government which gave me orders, was a refinement, I frankly say, unworthy of him.

ago I humbly co-operated with them for free trade. But free trade is only one of a nation's wants. "Man doth not live by bread alone," and the greatness of a nation cannot depend only on imports and exports.

The efforts in Parliament for the removal of unequal taxation adverse to Brazilian produce, and for the abandonment of our anti-slave-trade squadron, brought the two statesmen whom I have named, and Mr. Milner Gibson, Mr. Hutt, and others, into a position of co-operation with Brazil. We are all prone to believe what we wish; and a "Brazilian agent" found it easy to persuade these honourable men that all our difficulties with Brazil arose from the ill-usage of the English government, and that the government of Brazil voluntarily, and exclusively by its own efforts, suppressed the slave-trade, and did not do it sooner, not from want of will, but from regard for its own honour and dignity, offended by the proceedings of British cruisers. I am sure that Mr. Milner Gibson and Mr. Hutt, reading again in recent speeches and publications on Brazil the stereotyped histories of Brazilian perfection and British injustice, and comparing the information which they then saw no reason to distrust with what is now officially known to them, must be satisfied that they were formerly misled.]

In the year 1857, the question of our relations with Brazil, and of the "Aberdeen Act" in particular, was brought before the House of Commons by a member conspicuous for acuteness and force of eloquence, Mr. Roebuck. It is no reproach to the member for Sheffield that he was never in Brazil. He, doubtless, not only endeavoured to obtain the best information, but believed the information which he got to be trustworthy. His flattering account of the Brazilian government, given, no one will doubt, in perfect good faith, bears a strong family-likeness to those which have lately been given in Parliament by Lord Malmesbury, Mr. Fitzgerald, and Mr. Osborne. Your lordship said at the time to Mr. Roebuck that he evidently spoke "from information not gathered by himself, but furnished to him by interested parties."

Later, Mr. Roebuck became interested in Brazil as a Director of an Anglo-Luso-Brazilian Navigation Company, which for a time ran monthly screw-steamers to Rio. I remember, when passing through Lisbon at the end of 1859, on my way to Brazil, hearing that Mr. Roebuck was then in Lisbon on the affairs of that Company, in the management of which he took an active part. If the member for Sheffield, without personal knowledge of Brazil, could fall into error, who is acute enough to be proof against that dangerous thing, a little learning? No one would for one moment suspect Mr. Roebuck of knowledge of an act for which, as a Director of that Company, he was responsible—the conveyance of slaves from the northern ports of Brazil to Rio Janeiro by the Anglo-Luso-Brazilian steamers. This was brought to the knowledge of Lord Clarendon by Mr. Westwood, the Consul at Rio, on October 22d, 1860, in the following terms:—

"I think it my duty to report to your lordship, that the steamship 'Milford Haven' which arrived here on the 3rd instant from Liverpool, *viâ* Lisbon, St. Vincent, Pernambuco, and Bahia, brought from the two last-mentioned ports

44 slaves, as shown by the enclosed extracts from the daily report of the harbour-visit. The 'Milford Haven' is one of the vessels belonging to the Anglo-Luso-Brazilian Company, which established, about the end of last year, a line of steamers between Milford Haven and Brazil; but the Company has since altered the port of departure from Milford Haven to Liverpool. The vessels belonging to this Company are navigated under the Portuguese flag; but I believe that the enterprise is an English one, or, at any rate, that most of the shareholders are British, and residents in Great Britain. The steamers are officered and manned chiefly by Englishmen, having merely a flag-captain and a small portion of the crew Portuguese, so as to enable the ships to use the Portuguese flag. I understand that the undertaking has not turned out a successful speculation, and I believe that the Company is about to give up the line."

These slaves were carried to Rio Janeiro, as part of a slave-trading system which has for years past been remonstrated against by British Secretaries of State, beginning with Lord Malmesbury, denounced in the Brazilian Legislature, and censured by Brazilian Ministers,—of which Brazilian statesmen have said that it is attended with all the cruelties of the African slave-trade, and that it is, in fact, a disguised slave-trade. The same Mr. Consul Westwood thus described the traffic in one of his official reports:—"Many of these unfortunate beings are brought from estates where they were born, and torn away from relatives and old associations in the most inhuman and cruel manner possible." Sir Henry Howard thus described the system, April 8th, 1854:—

"All at once a slave-trader comes into the market from Rio de Janeiro, buys up from the needy or avaricious masters all those slaves he can obtain, and in most cases is the cause of the separation of a father from his wife and children, and *vice versâ*, the unfortunate African being, perhaps, sold at his ulterior destination to some harder master, or to some other unprincipled speculator."

It is unnecessary to say that Mr. Roebuck never imagined the possibility of the use of the steamers of his Company for the above purpose. There is none of our public men who would more abhor connexion with the sins of slavery. But is not this a striking example to prove how cautious should be those who are strangers to Brazil in accepting the information of persons connected with Brazilian enterprises, or of Brazilian agents? With the same honourable candour with which Mr. Roebuck not long since at Sheffield spoke about other questions, he will probably admit that, on this question also of Brazil, on which he once differed from your lordship, he has found that you were wiser than himself.

It is very important to make known some of the means by which Brazilian agency in England poisons the fountains of knowledge, confounds truth, obstructs good relations between the two governments, and is the enemy to both countries.

I have already mentioned that the person to whom your lordship's description of a "Brazilian agent" was generally understood by persons interested in Brazilian affairs to apply, is a member of the Reform Club, and that also he is notoriously the paid correspondent of the Rio *Jornal do Commercio*, and has been notoriously the inspirer of the *Daily News*, and informant of other English journals on Brazilian questions. It is easy for those who are familiar with his operations, to trace his hand in different journals, under various signatures. He may have co-operators and sub-agents. I cannot and do not accuse him individually of every one of the acts which I proceed to recount as specimens of the operation of Brazilian agency. But he is the chief workman.

The Brazilian public chiefly, if not almost exclusively, learn what passes in England about Brazil from the long letters of the paid London correspondent, translated into Portuguese, in the *Jornal do Commercio.* In those letters reappear the articles which the "Brazilian agent" has inspired, or the letters which, under different pseudonyms, he has written in English newspapers; and they are always represented as independent public opinion. It is well known that during the last year he constantly supplied materials and addressed letters to the daily Conservative organs as well as to the *Daily News.* He has not expected his statements in the *Jornal do Commercio* to be scrutinized here. I give an instance of misrepresentation. The "London correspondent" described the debate of last year on Lord Malmesbury's motion in the House of Lords as if he had been present, as he doubtless was, and he naturally described it to the advantage in every way of the defenders of the Brazilian government. Lord Stratford de Redcliffe happened to put a question to Lord Russell about Russia and Poland, just before Lord Malmesbury began; and the faithful chronicler represented Lord Stratford as prefacing his question with words conveying disapproval of the conduct of Her Majesty's government about Brazil. The newspapers of the day following generally reported Lord Stratford's observations at some length; not one of them reported the slightest allusion to the Brazilian question. Your lordship can judge whether it was likely that Lord Stratford, of all men, should have expressed incidentally an opinion on a foreign question which was immediately to be formally discussed. But it was important to make it believed by the Brazilian public, that the weighty opinion of the renowned diplomatist was in favour of Brazil; and the Brazilian public will probably never know the contradiction.

Completely contradictory statements on the same subject are made in the *Jornal do Commercio*, and in English newspapers. The Brazilian Legation has had part in the establishment and direction of three Brazilian railway companies organized in London, with a guarantee of 7 per cent. on the capitals from the Imperial and Provincial governments of Brazil; and the "Brazilian agent" actively assisted in the distribution of shares of these companies on their formation. One of these is the Bahia and San Francisco Company, the working of which has greatly disappointed the shareholders, who now find all or most of the guaranteed 7 per cent. swallowed up by excess of expenses over profits. A "communication" is made to the *Brazil and River Plate Mail*, a newspaper published in London, absolving the Brazilian government from all blame, and asserting that "the engagements of the Brazilian government have been fulfilled to the letter." * But the London correspondent of the *Jornal do Commercio* had shortly before, wishing to persuade the Brazilian

* *Brazil and River Plate Mail*, August 20th, 1864; "Communicated" article.

government to assist the shareholders in their difficulties, represented that the Brazilian government alonc was to blame, having sacrificed the interests of the Company to jobbery, and having broken its engagements. I quote one of the letters in the *Jornal do Commercio*:—

"For the direction of the railway the Imperial government is entirely responsible. It was made quite clear that the line ought to start from some point in the Reconcavo; and the government, moved by political and local considerations, and not by the interests of the undertaking, decided the contrary. Thus, then, the primitive mistake proceeds from the government, and not from the Company. It is not correct to say that the board trusted to vague calculations of receipts. An official report was presented to it, which minutely demonstrated a traffic of 130,000*l.* a year; and receipts of that amount, even with the actual expense of 65,000*l.* a year, would produce a gain of three and a half per cent. yearly to reduce the guarantee. The board, then, was deceived; not by their own imaginations, but by an official report. Besides, whose fault is it that there is a deficit on the Bahia line? Not certainly the Company's, which has, at all risks, fulfilled all its engagements, and which constructed within its guaranteed capital the ill-traced line which the government imposed on it, on condition of the 7 per cent. It was the fault of the government, which failed to fulfil its promise of opening, simultaneously, lateral lines to feed the line with district traffic."

At Rio it is represented that the Brazilian government has broken faith with the Company, which has, at all risks, fulfilled its engagements. In London it is asserted that the Brazilian government has fulfilled all its engagements to the letter. Before the British public, the

Brazilian government must, at all hazards, be defended; in Brazil, pecuniary interests must be pressed on the government, as responsible for mischief.

The letters of "C." in the *Daily News*, were replied to only in the columns of that journal by the "Friend to both Countries," who informed the public, or of whom the public was supposed to know, that the greater part of his replies were written from Germany. Last year, during the discussions which arose out of the reprisals, while the "Brazilian agent" was on English soil, elaborate statements and abusive letters, evidently from the same source, appeared in other journals. It is, perhaps, not surprising that the "Friend to both Countries" should extend the duality of his friendship, and be a friend to two parties and even two opinions. A long and elaborate statement on the subject of the British claims on Brazil, aud other Brazilian questions, appeared in the *Morning Herald* of August 19th, 1863, containing the same assertions and arguments which have lately come from the "Friend to both Countries." The substance is the same, but there is a difference of form and setting. In the letters in the *Daily News*, the writer has "the most profound respect for, and gratitude to, Earl Russell, for his great and illustrious services to England," and speaks of Lord Malmesbury as an inferior Minister, who has, however, understood Brazil better than abler men. In the *Morning Herald* it was naturally the other way. There Lord Russell was described as actuated by "petty persevering spite," and as "not of a stature to withstand the wish of Parliament," while Lord Malmesbury, "whose courtesy, candour, and liberality are acknowledged with gratitude by Brazil, as by every other foreign Power," would, by repealing the "Aberdeen Act," render the Foreign Office powerless. But, as I said before, the difference is only one of form and setting. The materials are the same in both places: but readers of different politics and predilections have to be coaxed into being taught, by flattery or by disparagement of the same person—

> "Ut pueris olim dant crustula blandi
> Doctores, elementa velint ut discere prima."

Character is not spared by this anonymous Brazilian agency. Mr. Reeves, the highly respectable British post-office agent at Rio, has been involved in a lawsuit with a Brazilian, the progress of which has revealed social immoralities, direct interference of a high official of the Ministry of Justice with the Judges, and great judicial corruption, and has also elicited remonstrances from Lord Russell and the British Legation. It became important to damage Mr. Reeves's reputation. At the end of last year, the Minister of Justice, Senhor Sinimbú, as he was retiring from office, issued a decree dismissing seven of the highest Judges in Brazil on a general allegation of corruption. So startling a sign of judicial corruption must be explained to the British public, and the innocence of Brazil demonstrated. It was, therefore, represented in English journals that the dismissed Judges were the last remains of Portuguese nomination, and that an Englishman, Mr. Reeves, had bribed them. One assertion is as untrue as the other. In three English journals it appeared in different forms, but evidently from the same informant, that the dismissal of the Judges was caused by bribery practised by an Englishman. Mr. Reeves was also contemptuously spoken of in one of these journals as "a dismissed Post-office servant." Another calumny! I abstain from naming the journals, for their Editors have, doubtless, long since regretted that they published calumnies on an honourable man, through credulous confidence in their informant. While the calumny was being circulated here, Senhor Sinimbú had indeed furnished a refutation by publicly stating in the Brazilian Senate that the dismissal of the Judges was in no way connected with Mr. Reeves's lawsuit. It has since become known that the dismissal, whether just or unjust, was immediately caused by another lawsuit, which had excited great interest, and in which both parties were Brazilians.

Not long since a circumstantial statement, full of falsehoods, appeared in the *Jornal do Commercio* from its London correspondent, about affairs of my household. I was able to trace this calumny to its origin in what was the Brazilian Legation, and is now the Brazilian Consulate, in Cavendish Square. I felt it right, under these circumstances, to make the calumnious statement known to Lord Russell, and point out to him, with proofs, or the means of proof, its several falsehoods. The London correspondent favoured the *Jornal do Commercio* at the same time with a statement of views of mine about the House of Commons and a particular constituency, in which

> "Some truth there was, but dashed and brewed with lies,"

and of which the portion that was truth was likely to be known to a "Brazilian agent," who is a member of the

Reform Club. The members of that society will probably be amazed to hear of one of their body purveying to a Brazilian journal calumnies on an English Minister, who offended the Brazilian government by the execution of a duty imposed on him for the protection of English interests, and whom Lord Russell has described as having executed his instructions "with fidelity, ability, and in a conciliatory manner."

A paper has been established not long since in London, devoted to South American affairs, and called the *Brazil and River Plate Mail*. The Editor has an undisguised partiality for the Brazilian government, but honestly opens his columns to different opinions. The London correspondent of the *Jornal do Commercio*, indignant at such honesty, writes out to the Brazilian journal that the Editor of the *Brazil and River Plate Mail* is pursuing a discreditable course, and trying to extort a subvention from the Brazilian government. It may be inferred, then, that subventions by the Brazilian government to newspapers are not unknown.*

These are a few specimens of the arts of Brazilian agency in this country. Honourable men, whether in

* Such subventions are notoriously given by the Brazilian government to European journals. See M. Expilly's statement, quoted at p. 104. I have received, on what I believe to be good authority, details as to Brazilian operations with the German press, which, since the reprisals, has been worked vehemently in abuse of Her Majesty's government and myself. A Hofrath at Potsdam receives an annual stipend from the Brazilian Legation in Berlin, and instructs the public for Brazil in the *Allgemeine Norddeutsche Zeitung*, and other papers. A German who has been Captain in the Brazilian army is similarly employed at Vienna, and is, I am told, formally attached to the Brazilian Legation there. At Hamburg the press is managed by a German doctor, who went out as a colonist to Brazil. The *General Emigration Gazette* of Rudolfstadt receives from the Brazilian government a subsidy of about 700*l*. a year.

Parliament or in the press, who have trusted to a "Brazilian agent," cannot know of, cannot suspect, such expedients. The combats of English political parties are ruled by a code of honour; and not less true is it of the press than of party, in words which, lately applied by the Chief Justice of England to the Bar, are likely to be historical, that ends are to be attained *per fas*, but not *per nefas*, and weapons wielded as by the warrior, and not as by the assassin.

It is obvious that a system of one-sided statement, exaggeration, and misrepresentation in Brazil of English opinion, coupled with calumnies, and again of studious misrepresentation in England of Brazilian affairs, must thwart and embarrass Her Majesty's government, mislead that of Brazil, and aggravate the difficulties for English interests in that Empire, and for good relations between the two countries.

Under these circumstances, I feel that I do a duty, in trying to make known to the English public some of the truth about Brazil, and the mischievous machinations of Brazilian agency. I have no thought of returning to Rio. Holding a diplomatic pension, I still eat the bread of the public. I remember, when Lord Howden returned from South America, that he was driven by misrepresentations of newspaper correspondents to expose them in the press under his signature. I feel assured that, so long as the system of Brazilian agency which has existed in London for many years in connexion with the Brazilian Legation continues its operations, there can be no permanent satisfactory diplomatic relations with Brazil, if an English Secretary of State for Foreign Affairs does not forego his functions, and if an English Minister at Rio does his duty, as your lordship and Lord Russell say that I did mine.

I have been accused of hostility to Brazil, but I have your lordship for a partner in the honours of this accusation. It is well known to your lordship, and many others, that I entered on my mission in Brazil with opinions favourable to its government, formed, before I knew the country, under the same influences which have so favourably impressed the general English public. The hostility of which I am accused is the conviction which I came to slowly and reluctantly, from a long and various experience, that the British public was misled and deceived,—that the Brazilian government would not do justice except through fear,—that all reasonable demands were met by excuses and delays, and in Lord Russell's words, "evasions, subterfuges, and unfounded assertions." This is my firm conviction, slowly and unwillingly arrived at. The same conviction is stamped on every one of Sir James Hudson's despatches during five years. That I neither showed offensive hostility to Brazil, nor was unpopular there before my duties brought me into direct conflict with the Brazilian government, cannot be better proved than by a statement made by the "Brazilian agent" himself, in one of his letters to the *Jornal do Commercio*, before the beginning of the long correspondence which ended in the reprisals, that I was the most impartial and industrious British Minister who had ever been sent to Rio. I can by no means admit that this high compliment, at the expense of my predecessors, was deserved.

Since the reprisals the same writer has used unsparingly his opportunities, in the English and Brazilian press, to abuse and defame me. Your lordship said, in the House of Commons: "It is a well-known practice in countries which are in that peculiar state of progress in which Brazil happens at the present moment to find itself, that, when their injustice or misconduct obliges a foreign government to use compulsion in order to obtain the redress which has been denied to friendly representations, they endeavour to take their revenge by pouring forth every sort of calumny on the agent who has been the instrument of the government using these means." A nobleman, who happened to be in Rio, to whom I am permitted to appeal by name,—the Marquis of Sligo,—the only member of either House of Parliament who visited Brazil during the three years of my mission, witnessed and can relate the daily incredible insults and annoyances of which I was the object after the reprisals. But what might not be possible, when one of the leading journals of Rio published a letter from a Brazilian gentleman describing his meeting Sir James Hudson at a ball, and expressing his regret that he had not inflicted personal chastisement on the miscreant?*

Several years ago an eminent English statesman, who had been a Cabinet Minister, had every expectation of being a Cabinet Minister again, and is now the Chancellor of the Exchequer in your lordship's government,

* This is related in Mr. Wilberforce's "Brazil viewed through a Naval Glass, with Notes on Slavery and the Slave-trade." Longmans. 1856. p. 224. Sir James Hudson was not then so well known as he is now. I find Mr. Bright complaining of his proceedings in Brazil as those "of a certain Mr. Hudson, who is now in Brazil, and who, I believe, pursued the right honourable baronet (Sir R. Peel) to Italy some fifteen years ago." (Hansard, April 24th, 1849.)

publicly addressed to Lord Aberdeen a startling account of abuses which he had ascertained for himself under the government of Naples, and dissipated and destroyed a network of fictions. It is time that the delusions prevailing in this country about Brazil should be destroyed —delusions propagated by an active and unscrupulous Brazilian agency, with the aid or willing belief of merchants, of trembling, hoping, or grateful holders of Brazilian investments, which have of late years, under Brazilian agency, rapidly accumulated in England, of great capitalists largely embarked in loans and speculations, who possess great social power.

The Messrs. Rothschild are the financial agents of the government of Brazil, and have negotiated Brazilian loans to the extent of several millions, and started two of three Brazilian Railway Companies organized in London. No one can doubt the value for the Brazilian government of the friendly wishes of the great house of Rothschild. Among the directors of the three Railway Companies referred to, are London merchants and bankers, and members of Parliament, of high standing and great influence, who have had at each of the three Boards the Brazilian Minister for a colleague. It is not in human nature that these gentlemen, for the most part personally unacquainted with Brazil, should not be disposed to receive favourably the representations of their Brazilian colleague and his agents, and to sympathize with a government on which largely depends the success of their great pecuniary enterprises. Several other Companies have in the last few years been established in London, with concessions of privilege from the Brazilian government.

But wherever else Brazilian agency, or the social power of mercantile and monetary influences, might directly or indirectly operate, it would not be expected that the *Edinburgh Review* should misrepresent the Brazilian question. The reprisals and suspension of diplomatic relations have been explained by published official documents, and by speeches of Ministers in parliament. A writer in the October number of the *Edinburgh Review*, alluding to our differences with Brazil, pronounces his judgment, that "diplomatic relations have been too long interrupted with a state with which England has certainly no reasonable ground of difference," and counsels Her Majesty's government to despatch a Minister to Brazil armed with the concession of the repeal of the "Aberdeen Act." I think I may safely assume that the writer is here your lordship's Mentor, and not your interpreter. Is he who thus seeks to guide, aware that the King of Portugal has been acting as mediator, and has he satisfied himself that it is by the fault of the English government that the mediation has not hitherto been successful? The writer does not seem aware that diplomatic relations were broken off by the Brazilian government, after an agreement made by them to give a pecuniary indemnity in the case of the "Prince of Wales," and to refer a part of the question of the officers of the "Forte" to arbitration, and that they were broken off, without waiting for the award in this case, on the ground that the reprisals were executed in Brazilian waters. But not a year passes before the Brazilian government proposes to coerce Monte Video by reprisals in Monte Videan territory, and proceeds to do so. The writer in the *Edinburgh*

*Review* is so little familiar with the question, as to describe the whole of our dispute with Brazil as having been referred to arbitration. He might, indeed, have been restrained from advising that, under present circumstances, the extraordinary step should be taken of sending a Minister to Rio to buy the restoration of diplomatic relations with the repeal of the "Aberdeen Act," by the declarations made by Lord Russell and your lordship at the close of last session. Lord Russell stated, when Lord Brougham suggested the repeal of the "Aberdeen Act" in the House of Lords; "The 'Aberdeen Act' had become inoperative, but if any party were to come into power which would endeavour to restore the slave-trade, they would have the opportunity of doing so if this Act were repealed. The Brazilian government had chosen to suspend diplomatic relations with this country, on a ground that could mean nothing else than objection to measures for the protection of the lives and property of British subjects in Brazil; and he could not think they were entitled, under the circumstances, to any great favour at the hands of this country." And your lordship said, a few days after in the House of Commons: "I am convinced that if the Act were repealed the Brazilian slave-trade would be revived."

Believe me,
My dear Lord Palmerston,
With sentiments of respect and gratitude,
Your faithful servant,
W. D. CHRISTIE.

*November* 15, 1864.

## CHAPTER I.

### THE STORY OF THE FREE AFRICANS.

CONVENTION OF 1826 FOR SUPPRESSION OF SLAVE-TRADE—STIPULATION FOR RELEASED AFRICANS—LORD PALMERSTON'S STATEMENT OF JULY 12, 1864—THE "DIARIO DO RIO."

IMMEDIATELY after the recognition by Portugal of the independence of Brazil in 1826, a Convention was concluded between Great Britain and Brazil for the suppression of the slave-trade, November 23, 1826, Mr. Canning being then Secretary for Foreign Affairs.

By the first article it was agreed and provided that, at the expiration of three years from the exchange of the ratifications of the Convention, the carrying on of slave-trade by Brazilian subjects, in any manner whatever, should be unlawful, and should be deemed and treated as piracy. The ratifications were exchanged March 13, 1827, and this article became operative in March, 1830.

In the remaining articles of the Convention the two parties adopted and renewed, *mutatis mutandis*, all the provisions as to right of search and Mixed Commissions for adjudication of captures contained in the existing Treaties between Great Britain and Portugal; viz. the Treaty of January 22, 1815, and the Additional Convention of July 28, 1817, and the several explanatory articles, instructions and regulations, and forms of instruments thereto annexed; and they agreed to appoint Mixed Commission Courts. Two such were appointed, one within British dominions at Sierra Leone, the other at Rio de Janeiro.

Among the regulations for the Mixed Commissions appended to the Additional Convention with Portugal of July 28, 1817, which became part and parcel of the Convention between Great Britain and Brazil, is the following as to the slaves which might be found in captured slave-trade vessels:—

"As to the slaves, they shall receive from the Mixed Commission a certificate of emancipation, and shall be delivered over to the government on whose territory the Commission which shall have so judged them shall be established, to be employed as servants or free labourers. Each of the two governments binds itself to guarantee the liberty of such portion of these individuals as shall be respectively consigned to it."

These words are the charter of liberty of the Africans in Brazil rescued from Brazilian slave-trade vessels by British cruisers, and handed over to the Brazilian government by the British and Brazilian Mixed Commission of Rio de Janeiro. These words give the British government the right to require from the government of Brazil the guaranteed freedom of these Africans.

A separate article, agreed upon September 11, 1817, was added to the Additional Convention between Great Britain and Portugal, providing that that Convention should remain in force until the expiration of fifteen years from the day on which the Portuguese government should abolish the slave-trade; and the Brazilian government claimed to interpret this article as terminating for them, on the 13th of March, 1845, fifteen years from the date at which Brazilian slave-trade became piracy, all the obligations of the Convention of 1817, as adopted and incorporated in the Convention between Great Britain and Brazil. The British government acquiesced in this interpretation ; and all that remained after 1845 of the British Convention with Brazil for the suppression of the slave-trade was the first article making slave-trade in Brazil piracy. The two Mixed Commission Courts, by agreement, continued to sit till September 13, 1845.

The free Africans, or *emancipados*, for whose liberty Brazil is responsible to Great Britain, are those handed over to the Brazilian government with certificates of freedom by the Mixed Commission Court of Rio de Janeiro between 1830 and 1845. In the absence of all authentic official information from the Brazilian government as to the number of these free Africans and their children, I stated to Lord Russell, in a despatch dated May 27, 1861, "I have found it difficult to obtain any certain estimate of the number of the free blacks in the country or of those released by the Slave-trade Commission ; but I think that these, with their children, would probably not exceed ten thousand."

Lord Palmerston, on July 12th of this year, having been asked in the House of Commons whether the Brazilian government had fulfilled their treaty-obligations with regard to these free Africans, made a remarkable statement. He said that the Brazilian government had flagrantly violated its treaty-engagements with regard to them, that frequent representations on the part of the

British government had not been attended to, that lists of the negroes had been asked for and never obtained. Lord Palmerston read an account of the mode of proceeding of the Brazilian government for granting letters of emancipation to these free blacks, taken from a Rio newspaper, the *Diario do Rio*, which had been printed in a parliamentary paper, "Correspondence respecting Liberated Slaves in Brazil, 1863," and again in the Slave-trade Correspondence, class B, presented to Parliament in 1864. The statement in the *Diario do Rio*, a paper edited by a Brazilian Deputy, is not the less true because it is a censure of the practice of the Brazilian government. The course of proceeding in the government offices, when one of the free Africans petitions for a letter of emancipation, was described as follows:—

"1. To ask from the Clerk of the Africans the positive attestation that the term [of apprenticeship] has elapsed.

"2. Petition the Imperial government through the Minister of Justice.

"3. The Minister of Justice refers to the Judge of Orphans.

"4. The Judge of Orphans gives information, and returns the petition to the Minister.

"5. The Minister refers to the Chief of Police.

"6. The Chief of Police refers to the general Guardian (Curador).

"7. The Guardian gives information, and returns the petition to the Chief of Police.

"8. The Chief of Police refers to the Director of the House of Correction.

"9. The Director of the House of Correction gives information, and sends back to the Chief of Police.

"10. The Chief of Police gives information, and sends back to the office of the Secretary of Justice.

"11. The Secretary's office makes a *précis* of the information to be acted on by the Minister.

"12. Finally, the Minister acts, ordering a letter of freedom to be issued.

"13. The petition returns to the Judge of Orphans.

"14. Notification of the decision is sent to the Chief of Police.

"15. The Judge of Orphans refers the petition to the Clerk, and orders a letter of freedom to be given; but retains it in his possession until the party pays the required fees.

"16. The letter is made over to the Chief of Police.

"17. The Chief of Police communicates with the Director of the House of Correction, ordering the African to appear.

"18. The Director sends for him, and the Chief designates his place of residence.

"19. The Chief of Police of the city of Rio de Janeiro communicates with the Provincial Chief of Police to whom the place designated belongs, and hands over the free African with the letter.

"20. The Provincial Chief of Police hands over the wretched man and his letter to the police authority of the place approved by the Chief of Police of Rio de Janeiro, as place of banishment for a free man condemned for no crime.

"And after all this work and expense incurred with procurators and intermediaries, in order that the petition may not remain buried in the great ocean of our departments, the wretched African succeeds in being banished from the place where he has lived ten, fifteen, or twenty years, in which he had taken root, where he had begun to found his future, his hopes.

"This is Brazil, in the year of grace 1863. This is not a censure on authorities or functionaries; it is an evil which is exclaimed against, and for which we claim the attention of the Imperial government."

Lord Palmerston concluded his statement as follows :—

"All the efforts we have made to obtain justice for these *emancipados* have failed, and we have not been able to obtain a list of them. We know that when they have been assigned to an owner, he has employed them in conjunction with his slaves, and that, when a slave died, he put an *emancipado* in his place, and reported the death of the *emancipado*, and not the death of the slave."

This statement of Lord Palmerston excited great surprise and much hostile criticism. On July 14th appeared a leading article in the *Daily News* condemning Lord Palmerston's speech. This article led me to address the Editor for the first time. My letter was immediately replied to in a letter signed, "A Friend to both Countries," the writer of which seemed to own himself the author of the leading article of July 14th, and had doubtless furnished the materials for it. My letters being continued, the so-called "Friend to both Countries" continued to reply. I tell no secret, and I am sure that I tell the truth, when I say that the "Friend to both Countries" is the same person as the paid London correspondent of the *Jornal do Commercio* of Rio de Janeiro, and as the Brazilian agent alluded to by Lord Palmerston in his reply to Mr. Osborne on July 18th: "I know, everybody knows, the source whence the honourable gentleman draws his information. He is indebted to an active Brazilian agent."

## CHAPTER II.

### THE STORY OF THE FREE AFRICANS.

REPLY TO CRITICISM ON LORD PALMERSTON'S STATEMENT—SIR JAMES HUDSON'S REPRESENTATIONS, 1846–1850—LORD RUSSELL'S INSTRUCTIONS AND MY REPRESENTATIONS, 1861.

A LEADING article in the *Daily News* of July 14th, on Lord Palmerston's statement about the free Africans in Brazil, contained the following passage :—

"The occasion of this painful display was an inquiry as to the fate or condition of the *emancipados,* or liberated Africans, about which the Foreign Office cannot, it says, get from Brazil all the information it wants. And why? Simply because it asks for impossibilities. The last of these Africans was admitted into Brazil in 1845, or nearly twenty years ago. They were, under the Treaty which was terminated in that year, apprenticed to planters in an Empire as large as Russia, scattered over provinces imperfectly organized, and distributed amongst slave-owners. For this distribution of them the English government is far more responsible than the Brazilian government, for it ought to have had the foresight, in making the Treaty, to make arrangements in it for carrying these coloured men to its own tropical colonies or restored them to Africa, instead of leaving them in a country panting at the time for slave-labour. There, however, they were left; and now, twenty years after the last of them were so disposed of, and thirty-four years after the first were apprenticed, the

British government insists on their identification from amongst three millions of slaves, on the delivery of lists of them, and on their restoration to freedom. Would that it were possible for the Brazilian government to fulfil these requirements. No doubt the planters who received these Africans have consigned many of them to slavery; but how is the Brazilian government to recover them?"

Now, what the Foreign Office says is, not that it "cannot get from Brazil all the information it wants," but that it has really not been able to get any information at all from the Brazilian government.

It does not "ask for impossibilities," for it only asks the Brazilian government to give what information it can, and to free those who are known and can be found. There is a very considerable number of these poor creatures now known, and to be found in the service of private individuals and in government establishments.

It does not now, in the year 1864, "twenty years after the last of them were disposed of, and thirty-four years after the first were apprenticed," ask for the first time; it has been asking without success for at least eighteen years past, and I need not say that eighteen years ago what may now be impossible might have been easy, and individuals who cannot now be traced might have been found.

On the 17th of November, 1846, all but eighteen years ago, Sir James Hudson reported as follows to Lord Palmerston the neglect and ill-treatment of the liberated Africans, and that it was easy for the Brazilian government, if they wished it, to exercise an effectual superintendence:—

"Tricks are practised with respect to these Africans, in transferring them from one master to another until they are lost sight of and forgotten, in sending them to considerable distances from Rio de Janeiro, in supplying certain influential politicians and men in authority and of influence with them as a means of ensuring a certain line of conduot, in jobbing with them in one way or another, in giving false certificates of death or disappearance, against all of which it requires constant watchfulness and care. That a complete superintendence might be attained over these liberated Africans is now clear from the circumstance that on the 1st instant ninety-seven Africans of the 'Flor de Loanda' received their full and entire liberty, and exercised their free choice of remaining in Brazil or of going to a British colony. Of every African of that cargo a full and satisfactory account can be given, and it appears to me that Her Majesty's government ought to receive an equally full and clear account of all Africans to whose emancipation they have been or may be accessories."

On the 26th of June, 1848, application was made by Mr. Hudson to the Brazilian government in the following inoffensive terms for a list, which was never given :—

"Her Majesty's government would be glad to know what is the present number of these emancipated negroes, where they are, and how they are employed, and especially what arrangements have been made for giving them moral and industrial instruction, according to the engagements contained in the Treaty, under the provisions of which they were captured ; and as the greatest portion of the negroes so captured and decreed by the Mixed Commission to be free, must by this time have been for several years in Brazil, and have become entitled to their entire and unrestricted freedom, Her Majesty's government would wish to have a list of those who have been placed in the full enjoyment of liberty."

Two years afterwards, in 1850, Sir James Hudson, by

Lord Palmerston's instruction, proposed to the Brazilian government the appointment of a Mixed British and Brazilian Commission to inquire after these liberated Africans and emancipate them. This proposal was absolutely declined.

Afterwards the Brazilian government proposed to send to Liberia such of the free Africans as wished to return to Africa; but they ultimately refused to carry out this arrangement on Lord Palmerston's proposing to them to sign a protocol of agreement.

All this I state to show that it is not now for the first time, "twenty years after the last of them were disposed of, and thirty-four years after the first were apprenticed, the British government insists on their identification from amongst three millions of slaves, on the delivery of lists of them, and on their restitution to freedom."

"Far be it from us," it was said in the same article, "to maintain that in this question Brazil is right in all that is done; but we are sure the English government is wrong in the manner and temper in which it deals with Brazilian errors and shortcomings."

Lord Russell instructed me, for the first time, to address myself to the Brazilian government on the subject of the free Africans, in a despatch dated February 8, 1861, which I give entire. It will show the conciliatory spirit in which he desired the question to be treated, and I think no one can here find fault with "manner and temper."

"Foreign Office, February 8, 1861.

"Sir,—I have received your despatch of the 20th of December last, suggesting that you should be authorized to apply to the Brazilian government for a detailed list of the free blacks who have been handed over by the Mixed Commission Court to the care of the Brazilian authorities, specifying what has become of them, whether dead, emancipated, or still in service, with a view to a demand being made by Her Majesty's government for the emancipation of all those negroes who have served beyond the term of apprenticeship prescribed by the Brazilian laws.

"I have, in reply, to acquaint you that I approve of your making a communication to the Brazilian government in the sense suggested by you, and in doing so you will at the same time state that, inasmuch as it was under the authority of a joint British and Brazilian Commission that these blacks were emancipated, Her Majesty's government feel that they are entitled to ask for this information respecting them, and are bound to look to their welfare; and you will add, that Her Majesty's government do not doubt that the same good faith which the government of Brazil has evinced in putting a stop to the African slave-trade, will equally lead them to render justice to the unfortunate victims of the traffic by restoring them to the full amount of liberty to which they are entitled.

"I think it right to observe, for your information and guidance, that, as the government of Brazil has of late acted in perfect good faith in regard to the suppression of the trade in slaves between Africa and Brazil, it would be advisable, in any communications which you may have on this question of the emancipated negroes, to avoid as much as possible any discussions which may tend to continue the feeling of irritation which has so long existed in the public mind in Brazil against this country in connexion with the slave-trade.

"I am, &c.
(Signed) "J. RUSSELL."

I obeyed Lord Russell's instructions in a note to Senhor Paranhos, written May 18, 1861. There had just been a change of government, and I had received from Senhor

Sinimbú, the predecessor of Senhor Paranhos, a note, of which the tone and professions appeared satisfactory. The following is the main part of my note of May 18, 1861, asking for a list such as Sir James Hudson had asked for in 1848, and I think it cannot be said that there is anything objectionable in respect of "manner and temper" in this note :—

"I have been instructed by Her Majesty's government to request the government of the Emperor to furnish it with a list of the free blacks who were handed over by the Mixed Commission to the care of the Brazilian authorities, specifying what has become of them, whether dead, emancipated, or still in service; and I have been further instructed to state that, as it was under the authority of a joint British and Brazilian Commission that these blacks were emancipated, Her Majesty's government feel that they are entitled to ask for this information respecting them, and are bound to look to their welfare. I have also been instructed to say that Her Majesty's government do not doubt, that the same good faith which the government of Brazil have evinced in putting a stop to the African slave-trade, will equally lead them to render justice to the unfortunate victims of this traffic by restoring them to the full liberty to which they are entitled. The instructions which I thus fulfil were necessarily sent me without knowledge or expectation of Senhor Sinimbú's note of February 28th. This note, when known to Her Majesty's government, will confirm their confidence in the intentions of the government of Brazil, and their expectation of a ready compliance with the request which I have been instructed to make."

On the 27th of May, 1861, I wrote to Lord Russell an account of my conversations with the Brazilian Ministers on the subject of the liberated Africans; and I again ask whether there is anything objectionable in this report in respect of "manner and temper," and whether this is asking the Brazilian government "for impossibilities?"

"In my conversations with Senhor Paranhos and with the present Minister for Foreign Affairs, I have held this language: that Her Majesty's government wish this question settled, and see no reason why it should not be settled as they wish, amiably and amicably; that the object of the list which has been asked for is the complete emancipation of all those free Africans now serving the Brazilian government or private individuals, every one of whom must now have served more than fourteen years, the term of service prescribed by Brazilian laws; that Her Majesty's government give full praise to the proceedings of the Brazilian government which have extinguished the slave-trade, and will be equally ready to praise them for a settlement of this question, such as is required by treaty-obligations and by humanity; that Her Majesty's government have the greatest desire to avoid angry correspondence, and that no good object can be gained by opening old sores and raking up past abuses, if any such there be, which cannot now be remedied; that the great object is to place in freedom all the free Africans now living who can be traced, and that it would be desirable if the Brazilian government, while preparing the list asked for, would also consider and frankly discuss with Her Majesty's government the measures best to be taken for disposing of these free Africans when emancipated. I have told them also that this is a question in which Her Majesty's government simply call on that of Brazil to fulfil a duty prescribed by treaty-engagements, and that it is not a case in which they can be fairly called upon to trust to good intentions. My remarks were apparently well taken. In a speech lately made in the House of Commons by Mr. Cave, reported in the *Times* of February 27, it is said that there are in Brazil 25,000 *emancipados* who are entitled to their liberty, having been set free by British cruisers, and who, notwithstanding the period of their apprenticeship had expired, are still kept in slavery. I have found it difficult to obtain any certain estimate of the number of the free blacks in the country, or of those released by the Slave-trade Commission, but I think that these, with their children, would probably not exceed ten thousand."

The writer in the *Daily News* says that the planters have consigned many of these liberated Africans to slavery, and asks how the Brazilian government is to recover them. Several of those perhaps they cannot now recover; but let them try to do their best. Let them, at any rate, give lists of those who are known, and place in freedom all those who can be traced. The Brazilian government, however, have not admitted any difficulty, and claim to be blameless. Senhor Sinimbú made the following statements on the 28th of February, 1861:—

"The Undersigned, &c. has the honour to inform Mr. Christie, &c. that the Imperial government, desirous, as it always has been, to place the free Africans in a more advantageous position, has promoted, and continues to promote on a larger scale, the emancipation of those who, having completed the term of service fixed in the decree of the 28th of December, 1853, are entitled to the full enjoyment of their liberty. And in order that this measure may be generally extended to all who are entitled to it, the same Ministry has ordered the Judge of the Orphans' Court to furnish a list of all the free Africans who were first captured and adjudicated as such by the Mixed Brazilian and English Commission, and who were distributed for service. The Undersigned has the satisfaction to assure Mr. Christie that the Imperial government, in the performance of its duty, moved by its own sentiments of justice, will do all it can within the sphere of its attributions to better the condition of these Africans by promoting their emancipation and the most suitable measures for procuring useful and profitable employment for them."

The writer blames the English government for want of foresight in handing over these liberated Africans to the Brazilian government, and says that arrangements should have been made for carrying them to our own tropical colonies or to Africa. The regulations of the Conventions with Portugal and Brazil were reciprocal and equitable, and Brazil would probably have been dissatisfied with any other arrangement. The Africans were to be "delivered over to the government on whose territory the Commission which shall have so judged them shall be established." There were two Mixed Commissions, one at Sierra Leone, the other at Rio de Janeiro; those judged at Sierra Leone were to remain with the British government, and those judged at Rio with the Brazilian. "Each of the two governments binds itself to guarantee the liberty of such portion of these individuals as shall be respectively consigned to it." Here is a solemn guarantee given by Brazil in a treaty. Great Britain may or may not have shown want of foresight, but that does not nullify or excuse breach of faith on the other side. Mr. Canning appears to be blamed for want of foresight, because he did not expect that Brazil would be faithless to treaty-engagements.

The writer in the *Daily News* has found fault with the "manner and temper" of the English government. The correspondence on the subject of the free Africans in the Blue-books of 1861 and 1862 was reviewed in July, 1862, in one of the leading papers of Rio de Janeiro, the *Cor-*

*reio Mercantil*, edited by a well-known Deputy of the Liberal party, Dr. Octaviano, who expressed a different opinion. I sent Dr. Octaviano's article to Lord Russell, July 21, 1862, and said, "The writer observes that no information as to this correspondence has been given in the annual Report of the Foreign Minister of Brazil, and commends the courteous tone of your lordship's despatches and of the notes of this Legation."*

But a conciliatory tone had no effect on the Brazilian government, and Lord Russell's language afterwards became strong.

The writer in the *Daily News* thinks that the English government should have made arrangements for carrying these released Africans to our own tropical colonies. Some were so disposed of while Sir James Hudson and Mr. Southern were our Ministers at Rio. In a despatch of mine to Lord Russell, of May 27, 1861, I said, "In former years many of these blacks were taken to British West India colonies, among others, Demerara and Jamaica; and perhaps Her Majesty's government may be glad to consider whether some of them might not now be transported to the colonies which are demanding coolies." This suggestion of mine was altogether ridiculed in 1862 by the paid London correspondent of the *Jornal do Commercio* of Rio.

* As this goes through the press, I receive an article in the same Brazilian newspaper by the same writer, September 8, 1864, relating the most recent proceedings of the Brazilian government for emancipation of free Africans, stating that in the previous seven months, while Senhor Zacarias was Minister, 848 letters of emancipation had been given,—about as many as had been given in the preceding ten years. The writer ascribes the little done in the preceding ten years to "the pride and inconvenient language of uncourteous English Ministers;" he refers to his article of 1862 mentioned in the text, but seems to forget that he there praised the courteous tone of my notes, which, like Sir James Hudson's, were unavailing.

## CHAPTER III.

### THE STORY OF THE FREE AFRICANS.

RECENT EMANCIPATIONS OF FREE AFRICANS—INATTENTION OF BRAZILIAN GOVERNMENT TO BRITISH REPRESENTATIONS—EFFECT OF THE REPRISALS—BRAZILIAN DECREES—COMPLAINTS BY BRAZILIAN SENATORS AND DEPUTIES—MR. SEYMOUR FITZGERALD—"REVUE DES DEUX MONDES."

APPEAL was made, in a letter in the *Daily News* of July 29th, from "quotations from English diplomatic despatches," to "Brazilian documents quite as authentic," which, the writer said, show that the Brazilian government "is doing its duty" about the *emancipados*. The writer stated from these Brazilian documents that in the last four years four hundred *emancipados* had received freedom, and that Senhor Zacarias, the present Minister of Justice,* has said that he is completing arrangements begun by his predecessor, and "hopes to have the information ready by the next session of the Legislature."

The information as to the *emancipados* freed in the three years from April 30, 1859, to April 30, 1862, is all faithfully given, and I think with no unfairness to the Brazilian government, in my despatches to Lord Russell, published in the Slave-trade Correspondence, Class B.

On February 4, 1861, I reported to Lord Russell that

* Senhor Zacarias, having become President of the Council and Minister of Justice in January, 1864, resigned, with all his colleagues, in the beginning of September. A new Ministry has been formed.

the provisions of a decree of December, 1853, for giving freedom, on their petition, to privately employed *emancipados* after fourteen years' service, had been extended to *emancipados* employed in government-establishments. I wrote as follows :—

"Your lordship will see that the Minister of Justice announces that the Council of State had, on his application, interpreted the decree of December, 1853, in such a manner as to extend its benefits to free Africans employed in government-establishments. Your lordship is aware that Mr. Howard strongly remonstrated at the time against that decree, as enabling only such of the free Africans as served private individuals to obtain emancipation after fourteen years' service. I am happy to be able to state that the Minister of Justice is giving some effect to the new interpretation of the decree, and that generally he is granting more letters of emancipation. During the whole of the twelve months from April 30, 1859, to May 1, 1860, letters of emancipation were granted only to thirty-eight. I have been furnished with a list of such letters granted from December 28, 1859, to July 17, 1860, less than eight months. The total number is sixty-four, of which thirty-nine are free blacks employed in government-establishments."

On June 20, 1861, I informed Lord Russell from the annual Report of the Minister of Justice :—

"It is stated that during the past year letters of emancipation have been given to one hundred and ten free Africans. This is a larger number than in previous years, but still a very small number."

On July 21, 1862, I reported :—

"Letters of emancipation have been given to one hundred and five free Africans during the past year,—not a very large number. Senhor Lobato states that he has given orders to the Chief of Police to collect in the House of Correction,—it is to be presumed with a view to giving them freedom,—all the free Africans assigned to private individuals who have served for fourteen years. The Mixed Commission, which consigned these free Africans to the care of the Brazilian government, having ceased to exist in 1845, seventeen years ago, there cannot be one of them who has not served more than fourteen years. The measure ordered by Senhor Lobato, if applied to all the free Africans, whether serving private individuals or the government, would cause the emancipation of the whole class."

$38 + 64 + 110 + 105 = 317$; and the difference between this and 400, viz. eighty-three, is, I suppose, the number freed in 1862-3, of which there is no report in the English Blue-book, diplomatic relations having been suspended in July, 1863. However, the four hundred admitted, what are they among so many?

Out of a total number moderately estimated at about ten thousand (Mr. Cave, a very intelligent member of the House of Commons, said twenty-five thousand,) all of whom should have been in freedom at latest in 1859 (for fourteen years' apprenticeship must then have expired for the last of the *emancipados* of the Rio Mixed Commission Court,) four hundred have been freed during the last four years, when, under Lord Russell's instructions, I was perseveringly pressing the question on the Brazilian government; and previously to these four years there is little or nothing to show: and during these four years I could get no lists in answer to courteously and temperately worded requests, nor could I, as may be seen by reference to the Blue-books, get attention to many representations and inquiries about the *emancipados* employed in government-establishments, about which there could not have been difficulty in giving information, if there were the will to give it.

Can we consider this tardy bit-by-bit emancipation of four hundred in the last four years a refutation of Lord Palmerston's statement? All that is proved is, that late in the day the Brazilian government has begun to do a little of what should all have been done long ago.

Lord Palmerston said on July 12th :—

"This matter has been the subject of frequent representations on the part of the British government; but these representations have not been attended to. We have asked for lists of these negroes, but have not succeeded in obtaining them. . . . . All the efforts we have made to obtain justice for those *emancipados* have failed, and we have not been able to obtain a list of them. We know that when they are assigned to an owner, he has employed them in conjunction with his slaves; and when a slave died he put an *emancipado* in his place, and reported the death of the *emancipado*, and not the death of the slave."

The accuracy of all this is not disputed.

Mr. Baillie, Chargé d'affaires at Rio, wrote to Lord Russell, December 30, 1861 :—

"Numbers of these Africans have been, *and are still being*, fraudulently consigned to hopeless and irretrievable slavery. The conduct of the government in conniving at such a state of things will, perhaps, be less wondered at when it is remembered that members of the Cabinet are frequently personally interested. For instance, I am informed that the head of the present Administration, the Marquis of Caxias, has not less than twenty-three or twenty-four blacks in his service, and the same may be said of many other Brazilians distinguished by their position and influence in this country."

Lord Russell wrote on the 6th of June, 1863, with special reference to the neglect of the Brazilian government in not answering my representations and inquiries, some of them a renewal of inquiries of Sir James Hudson as old as 1848:—

"It is notorious that the government of Brazil has for a long course of time habitually disregarded the representations made to it by Her Majesty's diplomatic agents in Brazil; and as one instance of this, it may be mentioned that six notes addressed to the Brazilian government between the 19th of December, 1860, and the 17th of April, 1862, have remained, if not unnoticed, at all events without satisfactory answers. These notes, written under instructions from Her Majesty's government, asked the Brazilian government for returns as to the number, and explanations as to the condition, of some thousands of negroes captured in slave-trading vessels, and decreed many years ago by the Mixed Commission at Rio to be entitled to freedom, but who, there is good reason to believe, are up to the present time held in bondage, contrary to law, and in violation of treaty-engagements. I may also refer to Mr. Christie's note to the Marquis of Abrantes of the 12th February last, in which, in obedience to instructions from Her Majesty's government, he called the attention of the Brazilian government to the various communications which he had addressed to them, and which remained unanswered, and claimed for all the Africans who had been liberated by the late Mixed Commission Court unconditional freedom. To this note, it is true, a reply was returned by the Brazilian government, but the Marquis of Abrantes' note of the 28th of February cannot, under the circumstances, and taking into account previous delays, be considered as satisfactory. In this note the Marquis of Abrantes states that the Brazilian government were studying with earnestness and solicitude the question as to the free Africans, in order to proceed with such discretion and prudence as the case required. But the result is that Her Majesty's government are as far as ever from receiving the information repeatedly asked for, and which the treaty-engagements in favour of the liberated Africans justify them in demanding."

Can it be a triumphant or sufficient answer to all this that four hundred *emancipados* have been set free during the last four years, and that the present Minister of Justice has reported that he continues to work at what the Marquis of Abrantes and his colleagues were studying with earnestness and solicitude in February, 1863, and hopes next year to give the information which during eighteen years Her Majesty's government have vainly asked for?

There is no doubt that the reprisals have had an effect on the Brazilian government. I wrote to Lord Russell, February 26, 1862, after the reprisals: "The attention of the Brazilian government is, I have reason to believe, seriously turned to this subject of the free Africans." And on March 5, I wrote, sending an answer which I had then quickly obtained: "Your lordship will observe that on this occasion I have received a sufficiently prompt answer: since the reprisals the Marquis of Abrantes has become very prompt in answering."

The writer went on to make further statements in praise of the conduct of the Brazilian government towards the free Africans:—

"It (the Brazilian government) has made decree after

decree for their advantage and ultimate freedom; it has limited the period of apprenticeship; it now directly intervenes when the *emancipados* are known to be apprenticed to private persons to ensure their freedom when the term of service is over; in many and increasing instances, as for example, when the conduct of the Africans apprenticed to public establishments is good, it gives them freedom before the expiration of their apprenticeship. I have before me in public documents particulars of a considerable number so restored to freedom by Senhor Sinimbú in 1862."

These, restored to freedom by Senhor Sinimbú in 1862, are of course included in the famous four hundred already mentioned, so that this is not an additional merit. But what means the giving them freedom before the expiration of their apprenticeship, the fourteen years' apprenticeship having expired for the very last of those liberated by the Anglo-Brazilian Mixed Commission five years ago, in 1859? The writer proceeds:—

"No later than June 4, 1861, I find an order of the government to the effect that whenever and wherever Africans under apprenticeship either present themselves or are presented by others to the police tribunal, they are retained by the State, and not allowed to go back to private persons, in order that, their apprenticeship over, their freedom may be effectually secured. And of this order the *emancipados* are taking advantage."

Those who have taken advantage of this order are also included, of course, in the famous four hundred.

Such a regulation, made known to me by Senhor Sinimbú, I reported to Lord Russell in a despatch of March 23, 1861, and I gave full credit to Senhor Sinimbú's statement. Again, on July 21, 1862, in a passage already quoted, I mentioned orders given by the then Minister of Justice (Lobato) to collect *emancipados* at the House of Correction, with a view to their being freed.

But while such regulations are cited as proof of the unreasonableness of the English government in complaining of anything, there are Brazilians, and Brazilians of high position, greatly dissatisfied about the *emancipados.*

I reported, September 30, 1862, that a distinguished Senator, the Viscount Jequitinhona, "complained of the great difficulties in the way of their obtaining letters of emancipation, and to the fact of their having now generally exceeded the fourteen years of apprenticeship prescribed by Brazilian legislation."

Senhor Madureira, a Deputy, thus spoke on June 6, 1862:—

"The slavery of free Africans still continues; the Africans taken in Brazil have all a right to their liberty. The decree of 1853, which mentioned fourteen years for their emancipation, was a provisional decree, which cannot be regarded as a permanent law. There are, then, at this day in Brazil free Africans who cannot be entirely free, who must be subject to the individuals to whom they have been assigned, subject to the administrators of public works, &c. How do all these live? Well, then, does the Brazilian nation require the services of these poor men? Is the nation not able to pay wages to free men for their labour? I hope that the Minister of Justice will revoke that decree; will declare all the free Africans really free, and will order their passes to be given in order to live as they may think fit. I have read even with disgust in the Report of the Minister of Justice of this year, that those

Africans who had completed the fourteen years were to go to the House of Correction, and there be at the order of nobody knows whom. I do not know what the Africans have to do in that house when they are entitled to their liberty. Are they not free?"

In sending home this speech to Lord Russell, I observed that "it does its author high honour, and its sentiments are perfect." And I think that most Englishmen will concur in this praise.

No one doubts that the Brazilian government have made many decrees, or that they have limited apprenticeship. What is the particular merit of the limitation of fourteen years' apprenticeship, which has generally not been observed? Are the decrees which have been made good decrees, and have they been observed in practice?

The decree of 1853 was strongly but fruitlessly remonstrated against by Mr. (now Sir Henry) Howard, the then English Minister at Rio, because it was confined in its operation to *emancipados* in private service, and because it threw even on them the burden of a petition and its expenses before they could get freedom at the end of fourteen years' apprenticeship.

At last, in 1861, when I had begun to press the Brazilian government on this question, the decree of 1853 was extended to the *emancipados* employed in government service. Why was not this done sooner? Why not at once? Why were Sir Henry Howard's remonstrances not attended to?

In May, 1861, the Senator Carneiro de Campos, who was named Minister for Foreign Affairs in the short-lived administration formed by Senhor Zacarias in 1862,* spoke thus in the Brazilian Senate :—

"I appeal briefly to the government in reference to a fact which I believe is still practised in our country, not in regard to slaves, but respecting Africans whom I consider to be worse off, and unduly so, than slaves—I mean the Africans who were destined to serve the State. The free Africans who were distributed among the public departments are destined, by an order of the government, to serve until they die. I make this appeal to the government, because it appears to me that a man declared free, and who is serving in the public establishments, cannot be considered as a slave until he dies, thus remaining worse off than those who were distributed to private persons."

In a communication from a Brazilian, which I forwarded to Lord Russell, May 27, 1861, it is said :—

"Does not all the world know that the lot of the Africans delivered to public departments is much worse, even in this capital, than that of those confided to private individuals? In the public departments no care is taken of their education; they are only taught the necessity of being obedient; their faults are punished with military rigour, and the civil authorities have nothing to do with their condition."

In 1863 a parliamentary paper, entitled "Correspondence respecting Liberated Slaves in Brazil," was presented to both Houses of Parliament, having been moved for by Lord Brougham in the House of Lords, which contained almost the whole of the correspondence printed this year under the head of Brazil in the annual

* While this is passing through the press, I learn that Senhor Carneiro de Campos has, on a change of Ministry, become Minister of Finance.

Blue-book, Class B, and contained that account taken from the *Diario do Rio* of the difficulties in the way of freedom for an *emancipado* which Lord Palmerston lately produced in the House of Commons, and which Mr. Seymour Fitzgerald had never heard of. I may here mention, by way of parenthesis, that Mr. Fitzgerald's excuse, that the document had appeared only in a Blue-book which is not usually distributed to members, does not avail him, as the parliamentary paper of 1863 was distributed to members of both Houses; but it might, I think, be expected that one who has been Under Secretary of State for Foreign Affairs, who now takes so prominent a part in questions of foreign policy as member of the Opposition, and who has also put himself forward as the protector of Brazil, might consider it his duty to ask for and obtain every year from the proper office in the House of Commons the annual Blue-book of Slave-Trade Correspondence. On the appearance, last year, of the "Correspondence respecting Liberated Slaves in Brazil," the paid London correspondent of the *Jornal do Commercio* wrote to that Brazilian journal that public opinion in England condemned the Brazilian government in the matter of the *emancipados,* that freedom was clearly their right, and that the Brazilian government was altogether in the wrong.

Lord Palmerston's statement as to false reports made of deaths of *emancipados* who were really made slaves of, had lately appeared in the *Revue des Deux Mondes,* in an article on "Brazil and Colonization," July 15, 1862. The writer, M. Elisée Reclus, says:—

"A clause in the treaty with England provided that the

blacks rescued from slavery should receive their liberty only after having served an apprenticeship under the guardianship of the Brazilian government. These agents were themselves planters, who received on their properties the newly-landed slaves; and, in order to escape from the embarrassing obligation to give them liberty, took care to exchange their names with labourers old or sick. Whenever one of these last died, they placed one of the newcomers' names on the list of deaths, and thus they made it all square with the government, which amiably closed its eyes to these peccadilloes."

# CHAPTER IV.

## THE STORY OF THE FREE AFRICANS.

HISTORICAL SKETCH—LORD ABERDEEN'S INQUIRIES, 1846—LORD HOWDEN—SIR JAMES HUDSON—MR. CONSUL HESKETH'S LIST OF 857 FREE AFRICANS, 1851—MR. SOUTHERN—SIR HENRY HOWARD—MYSELF—LIST OF 1301 FREE AFRICANS, 1860—FREE AFRICANS OF ITAPURA—WAGES DUE TO THE FREE AFRICANS NOT PAID.

THE public will be best put in possession of "the truth, the whole truth, and nothing but the truth," about the *emancipados* or free Africans in Brazil liberated by British cruisers, by a continuous historical narrative from our parliamentary series of Slave-trade Correspondence, Class B.

The Convention of Great Britain with Brazil of November 23, 1826, which provided for the suppression of Brazilian slave-trade, incorporated all the provisions and regulations of the existing Conventions with Portugal, among which was the following as to the negroes taken from captured slave vessels:—

"As to the slaves, they shall receive from the Mixed Commission a certificate of emancipation, and shall be delivered over to the government on whose territory the Commission which shall have so judged them shall be established, to be employed as servants or free labourers. Each of the two governments binds itself to guarantee the liberty of such portion of these individuals as shall be respectively consigned to it."—(Art. 7 of Regulations appended to the Convention with Portugal of July 28, 1817.)

The Brazilian government passed a law, on the 7th of November, 1831, for the supervision of the free Africans who came into their care under the above stipulations, placing them under the Court of Orphans, with a Curator specially appointed to look after them, and making regulations for their employment under government, and treatment until they should be re-exported to Africa.

On October 29, 1834, an *aviso* (order of government) was issued setting forth difficulties as to re-exportation, and directing, for "the better treatment and civilization" of the *emancipados*, that the Judge of Orphans and Chief of Police should dispose of their services by auction within the municipality of Rio de Janeiro, those who took them on hire being bound to give them up whenever the Legislature decided on their fate or the government determined to re-export them.

Another *aviso* of the following year (November 19, 1835) extended the letting out by competition of the services of the *emancipados* to the Provinces, the acceptance of tenders being made dependent on the permission of the government or of the Presidents of Provinces.

It was specially prescribed that the wages paid to the state for these *emancipados* should form a fund towards meeting the expenses of re-exportation, and a separate coffer was established, with Treasurer, Clerk, &c.

On the 13th of August, 1846, Lord Aberdeen directed our Minister at Rio, Mr. Hamilton, to obtain from the Brazilian government information about the condition and prospects of the free Africans who had been consigned to their care under the provisions of the Convention of 1826. It fell to Lord Howden to send to Lord Palmerston, on the 11th of December, 1847, an answer from the Brazilian government to the inquiry ordered by Lord Aberdeen.

"On the 22d of last March," said Lord Howden, "Mr. Hudson addressed a note to the Imperial government, but, as no notice was taken of it, he renewed the demand for this information on the 3d of August last. I have the pleasure at length of being able to transmit a note from the Minister for Foreign Affairs, in answer to these several applications. The assurances, as well as the account of the manner in which the supervision over these liberated Africans is exercised, are sufficiently satisfactory; but I have considerable misgivings as to the practical part of the question, and the way in which these paternal intentions of this government, as described, are worked out."

Then, seventeen years ago, only eleven or twelve years after the beginning of the letting out of the Africans to private individuals in the provinces, there could not have been any of that "impossibility" of identifying free Africans or preventing their being made slaves of, which has been alleged, and the Brazilian government declared that all was right.

The Brazilian Minister for Foreign Affairs, Senhor Saturnino de Souza e Oliveira, told Lord Howden, on November 16, 1847, that the *emancipados* in question were looked after by the Court of Orphans and a special Guardian or Curator; that this post of Curator was always conferred on a doctor of laws; that it was part of his duty, on the death of any of them, "to cause a certificate of decease, in the presence of witnesses and of the Judge of Orphans, and of his clerk, to be drawn up, verifying the identity of the individual, and that the person who may announce the death of an African taken as a servant can only in that way be exonerated." Senhor Saturnino proceeded to tell Lord Howden :—

"The Imperial government knows that the Guardian is frequently called upon by the said Africans with representations of ill-treatment, and that many of them have been withdrawn from the persons to whom they were confided, on its having been ascertained by their Guardian that they were not well treated. The Imperial government, faithful to the obligation it contracted, to guarantee the liberty of the Africans given up to it, has carefully endeavoured to fulfil this obligation by adopting divers measures, which have been communicated to the government of Her Britannic Majesty, to the end of guaranteeing that liberty, and of giving employment to the said Africans. . . . . It is possible that, in the practical execution of those measures, abuses incompatible with the condition of free men may be met with : in that case it appertains to the government, and to the authorities charged with the execution of those measures, to put a stop to any restriction which may perchance interfere with the liberty of the said Africans. The Imperial government has been careful in repressing those abuses ; those which it or the said authorities have had knowledge of have been repressed, because its protection is sufficient to cause them to cease from the moment in which their existence is known ; the administration which protects those individuals under the eye of the government, to which alone it can render an account of its management, has proceeded with regularity."

Lord Howden had misgivings as to the correctness of this cheerful statement. A year before, on November 17, 1846, Mr. Hudson had drawn a sad picture of the sufferings and wrongs of these *emancipados* in a despatch to Lord Palmerston, from which I have already quoted.

"Tricks are practised with these Africans, in transferring them from one master to another, until they are lost sight of and forgotten; in sending them to considerable distances from Rio de Janeiro, in supplying certain influential politicians, and men in authority and of influence, with them, as a means of ensuring a certain line of conduct, in jobbing with them in one way or another, in giving false certificates of death or disappearance, against all of which it requires constant watchfulness and care."

Lord Palmerston, on receiving the despatch of Lord Howden, of December 11, 1847, conveying Senhor Saturnino's general assurances, directed, on March 31, 1848, more particular inquiries to be addressed to the Brazilian government. Mr. Hudson, who had in the meantime become Chargé d'affaires at Rio, gave effect to Lord Palmerston's instructions on June 26, 1848, by asking the series of questions already quoted at page 9. To these questions no answer was ever given.

On February 27, 1850, Lord Palmerston furnished Mr. Hudson with the draft of a note to be presented to the Brazilian government on the general non-fulfilment of its treaty-obligations as to slave-trade; at the end of the note was a proposal for Commissioners to examine and free the *emancipados*. Lord Palmerston said:

"Those emancipated negroes ought by this time to be in the full enjoyment of their liberty. Her Majesty's government have reason to believe that they are not in such condition, but that the greater part of them are still practically held in bondage. Her Majesty's government propose, therefore, that British and Brazilian Commissioners should be appointed to examine personally these emancipated negroes, in order to give to them all the full and real enjoyment of that freedom which has been decreed to be their right."

Mr. Hudson gave effect to this instruction, and on

October 10, 1850, reported to Lord Palmerston that Senhor Paulino, then Minister for Foreign Affairs, had told him in conversation, "that the Imperial government will find no difficulty in giving complete and entire liberty to such of them as have served their time as apprentices."

No difficulty! Yet now we are told that it is, and always has been, an impossibility. No difficulty! Senhor Paulino still lives; he has now the title of Viscount Uruguay; he is now a diligent Senator and Councillor of State, one of the highest in reputation of Brazilian statesmen. Can he explain why that about which there was no difficulty in 1850, was not then done? Can he explain why it is not done even yet, fourteen years later? Will Viscount Uruguay assert that not a word is to be said against Brazil, because in the last four years 400 *emancipados* have been set free, and the present Minister of Justice hopes to give the English government some information next year?

Senhor Paulino on the same occasion proposed to hand over to the British Legation such of the *emancipados* as would wish to proceed to a British settlement, and send the rest to Liberia. Lord Palmerston eagerly accepted the proposal, but the Brazilian government then receded, and ultimately refused to execute their own plan.

On November 11, 1850, Mr. Hudson sent to Lord Palmerston another remarkable account of the pitiable condition of these *emancipados,* who, according to Senhor Saturnino, were so admirably overlooked by the Brazilian government, and who, according to Senhor Paulino, now Viscount Uruguay, could all without difficulty be placed in complete freedom.

"The position of these Africans is most wretched: they are ill-used, ill-fed, beaten without mercy and without reason, sold, false certificates given of their death, and, in short, every man's hand seems to be raised against them; they have no chance of real freedom in Brazil. I have endeavoured during many months past to counteract the gross injustice which is committed against these unhappy people, by instructing Her Majesty's Consul to receive their complaints, and to enter their names and the names of their masters in a register, so that I might have some check upon the latter, and afford some hope of justice to the former. I have never ceased to urge the claims of these Africans to their liberty; but five years of useless remonstrance appeared to me to be too much, and I told the Brazilian Minister for Foreign Affairs that the case of these Africans would some day be brought to an abrupt conclusion by their presenting themselves to the British Admiral and claiming his protection, which I knew would be granted to them."

I need not say that the Mr. Hudson from whom I have been quoting is the present Sir James Hudson. He was then comparatively unknown. His name is now an authority, and will command general respect. He did not believe the fine statements of the Brazilian government; he described to Lord Palmerston the truth; he could not get the Brazilian government to do its duty. The failure of duty on the part of the Brazilian government was, of course, Sir James Hudson's fault, and not the fault of the Brazilian government, which, we are told, requires "to be let alone by the Foreign-office, to be courteously treated by English Ministers, to have confidence substituted for distrust in its proceedings," and which does its duty, "not so fast as we may wish, because in a tropical country the mechanism of government moves rather slowly, but substantially and in good faith."

I have already mentioned that the Viscount Jequitinhonha complained in the Brazilian Senate in 1862 of the treatment of the *emancipados.* The same Senator, when bearing the name of Senhor Montezuma, had raised his voice in behalf of these poor creatures ten years before, in a speech of which Mr. Hudson forwarded a summary in a despatch to Lord Palmerston of October 14, 1851. Senhor Montezuma was very minute in his demands for information, and wanted to know, *inter alia,* the amount of the wages received for the services of the free Africans. He concluded his speech with a remark which is particularly deserving of attention :

"He did not mind its being said that in speaking in this manner he was extenuating the proceedings of England; he was as good a Brazilian as any of those who express that opinion, and the sentiments of Brazilian patriotism were as deeply implanted in his breast as in those of persons whose pens are productive of such flourishing articles."

On the 11th of December, 1851, just before leaving Brazil, Mr. Hudson forwarded to Lord Palmerston a most remarkable document,—a report of Mr. Hesketh, the Consul at Rio de Janeiro, on the state of the *emancipados.* Mr. Hesketh had been instructed by Mr. Hudson to open a register for the free Africans, and he had prepared with difficulty a list of 857. Mr. Hesketh wrote :—

"Not having access to any official record of their names, I was limited to the means afforded by notifying to the

Africans, through their comrades, to present themselves at this Consulate. This has been a tedious process, especially as many could only come by stealth, and some not at all, sending instead what particulars they could. However, the number emancipated by the Mixed Commission Court must have been much larger, and there is but too much reason to fear that many of these liberated Africans were removed far into the interior and sold, remaining in an even more helpless state of slavery than those whose names I now record. From the statements made by those who appeared at the Consulate, an opinion can be formed of their unprotected condition, and of the unjustifiable treatment to which a portion of them have been doomed. It will also be seen that several of the women have had offspring, and that a portion of these children have either been baptized as slaves or their births withheld from parish registration, and in all probability few reported to the Curator. Some of the Africans who presented themselves gave the names of their deceased comrades, in a few instances stating that they perished from barbarous treatment.

"The result of these individual reports is a deplorable picture of the unfeeling avarice actuating a portion of the individuals who undertook, as if in mockery, the welfare of those unfortunate Africans, some of whom declared to the unhappy beings they were bound to protect, that they have not even the safeguard of being held as their masters' property. These Africans appear to have been gradually distributed amongst the respectable classes; however, nearly the whole of them have long since finished the legal period of servitude to their actual masters.

"I have taken an opportunity of speaking to the Curator on this subject, when he acknowledged that his authority was set at nought by those who abused the Africans; for, when he has attended to their complaints, and removed an African, the master has had generally sufficient influence to obtain an order from superior authority to send back the identical African to the person who had abused his trust. There are three instances of the sale of these liberated Africans within what ought to be the personal inspection of the Curator; but I apprehend that to bring forward these accusations, before the three victims are in safety, might expose them to an immediate and worse fate.

"The list shows that a large number of Africans are employed in the House of Correction, at the department of Public Works, and at the Military Arsenal, all of whom complain of bad treatment. There are also several at the Dockyard who appear to be much better treated, being healthy, contented, and comfortably clothed and fed."

Mr. Hesketh began to make his list in November, 1849, and, under the difficulties he has described, by the 9th of July, 1851, he had made a list of 857. How much more might the Brazilian government have done by the same date, if they had begun when Mr. Hudson applied to them for a list on June 26, 1848! From that day to this they have given no list to Her Majesty's government.

Mr. Southern succeeded Mr. Hudson as Minister in Brazil at the end of 1851. He died at Rio a little more than a year after. On December 10, 1852, Mr. Southern called attention to the case of a poor free black who had served the Brazilian government for sixteen years in the Military Arsenal, and had received no wages.

I should mention that a law was made on September 4, 1850, prohibiting the further hiring out of the *emancipados* to private individuals, and prescribing that they should be employed under the guardianship of the government until they were re-exported at the expense of the State. Those at that time in the service of private individuals were, however, not withdrawn, and there has been no re-exportation.

On December 28, 1853, a decree was issued by the Brazilian government, ordering that the "liberated Africans who shall have served private individuals during the space of fourteen years are to be emancipated, upon their petitioning for the same." The term of apprenticeship had never yet been fixed. It was now fixed by this decree at fourteen years, the Brazilian government availing itself of a precedent in a Portuguese decree of 1815. But it will be seen that this decree was limited to free Africans serving private individuals. No term was fixed for the apprenticeship of free Africans serving the government. The decree also required the free Africans to petition. Mr. Howard (now Sir Henry Howard, and our Minister at Hanover) was then Minister in Brazil, and he addressed an able note to the Minister for Foreign Affairs, entreating the Brazilian government to extend the benefits of this decree to all the free Africans, those serving the government as well as those serving private individuals, and to dispense with the requirement of a petition. "It is to be feared," said Mr. Howard, "that the knowledge of their proposed release may be withheld from some of them by their masters, and that even when this is not the case, they may not know how to set about asking for their liberty. It would, therefore, be desirable that the Imperial government should dispense with that formality, and at once cause their manumission to be announced to them."

Mr. Howard was replied to on February 3, 1854, by the then Minister for Foreign Affairs, Senhor Limpo de Abreo, now the Viscount Abaeté, who, like his predecessor,

Paulino, Viscount Uruguay, is an active Senator, and member of the Council of State. Mark his reply. Referring to the *avisos* of 1834 and 1835, authorizing the letting out of the *emancipados*, he thus lauds the past:—

"The above-mentioned instructions, in ordering the services of the Africans to be farmed solely to persons of recognised probity and honour, and imposing on the latter the duty of clothing and taking care of them, and the responsibility for any abuse to which such persons might be guilty, had in view the double object of aiding, by means of their wages, the re-exportation of the Africans, and of keeping them in the meantime under a tutelar administration which might support and direct them in their state of ignorance."

Senhor Limpo de Abreo avoids in his note the question of extending the decree to free Africans employed by the government, but he says of all the free Africans in ques- that "it is certain that the term has now either expired, or is about to expire, for a large portion." But he objects to the dispensing with the requirement of a petition, because public order might be jeopardized by the speedy and simultaneous emancipation of "a large number in a body, tumultuously and without any formality," because he thinks that the Curator will protect their interests, and, lastly, because "the government of His Imperial Majesty, with the object of favouring and protecting these unfortunate persons, is disposed not to consent to the provisions of the decree being eluded." Again nothing is said of the impossibility or difficulty of identification.

To this note of Senhor Limpo de Abreo, now Viscount Abaeté, Mr. Howard replied on March 3, 1854.

He happily replied to the allegation of the danger to

public order which might arise from the immediate emancipation of a large number by the remark that, "if the Imperial government had gradually emancipated the Africans in question, any danger from simultaneous emancipation would have been obviated." The same allegation has several times been made since by Brazilian Ministers, while little or nothing has been done to give effect to the decree of December, 1853. Senhor Paranhos said the same thing to Mr. Scarlett in 1856. The Marquis of Abrantes said the same thing to me in 1863; and I replied, on March 4, 1863, much as, nine years before, Sir Henry Howard had replied to the Viscount Abaeté:—

"You speak of the inconveniences which may follow from a general sudden emancipation of the free Africans, who are without education and experience. Let me remind your Excellency that Her Majesty's government have been urging this question on the government of the Emperor, from time to time and in various ways, for the last seventeen years, and that similar language was held in 1856 to Mr. Scarlett, by Senhor Paranhos, who at the same time declared that it was the intention of the Imperial government to give all these free Africans their freedom. Had the interval been well employed in gradual emancipation, all might now be free. As it is, every free African who was liberated by the British and Brazilian Mixed Commission Court must have served more than fourteen years. And what was the object of this fourteen years' apprenticeship but to train them for the full enjoyment of freedom?"

Mr. Howard turned to account Senhor Limpo de Abreo's admission that the wages of the *emancipados* were destined to meet the expenses of re-exportation, and reminded him that the Brazilian *aviso* of 1835 had said, "the produce of the hiring shall be applied either in aid of the expenses of the re-exportation of the Africans, or for their benefit;" and he suggested that, as re-exportation seemed to be given up, the accumulated wages should be applied in some other way to the benefit of the poor creatures. He concluded by mentioning, as an instance of the difficulties which were in the way of the *emancipados* for obtaining freedom by petition, the case of one of them who had got the English Consul (Mr. Westwood) to prepare a petition for him, which was presented to the Curator—who was then required to procure a certificate that he had the means of leaving the Empire—who then presented a certificate from the Consul, which did not suffice—who then got a certificate from the captain who had agreed to take him to Africa, countersigned by the Consul—and who was then obliged to get and pay for a passport from the Ministry of Foreign Affairs.

"Claudio's certificate of liberty," says Mr. Howard, "was then delivered, but he was obliged to obtain from your Excellency's office a passport, which I understand he had to pay for, besides incurring other charges consequent on the necessity of employing an agent, and which it would have been impossible for him to meet had he not been assisted. I have not learnt that the Curator lent him any pecuniary aid; the question may therefore be asked, What became of the produce of his hiring? It is necessary to add that these various formalities, and the steps that Claudio was obliged to take, and of which I have only related a part, were not accomplished under several weeks, and required, it may be affirmed, more perseverance and energy to overcome than can be found among the generality of Africans."

"What became of the produce of his hiring?" That

is a question which the Brazilian government have yet to answer for all and each of the *emancipados* who have been either privately or publicly employed.

I hurriedly pass over the six years between Mr. Howard's correspondence with Senhor Limpo de Abreo and my arrival in Brazil. Mr. Howard, Mr. Jerningham (Chargé d'Affaires,) and Mr. Scarlett successively reminded the Brazilian government of their duties and their promises, under instructions from Lord Clarendon; and on October 13, 1856, Mr. Scarlett wrote to Lord Clarendon that Senhor Paranhos had promised to write him a note on the subject, and had stated that he did not think it desirable or safe to free all these blacks at once, but that it was the determination of the Brazilian government to abolish slavery, and they would be gradually placed in possession of liberty. But there is no trace in the Blue-books of this promised note, and no sign of effect given to the promise of gradual emancipation, till the subject begins to be treated in my despatches to Lord Russell in 1860.

How much might have been done in the fourteen years between Senhor Saturnino's fine professions to Lord Howden in 1846, and the beginning of my mission in 1860, if the Brazilian government had sincerely wished to do their duty towards the poor blacks and Her Majesty's government, and to fulfil the promises made by Senhor Saturnino, Viscount Uruguay, Viscount Abaeté, and Senhor Paranhos! The last-named gentleman is also living, and has lately been made a Senator.

I reported to Lord Russell, on May 17, 1860, that I had received a list, which had been for some time in preparation, having been ordered by Mr. Jerningham in 1856, of *emancipados* in the service of private individuals, comprising 1,301, with the monthly wages of each and length of service. I stated :—

"The monthly wages were generally from ten to eighteen milreis a month ;* low wages for this country. Many are hired out at as low a rate as four to six milreis a month, and, in some few cases, from forty to fifty milreis a month are given. Most of these blacks have been in their respective services from eighteen to twenty-six years ; very few indeed have served less than fourteen years. The persons whom the negroes serve are responsible to the government for these wages ; and I am informed that, if the government receive the wages, the negroes seldom, if ever, get anything, and that the sums go into the National Treasury. The blacks, I am informed, generally receive nothing but food and clothing."

I added, however, with caution, notwithstanding my alleged passionate desire to feed the fierceness of the Foreign Office :—

"It has taken a long time to prepare this list, and it has been made with much trouble and care ; but of course there may be some errors in it, and I do not make myself answerable for the correctness of the information which has been given me as to the negroes generally receiving no money, the wages not being always paid to the government, and, when paid, generally going into the National Treasury.

It is, however, all too true.

I added on this occasion that I was also informed that, beside the 1,301 in the list in the service of private individuals, there were about 2,000 in the service of the government in the two Provinces of Rio de Janeiro and

* The milreis is 2*s.* 3*d.*

St. Paul's, and probably 2,000 more serving in the other Provinces.

Now, why should not the Brazilian government have been able all this time to prepare for her Majesty's government a list like the list of 1,301 made under Mr. Jerningham's orders, and delivered to me in 1860? Why should not the Brazilian government up to this time have been able to give Her Majesty's government a list of at least those employed in government establishments, of which surely it must have been easy to make out a complete list in three years, to say nothing of sixteen years, counting from Sir James Hudson's formal request of 1848? As to the government-employed *emancipados*, one year should be amply sufficient to collect from all the provinces the lists of all the government establishments, even though "in a tropical country the mechanism of government moves rather slowly."

On July 24, 1860, I reported to Lord Russell that I had received some information about an intended forced removal of a number of the *emancipados* from a government establishment in the province of St. Paul's to another very distant one on the Upper Paraguay River; and here began a series of inquiries about these free blacks and others in government establishments in the provinces of St. Paul's and Mattogrosso, which, as Lord Russell declared in his despatch of June 6, 1863, "remained, if not unnoticed, at all events without satisfactory answers."

On November 12, 1862, I referred to a report of the Minister of Marine on one of these establishments:—

"The report mentions that of free Africans and slaves, thus mixing them together, there are in all 131 in the establishment of Itapura. The coupling in this way of free Africans and slaves will help to show your lordship how the free Africans are practically treated; and if no other motive existed, the inquiries which I have been making during the last two years should have led the Brazilian government to ascertain the number of free Africans in distinction from the slaves. But it seems as if the Brazilian government are determined not to give any of the desired information about the free Africans. Itapura is considered a most unhealthy place, and its great unhealthiness has been the subject of much discussion in the last session of the Legislature."

On the 24th of November, 1862, I sent to Lord Russell a copy of new regulations issued for the government of the free Africans at Itapura, and wrote as follows:—

"Your lordship will see that the free Africans in the Itapura naval establishment are to be organized under military discipline, with the name of 'Company of Itapura Workmen,' that they are to be employed in road-making and other public works, being clothed and fed, and receiving each man one hundred reis (about 2½*d.*) a day, and each woman or child fifty reis (1¼*d.*); that each is to have a small allotment of land and two days in the week for himself; that after six years of service and good conduct they are to receive letters of emancipation, and that any who in the meantime leave the colony will be subject to punishment. Every one of the free Africans made over to the Brazilian government by the Slave-trade Mixed Commission at Rio has already served more than fourteen years, and they are now to commence a new term of six years. The promised payment is nothing in a country where the price of ordinary labour is two or three milreis (4*s.* 6*d.* or 6*s.* 9*d.*) a day. In the meantime, though I have been endeavouring during the last two years to obtain for Her Majesty's government information about the free

Africans at Itapura, none has been given me; and I cannot inform your lordship of their number, or periods of service, or ages, or how they came to Itapura."

Lord Russell instructed me in reply, January 8, 1863:—

"The effect of the regulations recently issued for the government of the negroes at Itapura, is practically to consign to six years' forced servitude men, women, and children, who are free according to the showing of the Brazilian authorities themselves; and the government of Her Majesty are consequently bound to require that those Africans who were liberated under British auspices shall not be subjected to the regulations in question."

I conclude with the question of the wages due to the *emancipados*, whether privately or publicly employed. Has anything been paid by the Brazilian government to those who have been set free, to the famous four hundred, for instance? The wages of those who were let out to private individuals were received by the government. Those employed in government establishments were surely to receive some wages from the government. It has been seen that the apprenticeship of those working for government remained unlimited, long after fourteen years was nominally fixed as the term for those in private service. In the account of the necessary preliminaries for the freedom of the *emancipados*, lately produced in the House of Commons by Lord Palmerston, it is said that these poor creatures are required to pay the fees before they get their freedom. But what, as Sir Henry Howard asked in 1854, becomes of the produce of their hiring? The Viscount Abaeté told Sir H. Howard that the wages were funded for the expenses of re-exportation. A Brazilian writer, Tavares Bastos, whose statement was sent to Lord Russell by Mr. Baillie in December, 1861, says :—

"No account has ever been rendered of these deposits, nor with these means has any commencement been made of the re-exportation of those Africans who might choose to return. So clearly was this a formality, that from the budget of the 21st of October, 1843, until the present, those wages began to be classified among the items of the ordinary income of the State."

This appears to be too true. I have before me the budget of 1864–5, prepared by the Marquis of Abrantes. Among the extraordinary receipts, deposits, is put down, "Salary of free Africans," 1,608 milreis, about 180*l.* A modest calculation, supposing the number of men, women, and children to be anything like ten thousand! There is a report given by the Finance Minister of the state of all the other deposit funds, but no report of the "Free Africans' Fund." Yet during so many years there should have been a great accumulation. What has become of it? I wrote to Lord Russell, December 20, 1860 :—

"It was prescribed by treaty that these blacks should be employed 'as servants or free labourers,' and the Brazilian government guaranteed their liberty. A very important question for them is wages. . . . It seems to me that the Brazilian government are in every way bound, on emancipating them, to pay over to them for their benefit a fair balance of reasonable wages."

There is a despatch of Sir James Hudson to Lord Palmerston of June 24, 1847, stating that, on the emancipation of the free Africans of the "Flor de Loanda," he had paid to each of them, on behalf of Her Majesty's government, at the rate of one milreis (2*s.* 3*d.*) per month for the whole term of their apprenticeship, about eight years.

It is bad enough that those who have hitherto been set free by death or by the Brazilian government have received nothing, and that some ten thousand should remain in virtual slavery so long after the expiration of fourteen years for each and all. It is hardly conceivable that the Brazilian government should have kept no account of the money received and due for these blacks; but so it appears to be. The least that can now be done by that government is to follow the example of the English government in 1847, and pay to every one of those yet to be emancipated, and to every one already emancipated who is living, one milreis per month for the whole term of service. Little enough is one milreis per month to men employed as "free labourers."

One milreis per month for, say 5,000 only, would be 60,000 milreis a year; counting an average of twenty years' service, the sum due for 5,000, at this moderate estimate, would be 1,200,000 milreis, or about 135,000*l.* Double it, what is 270,000*l.* for the Brazilian Empire to pay, if it be a just debt to the poor *emancipados* otherwise so much wronged?*

* Since Lord Palmerston's speech, information has come from Rio of a considerable number of emancipations of free Africans made by Senhor Zacarias, while he was President of the Council and Minister of Justice, from January to September of this year; and the mail which arrived in October, leaving Rio on the 8th of September, brought evidence of a great public stimulus having been given to the Brazilian government in this question by Lord Palmerston's speech of July 12, which was known in Rio in the middle of August. The reprisals, and Lord Russell's despatch of June, 1863, had previously stimulated the Brazilian Cabinet. It is obvious that what has been lately done, might and should have been done

long ago. Much still remains to be done. It does not appear that anything is paid to the blacks on emancipation for wages during apprenticeship. It is said in an article in the *Correio Mercantil* of September 8, written evidently from official information, that Senhor Zacarias had issued 848 letters of emancipation since January 15, and that before he left office in the first days of September, he had proposed to his Cabinet a decree for the immediate emancipation of all the free Africans, whether in private or public employment, who had served for fourteen years; and there can be none of those released by the English and Brazilian Mixed Commission who have not served for more than fourteen years.

There appeared in the Rio *Jornal de Commercio* of July 12, a statement about a "free African" woman, which illustrates both past abuses and present difficulties. The woman is described as languishing in prison, having been there six months since the Minister of Justice granted her a letter of emancipation; her name had been in former years erased from the register of free Africans. The writer says—"The history of this poor woman is one of terrible injustice. A free African, her name was erased from the registers, and she was doomed to live and die in slavery. It was necessary for her to summon before the Judge the person in whose power she found herself, that he might exhibit the documents proving his right to detain her. No such documents were forthcoming, and, in spite of the strongest opposition, Dr. Silveira Martins, Municipal Judge, gave a sentence judicially declaring her to be a free African woman, but ordering her to be taken to the House of Correction, there to petition for her right. During a slight delay in the execution of the last part of this order, her late possessor presented himself to make an urgent demand for her, because, he said, he was interested. Her petition for emancipation was granted, but the poor Henriqueta is still in prison without crime or fault, and, from the moment the letter of emancipation was granted, illegally in prison. In the solitude of a prison poor Henriqueta has for six long months had the fear before her of returning to her old condition, uncertainty as to the future, and present bodily sufferings."

## CHAPTER V.

### THE ABERDEEN ACT AND ITS PROPOSED REPEAL.

LORD ABERDEEN'S NOTES BEFORE PASSING OF THE ABERDEEN ACT—BRAZILIAN REFUSALS OF ALL PROPOSALS—ANNUAL IMPORTATION OF 70,000 SLAVES—ABERDEEN ACT, 1845—DEFENDED BY SIR ROBERT PEEL AND SIR FREDERICK THESIGER, 1849—LORD ABERDEEN'S, SIR ROBERT PEEL'S, AND LORD PALMERSTON'S SPEECHES, 1845—LORD BROUGHAM'S SPEECH OF AUGUST 2, 1842—HIS PROPOSAL TO REPEAL THE ACT, 1864—LORD ABERDEEN'S LANGUAGE OF 1845; HIS DECLARATIONS IN 1856 AND 1858—MR. SEYMOUR FITZGERALD'S SPEECH IN 1858—LORD ABERDEEN'S PRIVATE COMMUNICATIONS TO LORD MALMESBURY—MR. OSBORNE'S MISSTATEMENTS.

It has been mentioned in Chapter I. that in the year 1845 the Brazilian government insisted on its right to denounce the whole of the British Slave-trade Convention with Brazil of 1826, except the first article, by which, from March, 1830, slave-trade in Brazil was to be deemed and treated as piracy. By this denunciation all the means provided by the Convention with Portugal of 1817, and adopted in the Convention with Brazil of 1826, of search, capture, and adjudication by Mixed Commission Courts, for the suppression of slave-trade, ceased to exist, and the Brazilian government altogether refused to enter into any new arrangements. The determination of the Brazilian government to denounce these provisions as soon as they could do so, had long been known to the British government. Lord Aberdeen, in a long and elaborate draft-note sent to

Mr. Hamilton, British Minister at Rio, June 4, 1845, to be presented to the government of Brazil, recounted his fruitless efforts to persuade the Brazilian government. The following is a part of Lord Aberdeen's statement :—

"Repeated representations were made to the Brazilian government on the continuance of the slave-trade, and the necessity of more active and powerful measures for suppressing it; and in the year 1835, articles additional to the Convention were actually signed by plenipotentiaries on the part of the contracting parties. Unfortunately these articles were never ratified by the Crown of Brazil.

"Again, on the 23rd of August, 1840, new propositions were made on the part of Great Britain, framed on memoranda drawn up by the Brazilian government; but when proposed by Great Britain, the Brazilian government declined to accept them.

"On August 26, 1841, the Brazilian government, on their part, proposed certain terms, and in April, 1842, the Undersigned submitted to the Imperial government proposals for modifying those terms so as to carry out effectually the intention of the parties to the Convention of 1826. But on the 17th of October in that year, the Brazilian government thought proper not only entirely to reject those modifications, but to declare by a note under that date from Senhor Aureliano to the Undersigned, that 'the Imperial government not only consider that other dispositions besides those which already exist, are now unnecessary in order to the total extinction of the traffic, but that they regard it as prudent not to adopt any others.'

"Accordingly, Senhor Aureliano returned to the Undersigned the draft of Convention, refusing peremptorily even to enter into negotiation on it. This occurred at a time in respect to which the British Commissioners had observed to Her Majesty's government that 'at no period has the Brazilian slave-trade been so extensively carried on as it is at the present moment in Rio de Janeiro itself.'"

At that time the annual importation of slaves into Brazil was moderately estimated at 70,000; and so said Lord Brougham in a speech in the House of Lords, August 2, 1842.

Mr. Hamilton was directed by Lord Aberdeen to inform the Brazilian government that they thus left the British government no alternative but to take matters into their own hands, under the terms of the first article of the Convention of 1826, which would remain in force. It was thus put in the draft-note sent to Mr. Hamilton, June 4, 1845:—

"The Undersigned is directed to observe that Her Majesty's government have no longer any course open to them under the Convention of November 23, 1826, than that of giving full effect to the stipulations of the first article of that Convention, under which Her Majesty has acquired the right to order the seizure of all Brazilian subjects found upon the high seas engaged in the slave-trade, of punishing them as pirates, and of disposing of the vessels in which they may be captured, together with the goods belonging to them, as *bona piratarum.*

"Her Majesty's government had hoped, to the very latest moment, that the Brazilian government would, by a renewal and extension of the engagements between the two countries, have offered to Great Britain some other means of giving effect by joint operations to the Convention of 1826. Unfortunately this has not been the case; and the vigour and success with which the slave-trade is now carried on under the Brazilian flag, leaves the British government no choice but to appeal to the rights and obligations which attach to Her Majesty under the first article of the above-mentioned Convention.

"The Undersigned is accordingly directed to declare that Her Majesty's government are prepared to exercise those rights, and that it is their intention immediately to propose to Parliament to pass the legislative enactments necessary for enabling Her Majesty to carry the provisions of that article into complete execution."

On July 2, 1845, Lord Aberdeen informed Mr. Hamilton that such a bill was prepared; this is the bill which was passed that year and is known as the Aberdeen Act. It is important to note Lord Aberdeen's language on this occasion to Mr. Hamilton, since it has frequently been, and is still, represented by the advocates of the Brazilian government as constituting a solemn obligation, absolutely binding on any and all of Lord Aberdeen's successors, to propose the repeal of the Act when there may have been no slave-trade in Brazil for a number of years.

"Her Majesty's government have prepared, and are about to submit to Parliament, a bill, giving to Her Majesty's Courts of Admiralty the power to take cognisance of, and to adjudicate upon, all vessels captured for carrying on the slave-trade contrary to the Convention of 1826, a power from which those Courts have hitherto been specially debarred by the act of Parliament originally passed for carrying that Convention into execution, in consideration that provisions were therein adopted for the maintenance of those mixed tribunals which the Brazilian government has now determined to dissolve.

"Her Majesty's government, however, are far from wishing this mode of adjudicating those vessels to be permanent. They will be ready, so soon as any measures of the Brazilian government shall enable them to do so, to recommend to parliament to repeal the bill now about to be brought forward; but whilst the present state of things continues, and until either the slave-trade of Brazil shall have entirely ceased, or the Brazilian government shall have entered into an engagement with Great Britain jointly to carry into execution the declared intentions of the parties to the Convention of 1826, that course will not be open to them.

"You are already aware that the measure by which, in the opinion of Her Majesty's government, the government of Brazil would best evince their determination to carry out the intention which they have so solemnly recorded, would be the negotiation of a treaty, similar either to that concluded between Great Britain and Spain in 1835, or to that between Great Britain and Portugal of 1842."

The "Aberdeen Act" was introduced into the House of Lords by Lord Aberdeen on the 7th of July, 1845. It passed through both Houses of Parliament in less than a month, without a single division. In the House of Lords no voice was raised in opposition; in the Commons Sir Thomas Wilde, afterwards Lord Truro and Lord Chancellor, stated some objections to the measure, but did not divide the House. It is needless to say that, whatever may have been Lord Truro's acumen and acquirements, his single authority can weigh for little against those of many other lawyers. The Lord Chancellor of the Cabinet which proposed the act was Lord Lyndhurst, its Attorney and Solicitor-general were Sir Frederick Pollock and Sir Frederick Thesiger.

Sir Robert Peel said on the occasion of a motion for the repeal of the act, April 24, 1849, by Mr. Milner Gibson, who cited the authority of Sir Thomas Wilde, then Chief Justice of the Common Pleas:—

"The highest authorities on international law were consulted by the government, and declared that, though without the consent of Parliament government could not give effect to the Convention, yet that there was nothing to offend against the principles of international law in the carrying out by statute of the objects intended by the Convention. The measure was brought before the House of Lords, and he was not aware that a single peer opposed the passing of the bill; he did not think that there was even a discussion upon it. The bill passed in the presence of the Lord Chancellor, the Lord Chief Justice, and others, the highest equity authorities and law lords of the greatest eminence; yet nothing fell from any one of them to the effect that it offended against some of the principles of international law. It was passed unanimously by the House of Lords; by the Commons without serious objection; and now this House was invited to repeal, virtually at least, by a single vote, a measure which passed with such general assent. Some reference had been made to an eminent lawyer, at present the Chief Justice of the Common Pleas, having called the bill a scandal; but that learned individual was a member of this House when the bill was passing; he offered some objections to the third clause, but did not oppose the bill either on the second or third reading."

And on this same occasion Sir Frederick Thesiger (now Lord Chelmsford) made a speech in favour of the act, and he was followed on the same side by Mr. Roundell Palmer, the present Attorney General.

Lord Aberdeen, in proposing this measure to the House of Lords, spoke as follows:—

"Your lordships are aware that the Brazilian government have always declined to fulfil their general engagements to cooperate with the British government for the abolition of the slave-trade. With rare and short exceptions, the treaty has been by them systematically violated from the period of its conclusion to the present time. Cargoes of slaves have been landed in open day in the streets of the capital, and bought and sold like cattle, without any obstacle whatever being imposed on the traffic. Our officers have been waylaid, maltreated, and even assassinated while in the execution of their duty, and justice in such cases, if not actually denied, has never been fairly granted. No doubt much has happened, in the course of the last ten or twelve years, which would have justified, and almost called for, an expression of national resentment."

Sir Robert Peel spoke as follows, July 24, 1845, in advocating the same measure in the House of Commons:—

"The government proposes this measure with regret. It would have been infinitely more satisfactory to them that the Brazilians should have consented to enter into a new engagement in substitution of the engagement of 1817, and should have acted in ready concert with us in the suppression of the slave-trade. Repeated exhortations were addressed to the Brazilian government for the purpose of inducing them to enter into amicable concert with us, and to enable us to search Brazilian vessels, and to punish those who were engaged in the slave-trade, under that act which had been agreed to by the Brazilian government of its own free will. But these efforts have failed. The Brazilian government have from time to time distinctly stated to us that her views on this subject are entirely at variance with ours, and from the Brazilian government we can expect no assistance or cooperation in the suppression of the slave-trade by her own subjects."

Lord Palmerston said on the same occasion:—

"I am sorry to say that it is impossible to state in exaggerated terms the just accusation against Brazil of bad faith as to the Conventions agreed to by it respecting the slave-trade. All our inducements, all our arguments, all our persuasions, were utterly fruitless, and whenever the subject of the slave-trade has been discussed here, the notoriously bad faith of the Brazilian government has been on all hands admitted and deplored."

It is important to adduce another testimony as to the conduct of the Brazilian government about the slave-trade, before the passing of the Aberdeen Act, and this is the testimony of Lord Brougham, taken from a speech of his in the House of Lords, August 2, 1842.

"In the first place, they have the recorded declaration of an honourable man in the Senate of Brazil, that the law abolishing the slave-trade was notoriously a dead letter, having fallen entirely into disuse. They have, in the next place, a petition or memorial from the Provincial Assembly of Bahia to the Senate, urging a repeal of the law; not that they gave themselves any trouble about the prohibition,—with that they could easily deal by wholly disregarding it,—but the provision that all slaves imported after 1830, the date of the law, should be free, embarrassed the operations of the purchaser, and made it very inconvenient to hold recently imported negroes. I find another Provincial Assembly, that of Minas Geraes, urging the same suit on the like grounds. After dwelling on the dangers resulting to the country from the want of negroes, the memorial adds:—'Above all, is the worst of all these perils, the immorality which is the result of our citizens being accustomed to violate the laws under the very eyes of the administration thereof.' I verily believe that the whole history of human effrontery presents no passage to match this—no second example of equal audacity. We have here a Provincial Legislature coming forward on behalf of pirates—for ever since March, 1830, slave trading is piracy by the law of Brazil; on behalf of pirates and their accomplices, the planters who profit by the piracy, purchasing its fruits; on behalf of these great criminals urging a repeal of the law which they openly avow is continually broken by them, and which they declare they will continue to set at nought as long as it continues unrepealed, but demanding its repeal on the ground that, while it remains, they, being resolved to break it, are thus under the necessity of committing the additional immorality of breaking it under the eye of the judges sworn to enforce it."

On June 28 of the present year, Lord Brougham, in the House of Lords, urged on Lord Russell the repeal of the Aberdeen Act, as due to Brazil for what, a few nights before, in giving notice of his motion, he had described as the "admirable conduct" of late years of the Brazilian government by which the African slave-trade had been suppressed, and as a graceful act with a view to a renewal of diplomatic relations with Brazil. Lord Russell declined to entertain the suggestion, observing that he was not convinced that the suppression of the slave-trade in Brazil had been entirely voluntary and from conviction; that the Aberdeen Act was a protection against possible renewal of the slave-trade; and that he did not think Brazil entitled to any act of grace or favour, when she had chosen to suspend diplomatic relations with England on the ground of measures taken by the English government to ensure safety for life and property of British citizens.

Lord Brougham's motion has revived discussion of the Aberdeen Act. It was asserted in the leading article, already referred to, of the *Daily News* of July 14, that a "solemn assurance" was given to the Brazilian government by Lord Aberdeen in 1845, "that the English government would propose its repeal when the African slave-trade was completely suppressed."

This is a misrepresentation of the following passage in Lord Aberdeen's note, written to the English Minister at Rio (Mr. Hamilton), on July 2, 1845:—

"Her Majesty's government will be ready, so soon as any measures of the Brazilian government shall enable them so to do, to recommend Parliament to repeal the bill now about to be brought forward; but, while the present state of things continues, and until either the slave-trade of Brazil shall have entirely ceased, or the Brazilian government shall have entered into an engagement with Great Britain jointly to carry into execution the declared intentions of the parties to the Convention of 1826, that course will not be open to them. You are aware that the measure by which, in the opinion of Her Majesty's government, the government of Brazil would best evince their determination to carry out the intention which they have so solemnly recorded, would be the negotiation of a treaty, similar either to that concluded between Great Britain and Spain in 1835, or to that between Great Britain and Portugal in 1842."

Such a treaty has not been made with us by Brazil. It cannot be contended that the above words of Lord Aberdeen constitute a solemn promise to Brazil absolutely binding on Lord Palmerston and Lord Russell, when they are of opinion, as they have both lately stated, that if the act were repealed, the slave-trade would or might be revived.

The writer proceeded to say that Lord Palmerston "disregards not only the solemn assurance made by Lord Aberdeen, but the opinion of all other well-informed men." I take exception to this sweeping statement. Lord Russell's ought to be the opinion of a well-informed man. He has now been at the head of the Foreign Office for nearly five years. His agents in Brazil should be comparatively well-informed on this subject. I quote, at present, only two of them. Mr. Callander, consul at St. Catharine's, wrote, June 23, 1860:—

"I believe I am justified in saying that the foreign slave-trade may be considered as having entirely ceased in this province; and, it is to be presumed, that no attempts are likely to be made to revive it, so long as the measures at present in force for its suppression are not relaxed."

Mr. Baillie, Chargé d'affaires at Rio de Janeiro, wrote, December 6, 1861:—

"As far as my own observations go, I have been unable to discern any desire or tendency towards the abolition of slavery in Brazil, or even the mitigation of its principal evils. The external slave-trade has undoubtedly ceased. There has been, I believe, no attempt to land slaves on the shores of Brazil for several years, and it is frequently said that a renewal of the traffic is impossible. This may turn out to be quite true; but how far the impossibility arises from any real aversion to slavery or sense of its moral wrong, or of the debasing influence it exercises wherever instituted, is quite another question, and I much fear that the feeling of a very large class in Brazil is rather a sullen acquiescence in a state of things which, owing to external pressure and public opinion, and other causes, cannot be helped, than from any conviction of the evils of the old system of negro importation."

The letter-writer in the *Daily News* made some further statements. He says:—

"The assurance Lord Aberdeen gave to Brazil in 1845, of the circumstances under which the Queen's government, in its corporate and enduring capacity,—not as a shifting succession of advisers—would repeal the Aberdeen Act, was either on the complete suppression of the slave-trade or on the conclusion of a new slave-trade treaty, and Lord Aberdeen himself, before his death, was of opinion, expressed both publicly and privately, that Brazil was entitled to the fulfilment of this engagement by having completely suppressed the slave-trade."

Lord Aberdeen spoke publicly on the subject twice after his last retirement from office,—on July 21, 1856, and on June 17, 1858; but I do not find that on either occasion he stated what is here represented.

On July 21, 1856, he said:—

"At the time of the passing of the act he had assured the Brazilian government of his regret at having to propose such a measure, and that nothing would give him greater pleasure than being able to move for the repeal of that act. He had even hoped that the time for repealing the act had come, but he regretted to find that what he had imagined had been completely effected by the Brazilian government had not taken place, and that there were some symptoms of a renewal of the slave-trade."

Well, but perhaps in June, 1858, two years after, Lord Aberdeen expressed himself differently. Not a bit. On June 17, 1858, he said in the House of Lords:—

"He would only say a word with regard to an act relative to Brazil which had been introduced by him, and was called by his name, but which he believed in Brazil was called the Algerine Act. When he brought in that act he assured the Brazilian government that nothing would give him so much pleasure as the arrival of the day when he should move the repeal of that act. He was not sure that that time had arrived yet."

Now for the solemn assurance given by Lord Aberdeen in 1845 for the Queen's government "in its corporate and enduring capacity, not as a shifting succession of advisers." How did his lordship express himself on this solemn subject? I should say, hardly becomingly, if *Hansard* reports correctly, and the "Friend to both Countries" has the true version of the solemn assurance. Lord Aberdeen said, on this last occasion, June 17, 1858:—"He would only recommend to the care of the government the realization of the hope which he had ventured to express when he introduced the act in question to that House." The realization of his hope, not the fulfilment of "a solemn assurance given for the Queen's government in its corporate and enduring capacity."

The government to which Lord Aberdeen addressed himself on June 17, 1858, was the government of Lord Derby. Lord Malmesbury, then Foreign Minister, took no notice of Lord Aberdeen's statement. A few weeks after there was a debate in the House of Commons on the slave-trade and the slave question and Brazil and the "Aberdeen Act," in which Mr. Cardwell and Sir John Pakington spoke hardly less strongly than Lord Palmerston of the good effect of the measures of 1850 and 1851 in the suppression of the Brazilian slave-trade, and in which Mr. Seymour Fitzgerald, Lord Malmesbury's Under Secretary, is reported to have observed:—

"If this country had not taken the firm position which we have occupied on this subject, or if at this moment we were to reverse our policy, does the House believe that countries like Brazil and Portugal would continue in the course which, following our example, they have adopted?

Does not the House rather believe that, if England were to exhibit any faltering in her policy, they would reverse their policy also, and the slave-trade become as general and rife as it was a few years ago?"

I am not aware of any public utterance of Lord Aberdeen on the subject of the "Aberdeen Act" after June 17, 1858. He died in December, 1860. But Lord Malmesbury has twice said in the House of Lords, that Lord Aberdeen, in a private conversation with him shortly before his death, declared that it would give him pleasure to see the act repealed. Lord Aberdeen said quite as much as this when he introduced the bill. Lord Malmesbury further said (July 14, 1863), that Lord Aberdeen had told him that "he had never felt satisfied in his mind that he was right in proposing that act." I doubt the accuracy of this statement, which is at variance with the public declarations of Lord Aberdeen and Sir Robert Peel.

I think that most readers, when they have before them the words of Lord Aberdeen in 1856 and 1858, as given by *Hansard*, will say that Mr. Osborne was not provided with the true explanation of why Lord Aberdeen did not propose the repeal of the act while he was Prime Minister from 1852 to 1855. Mr. Osborne said he did "not doubt that Lord Aberdeen would have repealed the act but for the presence in his cabinet of the noble lord (Lord Palmerston.)" Mr. Osborne also in his speech turned Lord Aberdeen's words of June 17, 1858, as given by *Hansard*, "He was not sure that *that time had arrived yet*," into "He was not sure that the proper time for its repeal *had not already arrived*."

It must be obvious to any man of sense that whatever

Lord Aberdeen may have said in 1845, even if it had been ten times stronger than it was, or whatever opinions he may have expressed after he ceased to be Premier, even if they had been stronger than there is any sign of, could not overbear the responsibility of succeeding Ministers to act according to conscience and conviction.

What may be fairly said about Lord Aberdeen is that, according to his own declarations, he proposed the "Aberdeen Act" in 1845 with the greatest reluctance, under an overwhelming sense of duty and necessity,—that he regarded it as a measure necessitated by a long course of conduct of the Brazilian government which he himself described as "systematic violation" of treaty engagements, and as "justifying, and almost calling for, an expression of national resentment,"—that he always hoped to be enabled to repeal the act by an entire suppression of the slave-trade or by the conclusion of a new Slave-trade Treaty,—that, after he ceased to be Premier, in 1856, he twice expressed, when out of office, his hope that the time for repealing the act was near at hand, but that on both occasions he spoke doubtingly, and on the last (June 17, 1858) said "he was not sure that the time had arrived yet," and recommended to the care of the government of Lord Derby, who, he said, "must have more information" than himself, the realization of the hope which he had ventured to express when he introduced the act in question.

Lord Aberdeen's hope will, doubtless, receive full care and attention from Lord Palmerston and Lord Russell, who can, however, hardly be expected to leave out of consideration the systematic violation for so many years of the treaty-engagements of the Brazilian government as to the *emancipados.* The "Story of the Free Africans," which has preceded, may lead many readers to think that the following passage of one of my despatches to Lord Russell is not intemperate, unreasonable, or unjust:—

"I have, on various occasions, suggested to your lordship the importance of endeavouring, if possible, to conciliate and persuade the Brazilian government to measures leading to the ultimate extinction of slavery, and in the meantime mitigating its evils. Her Majesty's government have certainly done ample justice to the Brazilian efforts for the extinction of the slave-trade. The conduct of the government about the free blacks is not to their honour, and is such as to throw doubts on the singleness and purity of their motives in the abolition of the slave-trade. When I first brought the subject of the free blacks to your lordship's notice in my despatch of May 17, 1860, I ventured respectfully to suggest that it would be well for Her Majesty's government, if they revived this question, to be prepared to persevere for the attainment of what they might demand, for I could not but see that this was a question likely to lead to angry correspondence and difficulties with the Brazilian government." (May 3, 1862, in Slave-Trade Correspondence, Class B, presented 1863.)

## CHAPTER VI.

### SLAVERY IN BRAZIL.

RECENT STATEMENTS THAT SLAVERY IS DOOMED IN BRAZIL—CORRESPONDENT OF "DAILY NEWS"—THREE MILLIONS OF SLAVES—NATIONAL SLAVES—PRESENT PRICES—ADDRESS OF BRITISH AND FOREIGN ANTI-SLAVERY SOCIETY TO EMPEROR OF BRAZIL—STATEMENTS OF SENHOR ANDRADA OF THE LATE BRAZILIAN LEGATION AND OF SENHOR ALMEIDA PORTUGAL—SEPARATION OF SLAVE FAMILIES BY SALE—"QUARTERLY REVIEW" ON BRAZIL—NO BEGINNING YET OF ABOLITION OF SLAVERY.

THE question with Brazil as to the repeal of the "Aberdeen Act" does not lie within the narrow limits of Lord Aberdeen's statement at the time when he proposed the act; it lies in the general character for faith and trustworthiness of the Brazilian government; in its systematic and flagrant violations to the last of treaty engagements and solemn professions and promises, made by a long succession of Ministers—Saturnino, Viscount Uruguay, Viscount Abaeté, Paranhos—each speaking for the Emperor's government "in its corporate and enduring character," as to thousands of *emancipados*, and in the present condition of slavery in Brazil, to which I now pass.

Some months ago, the "correspondent" of the *Daily News* at Rio de Janeiro reported the introduction into the Brazilian Senate by Senhor Silveira da Motta of a measure for compulsory emancipation of slaves belonging to foreigners and to religious bodies; and took occasion to observe that "it is becoming every day more evident that slavery is doomed in Brazil, and that, ere long, some measure will be taken having for its object the entire suppression of the system." (*Daily News*, of March 5.)

If the same correspondent has since reported that this measure met with little or no support and was quickly rejected, such a letter from him has escaped my eye. Senhor Silveira da Motta is a private Senator, not a member of the government. The measure which he proposed was for emancipation of all slaves belonging to foreigners of countries in which slavery is unlawful, belonging to convents and religious bodies, and belonging to the Brazilian nation or government. The same Senator has of late years several times proposed measures for prohibiting public auctions of slaves and separation of husband and wife, and parents and children, in sales; for facilitating manumissions on decease of owners in certain cases, and for indirectly discouraging the employment of slaves in domestic service in cities; and all his proposals have been quickly rejected, like his measure of the present year. These unsuccessful proposals of Senator Silveira da Motta are the only attempts that I know of which have been made to curtail or qualify the slavery system in Brazil, where the Rio correspondent of the *Daily News* has written that it is becoming every day more evident that slavery is doomed.

In a letter more lately published in the *Daily News* (August 5,) the Rio correspondent reverts to certain statements of his, which I had not seen, that "a great number of slaves are liberated voluntarily every year by their owners and by the government," mentions the recent emancipation by will of fourteen slaves by one proprietor "a similar act" in another case (number not stated), and the liberation of sixty-nine "slaves" by the Brazilian government on July 4; and he further promises "a statistical table and positive proof of the great number of slaves which are annually liberated in Brazil." I shall be very glad to see this statistical table, which I hope will be well authenticated, and these positive proofs of a large number of annual liberations. Hitherto I have seen in other journals positive statements of a large extent of emancipation proceeding in Brazil, but no statistics and no positive proofs.

There is no doubt, however, that this writer, in speaking of a number of slaves voluntarily liberated every year by the Brazilian government, and in recording the sixty-nine slaves liberated by the government on the 4th of July, has made the mistake common to the Brazilian government of regarding "free Africans" as slaves. The sixty-nine, as well as the others annually liberated by the government, are not slaves, but *emancipados,* whom the Brazilian government received to be treated as free labourers, and whose freedom they guaranteed to the English government. He does not say what has been paid by the Brazilian government, or that anything has been paid, to them, on account of wages.

Lord Palmerston stated, on the occasion of Mr. Osborne's late motion, that there were three millions of slaves in Brazil in a total population of seven millions and a half. There has never been a census in Brazil, and there is no official report known to me of the number of slaves. A laborious and well-informed writer in the *Revue des Deux Mondes* (July, 1862) says that the number of slaves in

Brazil is variously estimated at from four millions to two and a half, which is the lowest estimate, resting on "the evidence of the planters, who have an interest in concealing the number of slaves on account of the capitation tax."

Taking three millions as a mean number and moderate estimate, we require proof of a large number of annual manumissions in order to see our way therefrom to the ultimate doom of slavery in Brazil.

The whole number of slaves belonging to the Brazilian government or nation, whom the Senator Silveira da Motta has lately made an unsuccessful effort to free, is about 1,500; no more. It is mentioned in a report of mine, of February 4, 1861, from the annual Report of the Minister of Finance, that in the year 1859-60 twenty-one of the national or government slaves were emancipated. This at best is a mere drop in the ocean; but all or most of these might have been slaves past work and power of procreation.

The Finance Minister of 1862 (the Marquis of Abrantes) proposed in his report that he should be authorised by the Legislature to emancipate gratuitously "slaves of the nation when, by reason of advanced age or permanent infirmity of a grave character, they become unable to do work for the nation." Under such circumstances freedom is hardly a boon, and slaves by whose labour the government has profited so long as they could work, should be taken care of by the government, when from advanced age or permanent infirmity they can work no longer. Mr. Heywood quotes this curious passage in his paper on Brazil in the "Statistical Society's Journal" for June, and asks the natural question,—" But how are these infirm slaves to maintain themselves?"

The manumission of slaves past work and procreation is, of course, no real diminution of the number of slaves, and it will be most important, in any statistics of annual manumissions, to specify the numbers emancipated who are old and effete.

The present very high prices of slaves would not lead one to expect a very large, or, at any rate, an increasing number of manumissions. In the debate on Mr. Hutt's motion of July 12, 1858, for discontinuing our anti-slave-trade squadron, Mr. Charles Buxton, who opposed the motion, mentioned *70l.* as the price of a slave in Brazil, and as an immense temptation to the greed of the slave-trader. What is the price now? The last prices, as reported by our Consul at Rio, published in the Blue-books, viz. for July, 1863, are—

| | £ | s. | | £ | s. |
|---|---|---|---|---|---|
| Males (agricultural and mining) . . | 107 | 6 | to | 193 | 2 |
| Females ditto ditto . . | 107 | 6 | to | 160 | 18 |
| Males (domestic) . . . . . . . . | 129 | 3 | to | 214 | 2 |
| Females ditto . . . . . . . . | 107 | 6 | to | 193 | 2 |

It has been often said that so long as there is slavery there is danger of slave trade, and with the "institution" existing in such force in Brazil, with 3,000,000 of slaves there, prices at Rio reaching to *200l.* a-head, and the government resisting all proposals to mitigate or diminish slavery, it may occur to many that Lord Palmerston's and Lord Russell's fears of what might happen, if the "Aberdeen Act" were repealed, are not altogether chimerical.

I stated in a despatch to Earl Russell of August 5, 1860:— "The diminution in the number of slaves by emancipation, purchased or given, seems to be very trifling. The great increase in price of slaves since 1850 has necessarily made it more difficult to purchase freedom, and has diminished enfranchisements by testamentary disposition."

Mr. Baillie wrote to Earl Russell, December 6, 1861 :— "I have been unable to discern any desire or tendency towards the abolition of slavery in Brazil, or even the mitigation of its principal evils; the internal slave-trade is carried on as much as ever." I wrote in almost identical words on May 3, 1862. My last despatch, February 26, 1863, quoted lately by Lord Brougham as authority for the extinction of the slave-trade, states, what Lord Brougham did not quote, that "there is no sign of effort or preparation for the abolition of slavery."

On the 21st of March last a deputation, including Mr. Josiah Forster, and Mr. J. Cropper, of Liverpool, Professor Newman, and other excellent men, went with an address of the Committee of the British and Foreign Anti-Slavery Society for the Emperor of Brazil on the subject of slavery to No. 9. Cavendish-square, and were there received and addressed by Senhor Andrada, who has been for some years Secretary of the Brazilian Legation in London, and was then charged with the superintendence of the Brazilian Consulate and with the late Minister's railway directorships and financial business in London. A short account of this proceeding appeared at the time in several journals under the heading "Abolition of Slavery in Brazil." The address and the speeches were reported at length in the *Anti-Slavery Reporter* for April 1.

Senhor Andrada made several statements, which would be very gratifying, if correct; but which, I fear, were likely to mislead the excellent gentlemen whom he addressed.

Senhor Andrada having said what cannot be denied, that "the question is a very serious one," went on to say what I fear is not correct,—"It has been for some time under the consideration of the Imperial parliament; a great many measures have been proposed in both Chambers about the institution of slavery." And later he said,—"A great many steps have been taken there to give freedom to the slaves; every year the Minister has recourse to measures which give freedom to a great many of them."

I know of no measures which have been proposed or considered in the Imperial parliament except those proposed by the private Senator Silveira da Motta for preventing public auctions of slaves and separation of slave families by sale, or otherwise mitigating the evils of slavery, and for emancipating slaves of foreigners, religious bodies, and the Brazilian nation, which have all been summarily rejected, being opposed by the Brazilian government; and I think it strange that credit, under such circumstances, should be taken for the Brazilian government, parliament, and nation for long consideration of the question and proposal in both chambers of "a great many measures." As to "the great many steps already taken to give freedom to the slaves," and "the measures by which the Minister gives freedom every year to a great many," I do not know what can be alluded to except the annual emancipation of free Africans. But the free Africans are not, at least ought not to be, slaves.*

* The Rio correspondent of the *Daily News* has again, in a letter published in that journal of September 20, described the liberations of free

Senhor Andrada also said,—"We feel the wrongfulness of separating wives from husbands, and children from parents, and so forth." Does this mean that there is no separation by sales or otherwise of slave families in Brazil? How is it, then, if the Brazilians are all impressed with the wrongfulness of such separations, that, year after year, Senator Silveira da Motta proposes a bill for prohibiting such separations by sale, and that he finds little or no support for his proposal, which, year after year, is rejected?

Another Brazilian, Senhor Almeida Portugal, who has been a lieutenant of the Brazilian navy, made a speech at the anniversary meeting of the British and Foreign Anti-Slavery Society on the 20th of May, in which he even improved on Senhor Andrada's statements. The speech may be read in the *Anti-Slavery Reporter* of June 1. This gentleman said that "the leading parliamentary gentlemen had brought forward measures which would tend to an immediate extinction of slavery;" also that "the parliament in Brazil were now working, and the laws which had been brought forward would, he thought, meet their approval; these laws applied to slavery and to the emancipation of the slaves, granting them certain privileges." He also said that there was no such thing as separation of slave husband and wife, parents and children; these things were done in North America and in Russia, but not in Brazil. "In the Brazils slaves are treated in a very different way. They do not separate man and wife.

Africans which are now proceeding with increased rapidity, as emancipations of "slaves." He has not, up to the date at which this is passing through the press (October 20), sent any of his promised statistics of manumissions of slaves. This Rio correspondent of the *Daily News* is known to be a Mr. Tovey, closely connected with the bank of Baron Souto.

The owners in so doing acted according to their own feelings, and asked themselves the question how they would like to be separated from their wives and children."

"Immediate extinction of slavery" cannot be expected or desired where there are three millions of slaves in a population of seven and a half millions; but no measures at all, no "laws" for emancipation, have to the latest date from Rio been proposed by the government, or are being worked at by the Legislature.

As to no separation of slave families in Brazil, again I ask what is the meaning of Senhor Silveira da Motta's annual proposal of prohibition?

What is the meaning of this passage in a speech of Senator Silveira da Motta in the Senate on May 17, 1861, with reference to slaves belonging to the Brazilian nation, and to some slaves of the Emperor's stepmother, the Duchess of Braganza, residing in Lisbon?

"Is it a very worthy spectacle for a free nation that the government should take the mother and send her to one service, and take her small children and employ them elsewhere? Meanwhile all those slaves [of the government Botanical Garden] are threatened with this separation. We are now threatened with a great public sale of slaves belonging to the Duchess of Braganza, on an estate called 'Macaco,' her property. Orders have been received to sell that property; the slaves are to be sold by auction, and they are like those of the Botanical Garden. Almost the whole of them were born at that place; the fathers, mothers, children, and grandchildren are all to be put up to auction, and will be separated. It is a hardship to grant permission to sell the father and mother separately from the son not yet eighteen years old; it is a hardship, a profanation, and a disowning of the rite of our religion to allow the slaveowner to sunder those slaves who have been married in church."

What mean these words of Senator Silveira da Motta, in the same speech, in reference to a coasting slave-trade which goes on in Brazil to the extent of at least 5,000 a year, and which was the subject of several remonstrances ordered by Lord Malmesbury and Lord Clarendon?

"Among the slaves transported from the north I have seen some in the market of Rio de Janeiro who are children of ten and twelve years old, have left their parents in the north, and are sold here. I can assure the noble senator that a slave from the north told me that he was married in the province where he was sold, and that his wife remained there, and he was sent here."

Is it necessary to proceed with the refutation of the assertions of Senhor Almeida Portugal? I have read with feelings of sorrow and shame such a speech delivered at a meeting of the British and Foreign Anti-Slavery Society. This Brazilian advised the society to agitate for the repeal of the Aberdeen Act. He must have thought that he was addressing men entirely ignorant of Brazil, to whom he might say anything; and he told his tolerant hearers that "he did not think there were two countries more united and more sisterly in their views of freedom than were England and the Brazils." If the clear spirits of Clarkson, Wilberforce, and Buxton still hover over that Society, with which in life they laboured, and which yet has a borrowed lustre from their names, this speech must have made them shudder. The great men who have been among us to abolish slave trade and slavery were not wont to listen to slaveowners' bombast, or let slaveowners' agents into their camp.

I return for a moment to the statements of Senhor Andrada, whose connexion with the Brazilian government gives an official authority to what he says. Senhor Andrada mentioned that he had been Judge of Orphans in Brazil, and had so had the general supervision of all the free Africans. He knows, then, the history of the *emancipados* in Brazil which I have related. He said that there was "a very bad and erroneous opinion in England concerning the condition of our slaves," and that he had seen "a great many articles in the newspapers which very much misrepresent us in the matter." Senhor Andrada said that he had been applied to some time ago by the Editor of the *Quarterly Review* for information, and that he had given it to him "most conscientiously," and "stated what was really the condition of the slave, and also the social state of the black people after they were emancipated." I always supposed that the flattering article on Brazil in the *Quarterly Review* of October, 1860, was in some degree due to Brazilian inspirations. *Timeo Danaos et dona ferentes;* the Editor of the *Quarterly* asked the Brazilian Legation for aid. The article in question contained the following:—

"The condition of slaves in Brazil is highly creditable to the country. The facilities for the purchase of freedom are great, and when emancipated, if he should possess the requisite qualifications, there is scarcely an office in the State to which a liberated negro may not reasonably aspire .... By the Brazilian law, a slave can at any time appear before a magistrate, have his price fixed, and purchase his freedom. .... The moral aspect of slavery as it still exists in Brazil is in striking contrast to that of the United States. In the one it is an admitted evil, to be got rid of as speedily as practicable; in the other it is an institution, identified in the opinion of a large party with the interests and prosperity of the country. It is probable that before many generations have passed away slavery will cease to exist in Brazil; it exists now in a very mitigated form."

I thus commented on these statements in a despatch to Earl Russell of June 26, 1861:—

"There is no such law as is stated by the Reviewer, giving the slave a right to appear at any time before a magistrate, have his price fixed, and buy his freedom. This is a complete mistake. Slavery may be, and I believe is, with a considerable number of enlightened and respectable men in Brazil, 'an admitted evil;' but, as your lordship will have learnt from previous reports of mine, there are no signs whatever at present in Brazil of abolition of slavery, and there is no disposition even to entertain measures for mitigating its acknowledged evils, or for preparing for ultimate abolition. And slavery in Brazil certainly is, what the Reviewer says that it is not, 'an institution,' identified in the opinion of a large party with the interests and prosperity of the country. It would not certainly be inferred, from the Reviewer's account of slavery in Brazil, that there are more than 3,000,000 of slaves in a population of from 7,000,000 to 7,500,000. . . . . There is no doubt, as stated by the Reviewer, that colour is no obstacle to advancement, and the free-born son of an emancipated slave may attain to any position, if he has merits and abilities, and fortune favours him; but I do not know what is meant by saying that slavery 'exists in a very mitigated form.'"

Since the appearance of the article in the *Quarterly Review* in 1860, nothing has happened to test the alleged tendency to extinction of slavery, except the proposal of

Senator Silveira da Motta's measures already mentioned, and the rejection of all of them, the last in the spring of this year.

Senhor Andrada told the deputation of the Anti-Slavery Society that "the Emperor himself and all his Ministers, and all the Brazilian people, believe that it is a duty to humanity to abolish slavery." Again: "I can assure you that not only the Emperor, but his government, his advisers, and every Brazilian possessing the feelings of humanity, think that it is not only the duty, but that it will be for the interest of our country to abolish slavery." Again: "As I have already told you, the government and people of Brazil think that it is their duty and their interest, as soon as they possibly can, entirely to abolish slavery."

All I know is, that as yet there is no beginning, and as yet all the presumptions from public facts are the other way. However, the Committee of the British and Foreign Anti-Slavery Society state in their report, presented shortly after the interview with Senhor Andrada, that they "are assured that measures are in contemplation;" and they mention as under consideration, I presume in the Brazilian Cabinet, for there is no news of it in the Parliament, "one declaring free all slave children born from the date of the projected act." I trust that these assurances are better founded than many of the assertions of Senhores Andrada and Portugal.

## CHAPTER VII.

### SLAVERY IN BRAZIL.

SALE BY BRAZILIAN GOVERNMENT BY AUCTION OF UNCLAIMED SLAVES —SLAVES ILLEGALLY IMPORTED SINCE MARCH, 1830, AND THEIR CHILDREN--REJECTION OF LORD PALMERSTON'S PROPOSAL OF 1850 FOR A MIXED COMMISSION TO EMANCIPATE THESE NEGROES—NEWSPAPER ADVERTISEMENTS FOR SALE OR HIRE OF SUCH NEGROES—SIR H. HOWARD'S AND MR. CONSUL VEREKER'S REPORTS—BRAZILIAN GOVERNMENT DO NOTHING—STORY OF AN ENSLAVED FREE AFRICAN WOMAN AT BAHIA.

IN a Brazilian newspaper (the *Diario do Rio*) of February 4th, I read a paragraph headed "*Bens do Evento*," which means "eventual property," and enumerating thirteen slaves, male and female, who had been imprisoned, and, after a certain time, being unclaimed by their owners, lapsed to the State, and were ordered—to be set free? No—to be sold by auction!

How is it that slaves thus coming into possession of the Brazilian government are not set free, considering the account given by Senhor Andrada to the deputation of the Anti-slavery Committee of the feelings of the Emperor, Ministers, parliament, and people of Brazil as to abolition of slavery?

It will be satisfactory, in any statistics of Brazilian slavery, to know the number of slaves annually coming in this way into the power of the Brazilian government, and sold by auction.

Every slave introduced into the Brazilian empire after March, 1830, when the importation of slaves became unlawful under the stipulations of the Convention of 1826, and by the law of Brazil, is illegally a slave and legally free; so are his children, unless born of mothers who are lawful slaves. I need not say that, in spite of law and treaty, there was an immense importation of slaves into Brazil after 1830 till 1851 or 1852. The number of slaves illegally introduced during that period is estimated at a million. In a despatch of mine to Earl Russell, of May 27, 1861, I state that, of the 3,000,000 of Brazilian slaves, there may be 1,000,000 who are in illegal slavery. Does the Brazilian government, which is so zealous against slavery, and which should be the guardian and executor of Brazilian laws, do anything to rescue these victims of illegal slavery? The British government tried for some time to persuade the Brazilian government to do what was right in this matter,—respect their treaty engagements and execute their own laws, but, as in everything else, their efforts were ineffectual. Lord Palmerston in 1850 instructed Sir James Hudson to propose a Convention for a Mixed Commission to emancipate the negroes in illegal slavery. The Brazilian government refused. They pretended that any interference of the English government in the matter was an invasion of their national rights and dignity,—they would do their own duty themselves. They have not done it. "We have a treaty with Brazil," said Mr. Gladstone, in March, 1850, "which she has broken every day for the last twenty years. We have tried to secure the freedom of the *emancipados;* we endeavoured to make the Brazilians declare it a crime to import slaves into Brazil. This treaty has been repeatedly broken, and we have a perfect right to demand its fulfilment; and if we have the right to demand it, we have the right to do so at the point of the sword, in case of refusal. We have now a perfect right to go to Brazil and call upon her to emancipate every slave imported since 1830, and, on refusal, to make war with her even to extermination." The English government has never thought, and is not likely to think, of enforcing this right by war. But the right is here, and the duty is there; and when Brazil, or Lord Brougham, or Mr. Osborne, or a "Brazilian agent," comes forward to claim the repeal of the "Abcrdeen Act" as earned by the "admirable conduct" of the Brazilian government in suppressing the slave-trade, and as a fulfilment of an alleged promise of Lord Aberdeen, speaking for the Queen's government in its "corporate and enduring character," we have a right to reply: "First prove your admirable virtue by doing your duty completely, though tardily, as to thousands of free Africans and a million of illegal slaves, and fulfil your own 'corporate and enduring' treaty-engagements and promises, which involve the liberty, well-being, and happiness of upwards of a million of fellow-creatures, before talking to us of 'moral obligation' and the 'enduring and corporate character' of words of Lord Aberdeen's about the repeal of an act which your own extreme misconduct compelled him to pass, and which now only offends your pride."

These illegal slaves are at every moment and everywhere in presence of the Brazilian authorities, but are not seen. No step is ever taken to rescue them from their masters, who notoriously hold them, or publicly sell them, in defiance of the law. It may now be pretty safely taken for granted that any African-born slave fit for work is an illegal importation. Thirty-three years have passed since slave-importation became illegal in Brazil, in March, 1831. The slave-traders generally brought only grown men and women across the ocean, chiefly men. Thinking only of the moment, they did not waste space on children. The average term of life of a slave in Brazil is computed at thirty-five years, and of available service at twenty years. It may, therefore, be generally taken for granted that an African-born slave, or, as it is called in Brazil, slave *de naçao*, advertised in the journals for sale or hire, is an illegal slave. There is, at any rate, a strong presumption that it is so. Such advertisements occur every day. In the *Jornal do Commercio* of Rio, of May 28th, which is before me, I find seven such advertisements. In the same journal of June 15th, there is an advertisement of sale of slaves by auction, including four African-born slaves. The addresses are thus made known to the police, who make no inquiries and do nothing. But the Brazilian government, if asked, say that the government is on the alert, and that the police do their duty. Still nothing is done.

I wrote on this subject to Earl Russell, in a despatch dated June 24, 1861 :—

"Advertisements continually appear in the Rio journals for the sale of slaves, African-born, with a declaration of age, which, if true, renders obvious or probable their importation since 1831. I lately collected a few of these advertisements from the journals of three or four days, and directed inquiries to be made about the slaves advertised. Senhor Sá e Albuquerque having lately given me an opening for alluding to the subject, I mentioned to him the advertisements and the cases about which I had caused inquiry to be made. He stated that the police were always on the look-out for such advertisements, and that the slave-sellers had an interest in representing the slaves as younger than they really were. I replied to this last observation, that, by giving an age from which importation since 1831 was to be concluded, the sellers were incurring danger of criminal proceedings, if the police did their duty. Senhor Sá e Albuquerque, however, did not seek to deny the responsibility of the Brazilian government as to slaves imported since 1831, and he encouraged me to place in his hands a minute of the information contained in the inclosed report. I called his attention at the same time to an advertisement in the leading Rio newspaper of the 19th instant, of which I inclose a copy, for the sale of forty-five slaves, among whom those marked with a cross in the inclosed copy are, some of them certainly, and all probably, illegal importations. I explained to Senhor Sá e Albuquerque that I made these observations and gave this information unofficially, and that I did not undertake to keep him informed of evidence furnished by the Rio newspapers of probable infraction of Brazilian laws made in execution of a treaty with Great Britain. The Slave-trade Correspondence, Class B, furnishes instances of official communications made by my predecessors to the Brazilian government in similar cases."

Sir Henry Howard, when he was Minister in Brazil, did his best to get the Brazilian government to do their duty in this matter. He wrote to the Earl of Clarendon, August 12, 1854;—

"I have been induced to take up these cases with the Brazilian government, not from any exaggerated hope of really putting an end to similar illegal sales, but from the wish to deprive the slave-traders of that encouragement which so public and patent a violation of the law could not have failed to afford to them."

Mr. Consul Vereker alluded to this subject in a report on slavery in Rio Grande do Sul, addressed to Lord Clarendon on June 30, 1857:—

"The events which are taking place in this district, disclosing a ray of hope to the unfortunate negro race, are unquestionably the result rather of the inevitable force of circumstances than of the direct action of the authorities or of the heartfelt convictions of the people. No substantial impediments are offered to the clandestine sales, as slaves, of persons of colour entitled to their freedom; no efforts are made to wrench from their wrongful claimants those negroes who have been imported since 1831, and their children."

On the 7th of March of this year two slaves, stated to be natives of the coast of Africa, were tried and acquitted at Rio on a charge of theft, the government prosecuting. They are said not to have known their ages when asked. Did it ever occur to the authorities to ask themselves whether these two Africans, against whom the law was being pressed for suspected robbery, had themselves been robbed against the law of their liberty?

When the Emperor, Ministers, Parliament, and people of Brazil are all, according to Senhor Andrada of the Brazilian Legation, eager and impatient for the abolition of slavery, some beginning should be made of emancipation of the million of illegal slaves, some steps taken to put the authorities in motion to rescue these poor creatures from illegal slavery, when they come before the public in law courts and in newspaper advertisements of sales.

The full possible extent of the wrong arising from this illegal slavery may be best seen by a particular instance. The following tale of a free African was told to the Chief of Police at Bahia, in 1862, and published in the *Jornal da Bahia* of February 12, and April 2, 1862. A free African woman named Dido had been hired out by the authorities, in 1842, to a certain Councillor, named Rebouças; he sent her off to a distant sugar plantation, gave her a new name, Ritta, and transformed the free woman into a slave. She had seven children, who should all have been free, as the mother was, but who all grew up slaves of Councillor Rebouças. Two of these children, of the ages of eighteen and fifteen, presented themselves in 1862 to the Chief of Police of Bahia to claim their freedom. One of their sisters, they said, was then in the House of Correction, about to be sold; two others had been given by Rebouças as a marriage portion with one of his daughters.

Thus the evil does not stop with the one illegally enslaved. The wrong multiplies itself in the children and children's children.

## CHAPTER VIII.

### SLAVERY IN BRAZIL.

LORD MALMESBURY'S SUSPENSION OF SEIZURES IN BRAZILIAN PORTS AND WATERS, 1852—HIS INSTRUCTIONS AS TO COASTING SLAVE TRAFFIC—SLAVE-TRADE SUPPRESSED UNDER ENGLISH PRESSURE—TESTIMONIES OF MR. SOUTHERN AND MESSRS. CANDLER AND BURGESS—SIR HENRY HOWARD, MR. JERNINGHAM, LORD CLARENDON, AND MR. SCARLETT ON COASTING SLAVE-TRADE—FIVE THOUSAND SLAVES ANNUALLY TAKEN FROM NORTHERN PROVINCES TO RIO—SCARCITY OF LABOUR IN THE NORTH—MR. BRIGHT ON SLAVERY IN THE CONFEDERATE STATES—CONDEMNATIONS OF COASTING TRAFFIC BY BRAZILIAN STATESMEN—HORSEWHIPPING OF MOTHER AND SON BY A BRAZILIAN'S SLAVE AT JUIZ DA FORA, 1864—LORD BROUGHAM ON SLAVERY.

MR. OSBORNE lately informed the House of Commons of the suspension by Lord Malmesbury, when he came into office in the beginning of 1852, of the orders issued by Lord Palmerston in 1850, under which slavers had been captured by our cruisers in Brazilian waters. "Withdrawal," Mr. Osborne called it. "I find," said Mr. Osborne, "that Lord Malmesbury withdrew the order for British cruisers to enter the Brazilian ports and waters, and I must say that the conduct of Lord Malmesbury, who has been so much abused on this side of the House, in his management of our affairs with Brazil, has much redounded to his credit. The Brazilian Chambers, sensible of the kindness and conciliating disposition by which the conduct of the noble lord had been dictated, redoubled their efforts to suppress the slave-trade."

So effectual had been the work done under Lord Palmerston's orders by the end of 1851, that Lord Malmesbury was able to suspend the orders. I am happy to say that this suspension was not done with a "kindness and conciliating disposition" which involved a repudiation of the "Aberdeen Act," or of Lord Palmerston's mode of proceeding. On April 27, 1852, Lord Malmesbury communicated to Mr. Southern, then the Minister at Rio, the suspension of the orders of 1850. On June 18th, Lord Malmesbury wrote to Mr. Southern:—

"I have to instruct you to take every fitting opportunity of stating to the Brazilian government that if the African slave-traffic should not continue to be effectually kept down in the empire of Brazil, it will become your duty to report that circumstance to Her Majesty's government, who will, on the first demand from you, immediately renew the lately suspended orders which were issued by Her Majesty's government in 1850, authorising Her Majesty's cruisers to make captures within the Brazilian waters."

Lord Malmesbury, who came in for the death of the ocean slave-trade of Brazil, came in also for the birth of a coasting slave-traffic, which has gone on increasing to the present time; and he ordered remonstrances to be made to the Brazilian government against this coasting traffic, about which it is said by the "Friend to both Countries," that the English government worries the Emperor of Brazil "with no more right, morally or legally, to interfere than with the shoe-strings of the Khan of Tartary." "You will take every opportunity," he wrote to Mr. Southern, "of urging the Brazilian government to adopt some stringent and effective measures of police at the ports where these slaves are embarked as well as at Rio de Janeiro, in order to check these underhand attempts of the slave-traders to renew their traffic under cover of the coasting trade."

Mr. Southern duly informed Lord Malmesbury that the suppression of the slave-trade, had been forced on the Brazilian government by Sir James Hudson's execution of Lord Palmerston's orders. Mr. Southern wrote to Lord Malmesbury, August 10, 1852 :—

"I have the honour to inclose a translation of the speech of Senhor Eusebio Queiroz, the late Minister of Justice, in which that Deputy endeavours to show in a most laborious manner, that Mr. Hudson did not fairly report to Her Majesty's government the transactions in which he was so actively engaged during the last two years, when M. Eusebio was a prominent member of this government. The publication of Mr. Hudson's despatches in the Blue-book was considered a great blow to the Brazilian government, for by a perusal of Mr. Hudson's despatches it became manifest to all the world that the suppression of the slave-trade had been forced on this government. Now Senhor Eusebio and his colleagues rest their claims for the applause of the world on having spontaneously and on principle undertaken and carried through this most laudable enterprise."

There is another testimony on this subject which I desire to cite; it is that of two members of the Society of Friends, Messrs. John Candler and Wilson Burgess, who went to Rio in 1852 with an address to the Emperor on slave-trade and slavery; and their testimony is at this moment particularly valuable, when the Committee of the British and Foreign Anti-slavery Society are conveying in courtly phrases different sentiments to the Emperor of Brazil. They wrote on their return from Brazil :—

"Although viewing Christianity as a religion of peace, we cannot but deplore all resort to arms to further any cause, however righteous ; we must state our conviction that the late conduct of Great Britain in chasing the African slavers into the harbours of Brazil, and making seizures of them under its very forts, has contributed mainly to stimulate the government of Brazil to put down the African slave-trade to that country. It deeply wounded the pride of the nation to see its past insincerity and bad faith thus exposed to the whole world; the Emperor therefore resolved to take the matter at once into his own hands, and by bold measures to crush the traffic."

I observe that at the late interview of a deputation from the Anti-slavery Committee with Senhor Andrada, of the Brazilian Legation, Mr. Thomas Binns, one of the deputation, presented Senhor Andrada with a copy of Messrs. Candler and Burgess's book.

I return to the coasting traffic in slaves, against which, in 1852, Lord Malmesbury instructed the British Minister at Rio to remonstrate on every fitting occasion. Lord Clarendon, in 1854, instructed Sir Henry Howard "to call the attention of the Brazilian government to the cruelty of this system, and to suggest that it be put a stop to by some legislative enactment." Sir Henry Howard wrote to the Brazilian Minister, April 8, 1854 :—

"All at once a slave-trader comes into the market from Rio de Janeiro, buys up from the needy or avaricious masters all those slaves he can obtain, and in most cases is the cause of the separation of a father from his wife and children, and *vice versâ*, the unfortunate African being perhaps sold at his ulterior destination to some harder master, or to some other unprincipled speculator."

On July 14, 1856, Mr. Jerningham called Lord Clarendon's attention particularly to the increasing coasting trade, and pointed out its dangers. There were then landings and rumours of landings of slaves.

"Everything is possible on this line of coast, and although I have not had sufficient ground to believe that disembarcations occurred at Camamu, or at Cape Frio, one thing has rendered me distrustful for some months past; this is, the activity of the movements to the north and south of the coasting slave-dealers, who are continually on the wing between Bahia, Rio, and Santos. These men purchase slaves in the northern provinces, and bring them to Rio de Janeiro for sale, or take them to Santos, in the Province of St. Paul's; and this trade, unfortunately, is a legitimate one. I was told, on good authority, that between January 3d and June 3d of this year, 1,400 had been brought south from the northern provinces, where the cholera had been excessively severe. I have often asked myself the question, how comes it that these agriculturists and others, who complain so much of want of hands, can afford to increase that want by allowing so many blacks to be taken away from these provinces to the southern market? The only solution that appears to me to suggest itself is, that somehow or other, unknown to the government, Africans may be smuggled in by driblets to some secret northern point, and afterwards exchanged for coasting slaves who are brought up coastwise hither.

"I also find that Her Majesty's Consul at Maranham, Mr. Ovenden, copy of whose despatch to me respecting the late rumoured landing at Turyassy I here inclose, entertains the possibility of a similar manner of proceeding. Mr. Ovenden is of opinion that the slave-trade can never be extinct as long as it is allowed to convey slaves for sale from one Province to another; and he points out that it is the policy of the slave-dealer, both in a pecuniary point of view and in that of insuring success, to effect exchanges of Africans for coasters in the out-of-the-way places, where the farmers are poor and not over-trustworthy, which put him directly in possession of legal property, for which the provincial traffickers can get enormous prices in the richer and moneyed provinces of the south."

Again and again Lord Clarendon instructed Mr. Jerningham, and after him Mr. Scarlett, to make representations on the subject. Mr. Scarlett's last representation to the Brazilian Minister for Foreign Affairs was on January 8, 1858, and a copy of it was forwarded to the Earl of Clarendon in a despatch of April 1st, which found Lord Malmesbury again in office. Mr. Scarlett wrote to the Brazilian Minister in strong language:—

"The Undersigned, &c. has been instructed by his government to appeal strongly to the justice and humanity of the Imperial government on the subject of the coasting trade in Brazilian slaves, which has for some time been a disgrace to the country. . . . The Undersigned is convinced that the province of Maranham, on account of its latitude and burning climate, is the least likely to obtain hereafter the aid of white free labourers, instead of black slaves, and the consequent removal of the black creole population will only render it the more impossible to fill up the vacancy thus created by any other means than that of resorting to the still more iniquitous and illegal traffic in slaves from the continent of Africa, which, in spite of the government, the planters will be ultimately tempted to renew. The Undersigned trusts that the Imperial government will, on reflection, take the same view of this question as that taken by the government of the Queen, and that it will not hesitate, when the Legislature meets, to propose a law prohibiting the export or removal of slaves from the Provinces in which they were born, and, as a primary step, to interdict at once vessels subsidized by the government, carrying its mails, troops, &c. and commanded by officers of the Imperial marine, like the *Imperatriz* and others, from carrying these unfortunate people to other Provinces, for the purpose of being sold at a distance from their natural homes."

This trade remains unchecked. On September 30, 1862, I sent to Lord Russell a statistical table, showing that 34,688 slaves had been thus imported at Rio by sea in ten years and a half, from January 1, 1852, to July 1, 1862. To these importations are to be added those carried by land; and Senhor Soares, a Brazilian official and an authority beyond suspicion, estimates the average annual importation at 5,000. Senator Silveira da Motta has lately frequently called attention to this traffic, to its cruelties, its economical effects, and its bearings on the question of a possible revival of slave-trade in the north. "The north is being depopulated of slaves," said this Senator, May 17, 1861. Again, in 1862, he said:—

"The phenomenon to which the Minister should pay attention is the future of the north of the Empire. From the want of labourers, with a torrid climate, which is less inviting to colonization than that of the south, what is the condition in which the northern Provinces will remain in relation to those of the south? When the north shall have become entirely deprived of slave labour, when they shall have become at the mercy of the tardy and slow resources of colonization, what will be their destiny? Do they wish to live only at the cost of the south? And is the government to look on passively at the progress of that phenomenon, without having the courage to look its consequences in the face, when our neighbours in the northern division of this continent give us a sad example of its evil consequences?"

The draining of slaves by this unchecked coasting traffic from the north of Brazil, where African labour is more indispensable than in the south,—the draining of them from the part of Brazil nearest to Cuba, may be thought worthy of attention by the responsible Ministers of the Queen when asked to repeal the "Aberdeen Act."

On the occasion on which Lord Palmerston, in answer to a question from Mr. Hardcastle, described the misconduct of the Brazilian government about the *emancipados* in terms certainly not uncalled for, unwarrantable, or too severe, Mr. Bright urged on Lord Palmerston the repeal of the "Aberdeen Act," and asserted that that act was the sole cause of all our discontents and misunderstandings with Brazil,—"a nation," he said, "with which England had extensive commercial relations, and might have more extensive, if there was a government in this country at all disposed to meet the government of Brazil in a friendly spirit." If I might hope to be read by Mr. Bright, I should expect to shake him in his mistaken belief as to the causes of our endless troubles with Brazil. Presuming now to address myself to Mr. Bright individually, I beg him to review the conduct of the Brazilian government as I have described it with regard to the *emancipados,* and the facts, as I have stated them, as to the extent and condition of slavery in Brazil, and then to ask himself whether the Brazilian government is worthy of his sympathy and favour and protection, against the government of his own country. Is there no advice which, as an honest man and a Christian philanthropist, he will feel it his duty to give to the government of Brazil,—is there no action which he will require from the Brazilian government before again pressing on Lord Palmerston the repeal of the "Aberdeen Act" as an act of grace or an act of confidence for Brazil? Just before the beginning of the last session of Parliament Mr. Bright declared, at Birmingham, his views as to slavery in the Confederate States of North America. I quote some of his burning words:—

"I believe that in the providence of the Supreme the slaveholder, untaught and unteachable by fact, or argument, or Christian precept, has been permitted to commit —I will not call it the crime, but the act of suicide upon himself. (Cheers.) Whether President Lincoln will be in favour of abolition, whether the North are unanimous against slavery, whatever may be said or thought with regard to the transactions on that continent, he must be deaf and blind, and worse than deaf and blind, who does not perceive that through the instrumentality of this strife that most odious and most indescribable offence against man and against heaven, the slavery and bondage of four millions of our fellow-creatures, is coming to a certain and a rapid end. (Loud cheers.) I will say of this question that I look forward to the time when I shall stand on this platform with my honourable colleague, and when he will join with me,—for he is honest and frank enough to do that,—when he will join with me in rejoicing that there does not breathe a slave on the North American continent —(loud cheers)—that the Union has been completely restored; and not less will he rejoice that England did not in the remotest manner, by a word or a breath or the raising of a finger or the settling of a question, do one single thing to promote the atrocious object of the leaders of this accursed insurrection." (Continued cheering.)

These are not my words; they are Mr. Bright's. Well, then, while in all the surrounding Spanish American States there is no slavery, in Brazil there is "that most odious and most indescribable offence against man and against heaven, the slavery and bondage of three millions of our fellow-creatures." One million of these should have been long ago free by a treaty with Great Britain, which is disregarded and violated; there "breathe" in Brazil ten thousand "free Africans," "free" by name and by treaty, whose freedom is guaranteed to Great Britain, but who are kept by the Brazilian government in slavery, and receive, have received, and are to receive no wages, a great part of which has been confessedly received and spent by the Brazilian government. There is a coasting slave-trade, by which five thousand slaves a year are torn from their homes and families by the "atrocious" lust of lucre. This is the state of the "accursed" institution on the South American continent in Brazil; there also Mr. Bright must in his honest heart believe the slaveholder to be "untaught and unteachable by fact, or argument, or Christian precept;" and is it consistent in him, "in the remotest manner, by a word, or a breath, or the raising of a finger, or the settling of a question," to give countenance or encouragement or protection to a government which maintains this "accursed" state of things? It may at least occur to him that something else is wanted for setting things right than to get "a government in this country at all disposed to meet the government of Brazil in a friendly spirit."

To return once more for a moment to the coasting slave-traffic; it has frequently been condemned by Brazilian

Ministers in words, though it has not been prohibited or checked.

When Mr. Southern, serving under Lord Malmesbury, made the first remonstrance against this coasting traffic in a note to Senhor Paulino, July 3, 1852, he mentioned its antagonism to the principles laid down by Senhor Eusebio, the Brazilian Minister, for whom the credit of suppression of the slave-trade, after Sir James Hudson's strong measures, is specially claimed. Mr. Southern said: "The influx of slaves from the Provinces towards this capital is in direct opposition to the principles laid down for the guidance of the Imperial government in the Report of the late Minister of Justice."

In 1854, Senhor Wanderley, then President of Bahia, now Baron of Cotegibe, who has been a Minister and is a Senator, proposed a measure for dealing with this traffic as slave-trade, and subjecting it to the penalties of the African traffic. The measure was much supported, but was not carried. Sir Henry Howard reported at that time to Lord Clarendon that "one of the most distinguished public men" of Brazil had told him that "he considered the first thing that ought to be done was to put a stop to the transfer of slaves from one Province to another, then to remove them from the towns to the country, and attach them to the glebe, thus preparing the way for emancipation."

Sir Henry Howard, in a despatch dated January 24, 1855, wrote to Lord Clarendon of this coasting traffic, that it led to the importation into Rio of "slaves of notoriously bad characters, with the view of obtaining a better price for them than where they are known, as well as of negroes and others, of whom it may be presumed that they either have been, or are intended to be, illegally reduced to slavery." Sir H. Howard added: "It has been remarked that several assassinations of their masters, and suicides, have lately been committed in this Province by slaves imported from the northern Provinces."

On January 12, 1857, Mr. Scarlett reported that Senhor Paranhos, then Minister for Foreign Affairs, had spoken to him as follows about this traffic, which, according to the "Friend to both Countries," is "a great mitigation of the evil of slavery in Brazil, an advantage to the slaves removed, and a gain to humanity," and with which, according to the same cosmopolitan authority, the English Foreign Office has no more right to interfere than "with the shoestrings of the Khan of Tartary or with the fares of Brazilian railways." Mr. Scarlett writes:

"His Excellency (Senhor Paranhos) assured me that the Brazilian government would endeavour to mitigate, as much as possible, the evils by which this system of separating families was attended; and to show that although this traffic is permitted by law, it did not meet with his approbation or sympathy, he said that very recently he had caused a Brazilian naval officer commanding a ship of war to be dismissed from the service for taking slaves on board his vessel in a northern port to bring them to Rio de Janeiro, and, to indicate the opinion of the Imperial government, the circumstances of the case had been officially mentioned in a newspaper."

Mr. Scarlett added:

"As long, however, as this traffic in slaves is tolerated by law, and until the Legislature has resolved to put an end to this system altogether, I fear there is little chance of seriously ameliorating the condition of these unfortunate people."

The Senator Silveira da Motta has, during the present year, in the Brazilian Senate, described this coasting traffic in slaves as "in reality a disguised slave-trade."

The "Brazilian agent," however, who has for so long a time been misleading the *Daily News* and other English journals, and has latterly been writing in the *Daily News* as the "Friend to both Countries," asserted, in one of his letters, that this coasting slave-traffic is nothing but a transportation of labour, "made in obedience to economical laws," and further, "a great mitigation of the evil of slavery in Brazil, an advantage to the slaves removed, and a gain to humanity." One of his proofs of this is an alleged superior civilization of the southern Provinces, to which the slaves are taken:—

> "In the north, society is comparatively ill-organized, civilization is more backward, society is less sympathetic, the eye and supervision of the government are more distant: it is in the south that the immense progress and prosperity of Brazil are most evident; that the greatest advance in government and society has been made; that European habits and manners are more general; that humanity is more cared for; that public opinion has most influence; and that the ill-treatment of slaves is less probable."

A curious illustration of the state of manners and civilization in one of the southern Provinces to which many of those slaves are carried,—the Province of Minas Geraes,—reached England almost contemporaneously with the above statement. The following account of a Brazilian gentleman's employing a slave to horsewhip a young man who had given him offence, and of the slave's doing execution with his whip not only on the young man, but also on his aged mother, who came out on hearing her son's cries, was published in the *Jornal do Commercio* of Rio of July 30. The lady who was thus ill-treated is well known to me. She is by birth English, of a good English family, and the widow of a Brazilian diplomatist, Senhor Cerqueira de Lima. This scandal occurred in the civilized town of Juiz da Fora, the terminus of a splendid road which has lately been constructed at a great expense from Petropolis, from which it is about ten hours distant. It is in the Province of Minas Geraes, not far from the bordering Province of Rio de Janeiro. In that Province a large quantity of English capital is embarked in mines, and there are English Mining Companies employing a considerable number of slaves:—

"A most indescribable fact has lately occurred in the town of Juiz da Fora. There resides there Major Luis Pinto Coelho da Cunha, whose son Julio, from fourteen to sixteen years old, made it his constant practice to insult with the most opprobrious names a young man, Emilio de Cerqueira Lima, and his mother, Senhora Dona Henriqueta Cerqueira de Lima, to whom was entrusted the education of the daughters of the principal persons of the place. Emilio complained to the father, Major Cunha, in the presence of several persons. But this was of no use, for the next day the son repeated his insults. Emilio Cerqueira de Lima, enraged, gave Julio Cunha two or three taps with a thin cane, which did not hurt him in the least, as several witnesses assert. Julio went immediately to his father's house and came out with a whip, and at the door, in the presence of his mother and sisters, told Emilio that the next day he would have him punished with that whip. Francisco Alves da Cunha Horta, married to the boy's sister, declared that if he were the father, he would send two slaves to horsewhip Emilio. Two days after Emilio was barbarously flogged by the black man Romao, a slave of Francisco Horta, between one and two in the afternoon, in the principal street; and not only this, but the slave acted in the same way with Emilio's mother, who came out on hearing her son's cries. This proceeding was witnessed by some of the chief persons of the place, who did not, however, interfere, fearing that they might also be victims, as was indeed Dr. Nunes Lima, who cried out to the black to let his victims go. It is sad to have to record a fact which should have been possible only in a savage land."

I cite this simply as an illustration of the social habits of the higher class, in connexion with slavery, in one of the southern Provinces of Brazil, whose superior civilization has been vaunted by the "Brazilian agent." *

* I have not entered on the large and interesting question of the social, moral, and economical influences of slavery in Brazil. They are, and must be, the same as in all other countries where the "institution" has existed. There are good masters, and there are naturally many bad ones and much cruelty. Some incidental notices of the effects of slavery may be found in the despatches of Sir James Hudson and other British Ministers, in the series of Slave-trade Correspondence, Class B. There is no recent English work of value or authority on Brazil, treating this subject. The accounts of slavery in the work of Dr. Walsh, who accompanied Lord Strangford to Brazil as Chaplain, "Notices of Brazil in 1828 and 1829." are still worthy of perusal. For more modern accounts I must refer the reader to French publications; the valuable articles of M. Elisée Reclus, "Le Brésil et la Colonisation," in the *Revue des Deux Mondes* of June 15th and July 15th, 1862, the not less valuable and interesting articles of M. A. d'Assier, "Le Brésil et la Société Brésilienne," in the *Revue des Deux Mondes* of June 1st and 15th and July 1st, 1863, the chapter on "Slaves in Brazil" in M. Dabadie's "A Travers l'Amérique du Sud," (Paris, 1859,) and the work of M. Expilly, "Le Brésil tel qu'il est," (Paris, 2d edition, 1863).

Lord Brougham, in one of his celebrated speeches, lately reprinted in the collected edition of his works, Speech on Negro Slavery, July 13th, 1830, laid down two infallible tests of misery; decreasing or stationary population, and prevalence of crime. The slavery of three millions among the Brazilian population of seven millions and a half, may be judged by both these tests. I quote a part of Lord Brougham's speech :—"The two tests or criteria of happiness among any people which I will now resort to are the progress of population and the amount of crime. These, but the first especially, are of all others the most safely to be relied on. Wherever we see the number of men stationary, much more when we perceive them decreasing, we may rest assured that there is some fundamental vice in the community, that makes head against the most irresistible of all the impulses of our physical constitution. There cannot be a more appalling picture presented to the reflecting mind than that of a people decreasing in numbers. To him who can look beyond the abstract number, whose eye is not confined to the mere tables and returns of population, but ranges over the miseries of which such a diminution is the infallible symptom, it offers a view of all the forms of wretchedness, suffering in every shape, privations in unlimited measure, whatever is most contrary to the nature of human beings, most alien to their habits, most adverse to their happiness and comfort,—all beginning in slavery, the state most unnatural to man ; consummated through various channels in his degradation, and leading to one common end,—the grave. Show me but the simple fact that the people in any country are regularly decreasing, so as in half a century to be extinct ; and I want no other evidence that their lot is of the bitterest wretchedness ; nor will any other facts convince me that their general condition can be favourable or mild." In one of my latest despatches to Lord Russell, February 26th, 1863, I related, as the result of my inquiries during two years and a half, the opinion that "the slave population is decreasing, though not very considerably." I added, "The mortality among the children of slaves is very great ; and Brazilian proprietors do not appear to have given nearly so much attention as might have been expected, from obvious motives of self-interest, to marriages among slaves, or the care of mothers or children. There are no statistics as to the slave population, and the Government does not seem to care to have them." A most remarkable, and I believe unexaggerated, brief account of the "Social and Religious State of Brazil," may be read in "The Work of the Christian Church at Home and Abroad," No. 2, for April, 1863, published by A. Strahan and Co. Ludgate Hill, and to be bought for sixpence.

# CHAPTER IX.

## COMMERCIAL RELATIONS WITH BRAZIL.

LORD PALMERSTON CHARGED WITH SPITE TO BRAZIL — NEWSPAPERS IN EUROPE SUBSIDIZED BY BRAZIL—SECRET-SERVICE EXPENDITURE OF £30,000 A YEAR—MR. CANNING'S POLICY—THE TREATY OF COMMERCE OF 1827—FIFTEEN PER CENT. MAXIMUM OF BRAZILIAN DUTIES ON ENGLISH IMPORTS—CONSULAR ADMINISTRATION OF ENGLISH INTESTATE SUCCESSIONS — SIR HUGH CAIRNS AND BRITISH CLAIMANTS — EXCUSES FOR BRAZIL BY BRAZILIAN ADVOCATES—BRAZIL OBJECTS TO TREATIES OF COMMERCE WITH SUPERIOR NATIONS—HIGH IMPORT DUTIES AND SMUGGLING—CORRUPTION IN BRAZILIAN CUSTOM-HOUSES —MR. OSBORNE'S INFORMATION ABOUT BRAZIL.

EVERY member of Parliament who takes a different view of Brazilian affairs from Lord Palmerston and his colleagues, has been continually trumpeted by the "Brazilian agent," in his letters in the *Daily News*, as an "impartial public mau." Lord Palmerston and Lord Russell are biassed; Lord Malmesbury, Mr. Seymour Fitzgerald, Sir Hugh Cairns, and Mr. Osborne are "impartial public men." I do not know why members of the Opposition, hoping to be Ministers, should be more "impartial" than those who are charged with the responsibilities of government. Lord Palmerston is at any rate much better informed about Brazil than gentlemen out of office, who have more or less allowed themselves to be informed by the impartial "Brazilian agent," who, under the title of "Friend to both Countries," afterwards impartially lauds the impartiality of his instruments.

Sir Hugh Cairns, certainly not the least distinguished of these "impartial public men," said in the House of Commons, on the occasion of Mr. Osborne's late motion, that merchants in this country connected with Brazil were in despair on acccount of Lord Palmerston's "inveterate hostility to the government of Brazil." And Mr. Osborne, another "impartial," spoke of Lord Palmerston's "spite" against Brazil.

"Spite!" "Inveterate hostility!" Are these the feelings ascribed by "impartial" friends of Brazil to the Prime Minister of England?

A French writer, who knows Brazil well, M. Expilly, says that if one finds any fault with Brazil, speaks of the immorality of slavery, or anything else open to reproach, he is immediately and "necessarily an enemy of Brazil and deserves hanging."

The same writer makes some instructive statements as to the manner in which praises of Brazil have been manufactured in Europe; and it is a fact that something like 30,000*l.* is annually voted in the Brazilian budget for "secret expenses and the suppression of the slave-trade." But the slave-trade being suppressed, the inquiry naturally arises,—what is done with all this money? This question was asked not long ago in the Brazilian Senate, and Senhor Sinimbú, to whom, as a Minister, it fell to answer the inquiry, did not give so clear an answer as may be derived from the following statements of M. Expilly:—

"In Germany, France, Switzerland, and Italy, subsidized publications have undertaken an active propaganda.

. . . . In Paris, negotiations were opened with different organs of the press, with the avowed object of combating the sad impressions diffused by accounts which were declared to be 'calumnious' in the highest degree, and 'hostile' to Brazil. A vast plan had been conceived, by which several daily journals, and a still larger number of halfpenny sheets, were to exalt, in all tones, and under all forms which thought can assume, the progressive policy of Brazil, the mildness of its climate, the hospitality of its inhabitants, the varied productions of its fertile soil, and if not the benefits of slavery, which in Europe are not quite appreciated, at least the state of perfect happiness created for the blacks by this eminently patriarchal institution. This patriotic combination required, it seems, a little more money than was forthcoming; thus it failed almost entirely. One journal at present, is considered in Paris to have intimate relations with official Brazil." *

In a letter of the "Friend to both Countries," in the *Daily News* of August 23, is the following condemnation of a long succession of English Foreign Secretaries, with an explanation of his reason for adopting the signature:—

"What English interests, I ask, have they promoted in Brazil? They have not given us a Treaty of Commerce, they have not secured us a Consular Treaty such as France has obtained; they have not produced a settlement of the claims which the subjects of each country have on the government of the other, such as the United States long ago obtained. A very different policy in Mr. Canning's time made Brazil an Empire almost dependent on England. A subsequent policy of 'taunting' has converted it into an Empire on which the English government has not a particle of influence. It is because I wish to revive the policy of Canning in this part of South America, that

* Expilly, "Le Brésil tel qu'il est." Second Edition, 1863.

I have adopted the signature of 'A Friend to Both Countries.'"

But this Canning Redivivus had, in the course of his letters, and even in the very one which ended with this rhetorical flourish, assailed the two Treaties which Mr. Canning caused to be concluded with Brazil, quite forgetting, of course, that they were Mr. Canning's. These were the Conventions for the suppression of Slave-trade of 1826, and the Treaty of Commerce of 1827.

Mr. Canning recognised the independence of Brazil, and with much zeal and labour procured its recognition by Portugal. "He made Brazil," says the would-be reviver of his policy, "an Empire almost dependent on England." He might certainly have expected gratitude and fulfilment of treaty-obligations. But here, it appears, he made a great mistake. Indeed, we are told by Canning Redivivus, that he made two great blunders, two great faults. The first was the Slave-trade Convention of 1826, with its provisions as to the *emancipados*, which were forced into the Convention (I quote from the "Friend to both Countries") "simply to save England trouble and expense, and to escape from the responsibility of properly caring for those Africans;" and again the same writer says: "That those Africans were allowed to remain in the Brazilian Empire, was the consequence of the act and pleasure of the Foreign Office, in incorporating into the Convention of 1826, which it required from the Empire as part of the price of its recognition, the provisions of the pre-existing treaty with Portugal."

Here, then, was Mr. Canning's great fault No. 1, when he made Brazil "an Empire almost dependent on England."

He made a second fault in making a second Treaty, a Treaty of Commerce. The "Friend to Both Countries" reprobates the "injudicious stipulations of the English commercial treaty, which was the other part of the price paid for the recognition of the Empire by this country." Here is slap in the face No. 2 from young Canning for his great precursor.

> "We think our fathers fools, so wise we grow."

There were two very useful,—I should say judicious,—stipulations, which the English merchants valued, and the loss of which they have regretted ever since the Brazilian revocation of the Treaty in 1844, before the passing of the "Aberdeen Act;" and the Brazilian government had tried to assert an interpretation of the Treaty, which would have enabled them to revoke it two years earlier, in 1842.

The two stipulations of the extinct commercial Treaty which I refer to, were one confining duties in Brazilian custom-houses on English imports to fifteen per cent. *ad valorem*, and the other giving British Consuls a right of intervention in the administration of the estates of British subjects dying intestate in Brazil.

It is true that the Brazilian government did not observe the stipulation restricting the custom-house charges on English imports to fifteen per cent. In the list of unsettled British claims on the government of Brazil is a large number of claims arising out of violations and evasions of that stipulation of the Treaty of Commerce which Mr. Canning procured in 1827, and the Brazilian government revoked in 1844. The names of McCalmont and Cairns are well and honourably known among British merchants in Rio de Janeiro; and, if I am not mistaken, the special interest felt by Sir Hugh McCalmont Cairns in the question of Brazilian claims arises from private relations with merchants who are claimants. This is natural and proper; but it does not necessarily furnish additional proof of "impartiality." I wish to speak of Sir Hugh Cairns with the respect due to his splendid abilities and high personal character. He mentioned in his speech on Mr. Osborne's motion, that he received "communications from persons engaged in commerce between England and Brazil;" and with reference to the unsettled British claims on Brazil, he informed the House of Commons that "the merchants in this country who were interested in the question said they had long since ceased to importune the Foreign Office with regard to the resumption of diplomatic relations, because they were convinced of the inveterate hostility felt by the noble lord (Lord Palmerston) and the Foreign Office to the government of Brazil." Sir Hugh Cairns also said that "no person ever disputed the justice of those claims." This is saying rather too much. At any rate, the Brazilian government disputes their justice. But there are claims of Sir Hugh Cairns's friends anterior to 1844, anterior to the "Aberdeen Act" and Lord Palmerston's language about Brazil,—which, according to Sir Hugh Cairns in another part of his speech, are the two sole causes of difficulty,—for which the English government has never yet been able to obtain a solution. There is a large number of other claims of British subjects for loss of property and personal ill-treatment, some of them also of long standing, for which, during a long series of years, a long succession of British Foreign Secretaries and

British Ministers have been unable to obtain a hearing. May not the conduct of the Brazilian government towards these claimants have contributed to cause those angry feelings towards Brazil of which the Foreign Office and Lord Palmerston are accused? And is it fair, is it grateful, is it honest or patriotic in Sir Hugh Cairns's clients, if he correctly represents their sentiments, to turn round and side with Brazil in blaming Lord Palmerston and the Foreign Office for disapproval of the Brazilian government, partly caused, and amply justified, by Brazilian treatment of British claimants?

The stipulations of the extinct Treaty of Commerce with Brazil of 1827 are pronounced "injudicious," because they rendered the finances of the Empire insufficient for the requirements of the government. The fifteen per cent. maximum of customs-duties for Brazil was too low. The writer evidently speaks with authority for Brazil, and he has here told us a secret. We now know why the Brazilian government were so impatient to revoke that Treaty, why they would have revoked it even in 1842, but that Lord Palmerston's and Lord Aberdeen's determined resistance to the Brazilian interpretation of the denouncing clause obliged them to wait till 1844. It was not the Aberdeen Act, which did not then exist, nor was it Lord Palmerston's "spite," nor the "spite" of Lord Aberdeen, (for he was Foreign Minister in 1844, having succeeded Lord Palmerston in 1841;) it was the "injudicious" lowness of the maximum of fifteen per cent. import duties; and this revelation may help to explain also how it is that we have never since achieved another commercial Treaty with Brazil. Sir Robert Peel's government sent the late

Sir Henry Ellis on a special mission to Brazil in 1842, before the termination of the old Treaty, to endeavour to negotiate a new one. He failed altogether. It was made a reproach at the time to Sir Robert Peel's government, that Mr. Ellis's mission failed because Brazilian slave-grown produce was not admissible on the same terms as the produce of our own colonies. Not a bit of it. It would have been "injudicious" in Brazil to limit herself to import duties so low as fifteen per cent. *ad valorem.* That was the reason. There have been subsequent attempts made to negotiate a Treaty of Commerce, after differential duties against slave-grown produce were swept away, but the result has been equally unsuccessful. Then the "Aberdeen Act" has been put forward by "Brazilian agents" as the reason of failure, differential duties against Brazilian produce being no longer an available pretext. In fact, Brazilian agents have always been ready with some reason to show that Brazil is not in fault, and resents ill usage. It is at this moment the reprisals and Lord Palmerston's language. We may wait for ever if we wait for the end of this succession of pretexts, which is like an ever-running river.

> "Rusticus expectat dum defluat amnis, at ille
> Labitur et labetur in omne volubilis ævum."

The real fact is, that Brazil does not choose to make Treaties of Commerce with European nations, or nations stronger than herself. She has made several, and is eager to make them, with her neighbours, the Spanish American States, which are her equals or inferiors.

Lord Palmerston said long ago, in answer to Lord George Bentinck, March 21, 1848 :—

"I cannot hold out to the House any confident expectation that in the present state of the Brazils it is likely that any commercial Treaty with this country can take place, as the Brazilians are averse to any avoidable treaties with foreign countries, and as they have a notion that we look upon their trade as so valuable that we are willing to carry on the commerce with them on almost any terms they choose to fix."

France, most of the other European nations, and the United States, made Treaties of Commerce with Brazil, containing a stipulation similar to that of the English Treaty of 1827 against higher import duties than fifteen per cent. Brazil since 1844 has been free from this obligation towards all other states as well as towards England. None of these other states have since made a Treaty of Commerce with Brazil.

If, then, English governments since 1844 "have not given us a Treaty of Commerce with Brazil," we are so far not worse off than the United States or any European nation. As to their not having "secured us a Consular Treaty such as France has obtained," I will speak later.

Brazil having become free to impose what import duties she chose, established a tariff of generally thirty per cent. and ranging in some cases as high as fifty per cent. Would such a tariff necessarily increase her revenue? Would English commerce suffer more than Brazil from a tariff which provides a high premium for the smuggler, and a strong incitement to custom-house corruption?

The following statement occurs in a report of Mr. Baillie, Secretary of Legation, January, 1861, as to the smuggling of English goods into the southern Brazilian Province of Rio Grande do Sul through Monte Video, and has been quoted by Mr. James Heywood in his paper on Brazil in the *Statistical Society's Journal* for June :—

"A great deal of smuggling is carried on over the frontier from the River Plate States, which, according to the Report of the Minister of Finance for 1860, is rapidly increasing. This is the principal impediment to British trade direct to Rio Grande. The duties imposed in this port are so much higher than those in Monte Video, that British manufactures passing the overland frontier can be furnished in the interior of the province of Rio Grande do Sul twenty per cent. cheaper than the regular merchant can afford to sell them. The duties on British goods vary in fact from fifty to eighty per cent. on the cost price in England."

If high import duties contract English commerce with Brazil, Brazilian revenue does not gain proportionally by the higher duties (this is trite political economy,) and the development of Brazil is checked. Mr. Bates, whose delightful volumes on the Amazon have been widely read, points out the effects of high duties and a restrictive policy in the poor returns of imports and exports of Pará, the port of the mighty Amazon river.

It may be, then, that the stipulation of the English Treaty of Commerce, which restricted Brazilian import duties to fifteen per cent. was not so "injudicious" for Brazil, and that lower duties than those which now prevail might quicken prosperity and increase revenue.

There is a cause diminishing customs-receipts which doubtless compromised Brazilian resources, while the Treaties of Commerce were in force, more than the limitation of import duties, and which still is a corroding canker of Brazilian revenue. It is a cause which no Treaty of Commerce can directly touch, and which it would be most difficult to trace in any way either to the "Aberdeen Act" or to Lord Palmerston's language and hostility. The corruption of custom-house officials in Brazil is general. In 1862 there was an investigation into the Rio Custom-house by a parliamentary commission. Senhor Tolentino, the Inspector of Customs, a man of probity, when called upon by the Minister of Finance to make a report to him, reported the state of things as utterly hopeless. Senhor Tolentino had been appointed Inspector in 1861, and it is notorious that he tendered his resignation very soon after his appointment, seeing his inability to grapple with the abuses of the Custom-house, and fearing that his reputation might be compromised. He told the Minister that the fault was with the government, but still more with the nation, and that he felt himself powerless to do good. This report was published; here is an extract from it:—

"Your Excellency is accustomed to say loudly that the government is the plague. I will accept this remark, which in its restriction is invidiously partial; but I will admit it only as an effect, in order to ascend to the cause of the symptom, and to find it in the heart of our society, in the origin, the customs, the education of our people; after which, paraphrasing the sentiments of your Excellency, I will say with a greater extension, 'the plague is in the blood of the nation.' . . . . The acts of the government have the greatest part of the responsibility for the scandals which are ascribed to the Custom-house. . . . . Your Excellency asks me what are the measures which I propose to suggest for making this department moral? I answer, none, if the Imperial Government intends that that subservience to the unjust demands of patronage which has extorted all nominations for the Custom-houses is to continue to be the principle that governs."

The Commissioners, of whom the most prominent was Senhor Saldanha Marinho, a Deputy, and Editor of the *Diario* newspaper, (one of the leading political newspapers of Rio, which Mr. Osborne lately described in the House of Commons, never of course having seen it, as "a sort of half *Owl* and half *Punch*,") objected very much to Senhor Tolentino's wholesale condemnation of the nation, but affirmed "the existence of inveterate evils which only gigantic remedies could extirpate." They said in reply to Senhor Tolentino: "If corruption prevails in the Custom-house, the Custom-house does not represent the nation, and of the errors of a government the nation is almost always rather the victim than the cause." In consequence of the report of this Commission forty-five officers of the Custom-house of different ranks were dismissed, and about thirty merchants and despatchers were proclaimed as forbidden to enter the Custom-house. This may show how custom-house receipts would have been diminished, while the "injudicious" Treaty of Commerce of 1827 remained in force, by another cause than moderate import duties. I fear that Senhor Tolentino, who has ceased to be Inspector of Customs, would not say that the measures of 1862 have destroyed corruption even in the Rio Custom-house. If such was the state of things at Rio, what would it be in the other ports? The Count de la Hure, in his friendly account of Brazil, dedicated to the Brazilian Emperor, speaks of the general venality of Brazilian custom-house agents as notorious.*

* L'Empire du Brésil, par Victor L. Baril, Comte de la Hure. Paris, 1862.

Mr. Osborne spoke of the absence of a commercial Treaty with Brazil as a wonderful phenomenon, involving, of course, blame to the English government. "I believe," he said, "that the empire of Brazil is the one isolated example in the civilized world of a state with which we have numerous transactions of various kinds, and with which we have not a single commercial Treaty, or a Treaty of any kind, except the Convention of 1826 [the Slave-trade Convention, a part of which is still operative.]" If this be so, that Brazil is the only country of the civilized world with which we cannot make Treaties, one may suppose it is the fault of Brazil, if there is fault anywhere. However, we are not worse off as to a commercial treaty with Brazil than other nations. Mr. Osborne, however, announced that "Brazil would be too happy to enter into a commercial Treaty and a postal Convention," if the "Aberdeen Act" were repealed. He even went on to describe the sentiments of the new Brazilian Chamber of Deputies: "I believe it is well known that the temper of that assembly is such that, if you repealed the act of 1845, they would be ready to grant you anything in the way of commercial freedom." How does Mr. Osborne, who never was in Brazil, and whose speech does not show very full or accurate information, know all this? Who told him this? Lord Palmerston said, "An active Brazilian agent." I fear that Mr. Osborne was not well instructed. I doubt whether England wants, or would gain anything by, a postal Convention with Brazil. The Royal Mail Company's steamers, largely subsidized by the English government, and having no subsidy from Brazil, have rendered, and are rendering, incalculable benefits to Brazil: we have our own Post-office agents at the principal ports; the Brazilian Post-office is, if possible, worse than the Brazilian Custom-house. As to a commercial Treaty and commercial freedom, I trust so little to Mr. Osborne's information that I would suggest to him to advise, through his instructor, the Brazilian parliament to grant what he has been told they are so well disposed to, and what would be so much for their own interest, before the "Aberdeen Act" is repealed.

# CHAPTER X.

## COMMERCIAL RELATIONS WITH BRAZIL.

CONSULAR CONVENTIONS REFUSED TO ENGLAND AND AUSTRIA—ABSOLUTE EQUALITY AND RECIPROCITY REQUIRED—COMPLAINTS OF BRITISH RESIDENTS IN BRAZIL AFTER EXPIRY OF TREATY OF COMMERCE IN 1844—MR. GRIMSDITCH, MR. MILNER GIBSON, AND MR. BRIGHT, 1845—BUENOS AIRES AND MOST SOUTH AMERICAN STATES HAVE GRANTED WHAT BRAZIL REFUSES—LORD KINGSDOWN'S ACT, 1861—PROPOSED OPENING OF AMAZON RIVER—CORRUPTION OF ORPHANS' COURTS IN BRAZIL—ORPHANS' COURT OF PIRAHY—MISREPRESENTATION OF AN OPINION OF SIR CRESSWELL CRESSWELL—PRESENT CONTROVERSY BETWEEN BRAZIL AND THE FIVE EUROPEAN GOVERNMENTS WITH WHICH SHE HAS MADE CONSULAR CONVENTIONS.

HAVING shown in the last chapter that, if to be without a Treaty of Commerce with Brazil is a misfortune for England, we have all Europe and the United States for our companions in misfortune, I proceed to the subject of a Convention as to privileges and duties of Consuls, where, we are told by the letter-writer in the *Daily News*, France has got the start of us. Our government and diplomacy, he says, "have not secured us a Consular Treaty such as France has obtained." Here,—which is not usual with him,—he has really understated the case against the English government. Switzerland, Italy, Spain, and Portugal have, as well as France, obtained Consular Treaties. However, England is not quite alone in this second misfortune, even if singular in wickedness towards Brazil. Brazil has lately refused to England and Austria Consular

Treaties similar to those concluded with France, Switzerland, Italy, Spain, and Portugal. The Marquis of Abrantes, in his report to the Chambers as Foreign Minister, of 1863, gave the reason of the two refusals. After enumerating the nations with which Brazil had concluded Consular Treaties, he says :—

"Some governments have endeavoured to obtain for their Consuls the favours granted, or which may be granted, to the most favoured nation. In this sense the Imperial government received proposals from the government of her Britannic Majesty and from that of his Imperial and Royal Apostolic Majesty. These proposals could not be taken into consideration so as to come to an arrangement with the two powers mentioned, because there was wanting the essential basis in such agreements of treatment of the Consular Agents of the High Contracting Parties on the footing of the most perfect equality and reciprocity in the exercise of their functions."

I have mentioned in the last chapter that there was a valuable provision in the extinct Treaty of Commerce of 1827, giving our Consuls in Brazil the right of intervention in the administration of British intestate estates. The provision was reciprocal, and in these words :—

"They [English and Brazilian Consuls] shall exercise the right of administering to the property of subjects of their nation dying intestate, for the benefit of the legitimate heirs to such property, and of the creditors of the estate, so far as the laws of the respective countries will admit."

The loss of this right for British Consuls in Brazil was a serious loss to British merchants and residents in that country. Great trouble soon arose. It was attempted even to enforce the *droit d'aubaine* in cases of British subjects dying intestate, and to claim their property for the Brazilian crown. The corruptions, extortions, and harassing delays of the Brazilian Orphans' Courts were a plague and terror for British subjects who had lost the protection of their treaty. Complaints were made in the House of Commons. Mr. Milner Gibson and Mr. Bright again ascribed these troubles of Englishmen to the differential duties against Brazilian slave-grown produce maintained by Sir Robert Peel. Mr. Grimsditch, the member for Macclesfield, having brought forward the subject on the 28th of April, 1845, Mr. Milner Gibson said:—

"It was felt that the great difficulty of our recent relations had been owing to the unfortunate policy of this country towards Brazil upon the Brazilian sugar question. In fact, until the government should retrace their steps on that question, nothing else that they could do would have the effect of re-assuring the British subjects in that country that they were placed in the full enjoyment of their privileges which they had a right to enjoy."

Mr. Bright followed with even stronger language:—

"In the district from which he came there was the greatest possible dread that their trade with the Brazils, which amounted to a million and a half, was jeopardised and endangered by the course which our government had taken. This was characterized as an unfriendly act of the Brazilian government; but how could it be expected that that government should entertain any friendly feelings towards us, while under a pretence, which they all believe to be of a hypocritical character, this country was prevented from trading fairly with the Brazils? He would submit that this was an evil which was occasioned by that combination of monopolists under whom the right hon. baronet (Sir R. Peel) had, to some extent, subjected his government."

Well, that Brazilian grievance, whether reason or pretext, has long since disappeared; and Brazil still refuses to the English government a Convention comprising a reciprocal consular privilege of intervention in the administation of intestate estates on the basis of the extinct Treaty of 1827. That basis was "so far as the laws of the respective countries will admit." On that basis England has of late years had no difficulty in arranging for this consular privilege with most of the Spanish states of South and Central America: with Buenos Aires we have had the privilege by treaty since 1825. Brazil will not even treat with us for this privilege on the basis of reciprocity of treatment as of the most favoured nation. The Brazilian government require "the most perfect equality and reciprocity." What does this mean?

There are two points involved in the question. One is the right given to the Consul: it is required that the Brazilian Consul shall in England have the right of acting as administrator in all cases of Brazilian intestacy, without any option in the Court of Probate. This is one point. The other is, that children of English subjects born in Brazil, being by Brazilian law Brazilians, Brazil will not allow such children, being minors, to be included as English in the English Consul's administration of intestate properties, unless England will allow the children of Brazilians born in England, who by English law are English subjects, to be treated, while minors, as Brazilians.

But it may be asked, why has not England agreed to these two conditions of equality?

Until the passing of Lord Kingsdown's Act of 1861, as to the wills and domiciles of British subjects dying abroad and foreigners in British dominions (24 and 25 Vic. c. 121,) England could not possibly have agreed to either of these conditions without a special Act of Parliament, making an exception for Brazilians in our laws as to administration and as to nationality; and it was not likely that the English parliament would entertain an exceptional legislation in these matters for Brazil. Why should Brazil make difficulties when other South American states make none? Literal reciprocity after all is not essential equality. There is "no perfect equality" in the circumstances and conditions of the two nations. England derives no advantage from the residence of Brazilians equivalent to the gain of Brazil from English merchants, engineers, and artisans who go thither. There are no complaints of corruptions and abuses of our Court of Probate, as there is an universal outcry in Brazil against the abuses of Brazilian Courts of Orphans. It is the strong interest of Brazil to encourage foreigners. She ought not to insist, as a matter of pride, on a formal literal reciprocity when Brazilian subjects have no grievance in England to be rid of, and British subjects have great cause of complaint in Brazil. Practically, there would never be a difficulty in a Brazilian Consul's obtaining letters of administration from the Court if authorised to act for the absent representatives, or upon his application in the absence of representatives where action is urgent.

Lord Kingsdown's Act of 1861 enabled her Majesty to give effect by Order in Council to Conventions with foreign states, providing that the subjects of neither shall acquire domicile in the other except by a year's residence and a formal declaration of his intention of domicile, and also providing that the Consuls of either may administer in the other to a deceased countryman's estate, "when there shall be no person present at the time of such death who shall be rightfully entitled to administer to the estate of such deceased person." This act should have removed all difficulty as to the point of reciprocal right of Consuls to administer, and with common good will, if not common sense, on the part of Brazil, there should be no difficulty on the question of children's nationality. But *Dîs aliter visum.* The Brazilian Minister has announced that the proposal made by me under Lord Russell's instructions in 1862 could not be taken into consideration.

It is this privilege of consular administration of British intestate estates in Brazil, to rescue British subjects from the abuses and difficulties of the Brazilian Courts, which is the important point of a Consular Convention. All the rest is immaterial.

Our government and diplomacy, we are told, "have not secured us a Consular Treaty such as France has obtained." French legislation opposes no difficulty to the grant to Brazil of perfectly equal conditions. France always contended that the clause in her former Treaty of Commerce relating to consular administration of intestate estates was, with some other clauses of the treaty, permanent and not denunciable. France further insisted on the treatment of sons of Frenchmen born in Brazil as French subjects. Yet, under all these circumstances, and with all her facilities, it was with the greatest difficulty, and not without unmistakable intimation to Brazil of serious consequences of a refusal, that France, after long negotiation, at last, in 1860, obtained her Consular Convention.

The conclusion of the Consular Convention with France of 1860 (the first of the Brazilian Consular Conventions,) was preceded by a legislative enactment as to the civil *status* of children of foreigners born in Brazil, which was as follows :—

"The law which regulates in Brazil the civil *status* of foreigners residing in the country, not employed in the service of their nations, may be also applied (poderá ser tambem applicado) to the civil *status* of the children of the same foreigners born in the Empire, during minority only, and without prejudice to the nationality recognised by the sixth article of the Constitution. When these children reach the age of majority, they will enter into the exercise of the rights of Brazilian citizens, subject to the corresponding obligations imposed by the Constitution and laws."

When this enactment was made in 1860, Englishmen in Brazil rejoiced, believing that all their troubles, at any rate about the Brazilian nationality of their children born in Brazil, while minors, were at an end. No more trouble with the Orphans' Courts on account of Brazilian nationality of infants. No more liability for sons under age to compulsory service in the Brazilian militia. They soon found out their delusion. This decree did not settle the question; it only said that it might be done. "The law, &c. may be, or will be able to be, applied." The decree only empowered the executive to act, leaving it to act when and how it chose. The executive determined to proceed by Conventions framed on the basis of "most perfect equality and reciprocity;" so Englishmen in Brazil have as yet got nothing by the motion; which, we are required to believe, is not in any way the fault of Brazil, but the fault of a long series of English statesmen, beginning with Mr. Canning and ending with Lord Russell, who have none of them ever known how to treat Brazil with proper respect or tenderness.

One of the last misstatements of the "Friend to both Countries" in the *Daily News*, is that the Brazilian Legislature "affixed to the authority it gave its government this condition, that all such treaties between Brazil and other nations should contain reciprocal stipulations." This, like almost all his statements, is pure fiction. There was no such restriction imposed on the executive.

It is important at this moment to note the distinction between a Brazilian act which only empowers, and one which determines, as, if we are to rely on recent news from Brazil, the Legislature has been engaged in considering a merely enabling act for the opening of the Amazon to foreign navigation and commerce, by which it will be left to the executive to make its conditions for the concession to each nation.

Brazil will be morally entitled to claim to treat with Great Britain on a basis of "the most perfect equality and reciprocity," in a matter relating to courts of law, when her judicial system is on something like an equality with ours. We have heard lately of a sudden arbitrary removal of seven of the highest Brazilian judges, without trial, inquiry, or even specific accusation, on the ground of corruption. This fact is a proof of what I assert, that the following sentence of a remarkable letter from Mexico, which lately appeared in the *Times*, is applicable to Brazil.

"The first thing to be considered upon the institution

of a suit is, not whether you have justice on your side, but whether you can afford to outbid your opponent. Venality among the judges has been universal, and I could give you instances which would make the hair of English lawyers stand on end."

As to the Brazilian Orphans' Courts, which belong to my present subject, the following has very lately been published in the *Brazil and River Plate Mail* from Brazil:—

"Orphans' Court of Pirahy.—The Supreme Tribunal of Rio granted appeal, on April 27, in a cause displaying a scandalous conspiracy of the Judge of Orphans of Pirahy, with the Collector of taxes of the same place, and the Curator of the estate, to defraud the heirs of Dona Francisca Luisa de Assis, who died intestate, leaving a fortune of about 8,000*l*. One of the heirs had demanded possession the day after the funeral, but was refused, and the Judge of Orphans, pretending there were no heirs, had been enjoying the property ever since, dividing the spoils with his fellow-conspirators. The Court, consisting of nine members, granted the appeal. A writer in the *Correio Mercantil*, May 12, says: 'Who will compensate the heirs for the losses which the property has suffered in the hands of the authorised public agents? From twenty to thirty slaves have died in one year. The rest have become demoralised by the absence of a master. The rents no longer suffice for the expenses. The Judge, the Curator, the Doctor, and the Collector have been receiving many contos of reis (many hundred pounds) for commission, curatorship, doctoring, &c.; and they are to refund—but when? All this is the fault of the Judge of Orphans and Delegate of Police of Pirahy.'"

I have stated that there would be no practical difficulty in England in granting administration to the Brazilian

Consul, if he were authorised by the absent representatives, or on his application in a case of urgency.

The individual who has written so many letters in the *Daily News* under the signature of "A Friend to both Countries" has said, on the contrary, that the state of our law is very defective for Brazilians, and has invoked the authority of Sir Cresswell Cresswell. He has written as follows:—

"But our Foreign-office refuses to make an Anglo-Brazilian Consular Treaty reciprocal, as that of France is; it insists that it shall in this respect be unilateral. And why? Because it says no alteration is required in English law as to foreigners dying intestate in England; whereas in one of the very latest judgments delivered in the Court of Probate by Sir Cresswell Cresswell, that great Judge pointed out the present state of our law in such cases, as involving a great defect and immense risk to the property of intestate foreigners dying in England. Here, again, the fault is not, when looked into, with Brazil or its government."

This is, as usual with the writer, a complete misrepresentation. Let me tell the truth.

In the case of one Wyckoff, an American belonging to one of the Confederate States, who died on board an English vessel on his way to this country, and had bills of exchange payable to his order here, there was urgency, and a difficulty about a grant of administration, there being no relatives in England, and communication with the family of the deceased being cut off by the blockade of the Southern ports, and Sir Cresswell Cresswell, not satisfied to follow the course which, in a similar case, had been taken by Sir John Nicholl, of granting a restricted administration to a mere acquaintance of the deceased, wished the Queen's Proctor to act as administrator. The Queen's Proctor declined, and Sir Cresswell Cresswell remarked :—

> "In all cases of this sort it is better that there should be some public officer. We might have a scramble between different individuals ; some might get one part of the property, and others another part of it, and they might all say, 'Make me the administrator,' whereas here is the Queen's Proctor, a responsible party."

This *obiter dictum* is the "judgment" referred to ; and this is the whole of the "great defect and immense risk." It is clear that the Consul of the country of the deceased would have satisfied Sir Cresswell Cresswell's requirement. If the Brazilian Consul were authorised by the Brazilian government to act in such cases for Brazilians, or chose, as he probably might, to act without special authorisation, there would be no difficulty. Necessarily for Mr. Wyckoff, of the Confederate States, there was no Consul here to act. The case occurred in Michaelmas Term, 1862. It is the subject of an article in the *Law Magazine* of February, 1863.

It will be seen that Sir Cresswell Cresswell did not charge the English Court of Probate with any of those abuses and corruptions of which Brazilians and foreigners alike accuse the Brazilian Courts of Orphans.

The London paid correspondent of the *Jornal do Commercio* some time since informed the Brazilian public, in terms almost identical with those lately employed by the "Friend to both Countries" in the *Daily News*, of the great defects of the English law as regards administration of intestate successions of foreigners, as vouched for by Sir Cresswell Cresswell.

The Consular Conventions concluded by Brazil with France, Switzerland, Italy, Spain, and Portugal, are at present the subject of a warm controversy as to the interpretation of the clauses which concern administration of successions; the five European governments being unanimous, and their representatives at Rio having protested in a collective note against the proceedings of the Brazilian government in the matter.

# CHAPTER XI.

## COMMERCIAL RELATIONS WITH BRAZIL.

STATISTICS OF COMMERCE WITH BRAZIL—INCREASE OF COMMERCE SINCE SUSPENSION OF DIPLOMATIC RELATIONS—SIR HUGH CAIRNS—IMPROVEMENT IN BRAZILIAN GOVERNMENT SINCE THE REPRISALS—CHANGE OF COMMERCIAL POLICY NECESSARY IN BRAZIL—IMPORT AND EXPORT DUTIES—CUSTOMS REGULATIONS—ACTION OF SOME BRITISH SUBJECTS AGAINST THEIR OWN GOVERNMENT—STATEMENTS OF LORD BROUGHAM, LORD HOWDEN, SIR JAMES HUDSON, LORD PALMERSTON, AND MR. CONSUL COWPER—THE SECRETARY OF THE BRITISH AND FOREIGN ANTI-SLAVERY SOCIETY.

LORD PALMERSTON, in reply to Mr. Osborne's invective on a late occasion, produced statistics of our imports from and exports to Brazil, to show the growth of our Brazilian trade, especially of late years. From 1850 to 1852 he stated the value of the imports as about 2,000,000*l.* a year, and of the exports as varying from two to three millions. From 1860 to 1863 he gave the figures as follows:

| | 1860. | 1861. | 1862. | 1863. |
|---|---|---|---|---|
| Imports . . . | 2,200,000 | 2,600,000 | 4,400,000 | 4,500,000 |
| Exports . . . | 4,500,000 | 4,500,000 | 3,700,000 | 3,900,000 |

These figures certainly prove one thing, that the commerce between England and Brazil has even increased since the reprisals.

Sir Hugh Cairns, somewhat put out by these figures, said he knew from his friends among Brazilian merchants—

"That traders laboured under constant and serious apprehension with regard to the risks to which their property was exposed in Brazil, from the want of that protection which British commercial interests enjoyed in every other country, and that they stated in the most decided manner the conviction that the renewal of diplomatic relations would be followed by a considerable expansion of commerce. He trusted, therefore, that the Foreign Office would endeavour to ascertain whether or not this was a delusion under which the government laboured. He pronounced it an utter and complete delusion. (Lord Palmerston held up his paper of figures.) Could the noble lord contradict what he had stated,—that the merchants were filled with apprehension in regard to their property, and that they said the exports could be perhaps doubled if commerce received due protection?"

What are the apprehensions of British merchants trading with Brazil, and what is the protection which they want? Does Sir Hugh Cairns refer only to the want of a Minister at Rio? "It is notorious," Lord Russell has said in a published despatch, "that the government of Brazil has for a long course of time habitually disregarded the representations made to it by Her Majesty's diplomatic agents in Brazil." British Ministers at Rio have had the greatest possible difficulty even in getting answers to their notes. Of this there is abundant proof throughout the long series of published Slave-trade Correspondence, in the correspondence about the "Prince of Wales" and "Forte," and in what has lately transpired as to the question of the British claims and the case of Mr. Reeves.*

* Mr. Reeves is the British Post-office agent at Rio de Janeiro. He has had a law-suit with a Brazilian woman, and the Director General of the Ministry of Justice wrote to two Judges before whom the case was pending, asking them as a favour to vote for the Brazilian woman. The letter came into Mr. Reeves's possession. I brought the matter to the knowledge of the Brazilian Minister for Foreign Affairs (Marquis of Abrantes); my

But since the reprisals and the suspension of diplomatic relations our Consul has found a marked improvement. The lately deceased Consul, Mr. Westwood, had been some twenty years at Rio as Vice-Consul and Consul. A Brazilian Deputy, Senhor Nebias, stated, shortly after Mr. Westwood's death, in the Chamber of Deputies, on March 14th of this year:—"It is known that the English Consul, who has lately died, was in the habit of saying that his position had never been so good as since the suspension of diplomatic relations. His reclamations had never been so well attended to, and he had never seen so great a desire to oblige him." So far, then, Sir Hugh Cairns's friends may feel easy.

But perhaps it is the want of a commercial Treaty and Consular Convention and liberal commercial policy on the part of Brazil that Sir Hugh Cairns's friends complain of. But all that rests with Brazil. And does Sir Hugh Cairns feel convinced that Brazil would grant us a good commercial Treaty and reasonable Consular Convention on a renewal of diplomatic relations, even if the renewal were accompanied by a repeal of the "Aberdeen Act?" It was all refused to Mr. Ellis, sent, with the highest diplomatic rank, on a special mission, before the "Aberdeen Act" existed. He must remember, too, that Brazil stands, even

note was not answered. Lord Russell approved my note, and ordered me to write another. This elicited a reply of excuses from the Brazilian official, one of them being that the writing of such letters to Judges was a custom of the country. Senhor Sinimbú, who was then Minister of Justice, has lately, while the Portuguese mediation was proceeding, produced in the Brazilian Senate most of the correspondence, defended the official who solicited the judges, and described my notes, which were approved and ordered by Lord Russell, as "most impertinent." This case was referred to by Mr. Newdegate in the House of Commons, on the occasion of Mr. Osborne's motion, June 18, 1864.

at this moment, towards England, in the face of the world, in the unhappy position of violator of existing treaty obligations, and that she evaded and violated the stipulations of the former Treaty of Commerce. It is Brazil that must change her policy. If she will observe the faith of treaties and comity of nations, she will have no trouble from England; and the expansion of commerce must come from a change in the policy of Brazil, which it is her own interest to make, and which can be made without Treaty or Convention.

Moderate import duties, no export duties or very low ones, Custom-house regulations as little vexing as possible, honest Custom-house administration, fair and liberal treatment of foreigners, pure justice, a treatment of immigrants which will encourage immigration,—these are the cardinal points of a policy which will expand Brazilian commerce, which involves issues for Brazil much larger than a treaty with England, and which need not wait for the repeal of the "Aberdeen Act."

Import duties now average 30 per cent. This is a moderate statement. Export duties range from 5 to 10 per cent. The Provincial Assemblies, which are precluded by the Constitution from imposing import duties, are permitted to levy export duties. I have already spoken of Custom-house corruption and venality of judges. No one acquainted with Brazil will deny that the following extract from the work of a gentleman who cannot be accused of being hostile to Brazil, is still a correct account of the vexations for foreign traders in Brazilian ports. The work I refer to is Mr. Hadfield's "Brazil and River Plate," published in 1854:—

"In Brazil you have the ordeal of health-visits, police, and Custom-house searchers, before you can even leave the ship, and if a vessel arrives after dusk, no matter where from, coasting or otherwise, she must remain till morning for the visit, after which she is a kind of Custom-house prey, watched and pounced upon in every possible manner, if all is not found to be strictly in accordance with the long string of regulations, numbered like a criminal code; and woe betide the unfortunate shipmaster or merchant importing goods who innocently falls into the trap laid for him. It is a case of heavy fines, damages, and often confiscation of ship or property, although it can be clearly and satisfactorily proved that no one is to blame in the matter, and that there has been no fraudulent intention whatever. The stipulations of the Custom-house code are being continually infringed, and yet, like the laws of the Medes and Persians, it altereth not. All this is very sad, and unworthy of a country that looks to commerce for its intercourse with Europe, and as a main source of revenue and social progress."

The English government, in its relations with Brazil, has had two chief objects of attention and duty,—the slave-trade, and the interests of English merchants and residents. The latter comprises protection against wrongs and extension of commerce. It is a painful fact that one of its chief difficulties in dealing with the Brazilian government has always arisen from the opposing action of some Englishmen. The bulk of the English community in Brazil,—quiet, respectable men,—pursue their business and hold their tongues, knowing what they might suffer from open expression of opinion in support of their own government, against that of the country to which they have gone to make their fortunes. But unscrupulous, ill-conditioned Englishmen make it their business and find it their interest to side openly with Brazil, and curry favour with the Brazilian government by puffing it in every conceivable way, and throwing dirt on their own government and Ministers. This is sometimes done for a good substantial consideration. The general indifference to Brazil, and ignorance about it in this country (for beyond the circle of those connected with Brazil by commerce, the ignorance in England about that Empire is general,) have given great scope for the operations of interested puffers. A few misleaders make many misled, and the "Brazilian agent" knows how to employ

> "the tool
> That knaves do work with, called a fool."

Every laudatory speech or newspaper article is sent out to Brazil, translated into Portuguese, read by the public, who are told little or nothing of the other side, and they come to believe that Brazil is the object of universal European admiration, except in the British Cabinet, where the evil spirits of Lord Palmerston and Lord Russell predominate; and thus is the Brazilian government encouraged and incited to resist that of England in its endeavours to protect British subjects and promote British interests.

Lord Brougham, in a speech to which I have already had occasion to refer, delivered in the House of Lords on August 2, 1842, held up to scorn the conduct of English merchants at Rio as to the slave-trade. I quote a part of his invective:—

"A case lately came before the Privy Council on the claim of a Brazilian vessel condemned for slave-trading. The ship had been sent out on a slaving voyage, and the consignee of the cargo was a very well known slave-trader;

but, among other evidence which he produced, to avert the condemnation, was the certificate of twenty or thirty mercantile houses established in Brazil, all testifying to his high character for respectability and honour. Of these houses, about one half were British firms. These men scrupled not to join in bearing this testimony to the character of a person whose slave-trading must be as well known upon the 'Change of Rio as the name he is called by, slave-trading having been by the law of Brazil treated as piracy for the last ten years and upwards. Of the British houses that so certified I will say nothing, except that three of them are represented to me by persons on whose information I think reliance may be placed, as having lost together 12,000*l.* by some late condemnations of vessels for slave-trading; and I know that the despatch of the Commissioners to the Secretary of State, dated July 14, 1838, to which I have already referred, distinctly states 'British capital to have suffered severely in Rio from recent captures.' But if our merchants settled in Brazil thus vouch for the character of Brazilian slave-traders, see how mutual the voucher is; how freely the Brazilian slave-trader bears his testimony reciprocally to the character of the British merchant! In a journal believed to be under the patronage, and known to speak the sentiments, of a celebrated Brazilian Minister connected with the slave-trading party, I find this panegyric on our countrymen: 'We greatly respect the English merchants for their conduct in our internal concerns!' Whether the part of their conduct thus so greatly respected is their bearing judicial testimony to the honour of pirates, or only their importing from seventy to eighty negro slaves, in breach of the laws of England, I am not prepared to say. But the principal ground of respect is their conduct towards Africa, 'the way in which they there contribute to ransom the captive blacks by ordering goods fit for being employed in this work of humanity.' Whether the goods so humanely used are the coast guns, as they used to be called, which, being bought for twelve or fifteen pence, burst in the hands of the negroes the second or third time they are fired, or whether the allusion may be to the shackles, the manacles, the iron weights that form part of the cargo in the voyage of humanity, or whether the whips and goads invested are more darkly shadowed out under the tender phrases, I will not take upon me to decide. But on the next topic of praise there can be little doubt, 'the lending their money to the adventurer;' the humane adventurer, and 'insuring, as is said' (I make no doubt most truly said,) 'the vessels destined for the slave coast.' No doubt the insuring such vessels is naturally a matter of eulogy to the affectionate lovers of the unhappy African race, eagerly celebrating the praise of those engaged in their ransom."

Lord Howden wrote to Lord Palmerston, November 12, 1847, that he had no hope of seeing a notorious slave-trader punished for a proved crime, "because," said Lord Howden, "he has many friends among the English merchants, because he owes them money, and they have entreated the Brazilian government, which requires no pressing, not to send him away."

Sir James Hudson, battling bravely with the Brazilian government for the suppression of the slave-trade, wrote to Lord Palmerston of "the money-power of the slave-dealers and their hold on British commerce," and of "threatened deputations to myself from British merchants under pretence of seeking the protection of the Legation," which, Sir James Hudson says, was "too flimsy a pretext and too thin a shield."

Lord Palmerston addressed this instruction to Sir J. Hudson, March 29, 1851:—

"I have to instruct you to warn such of the British

merchants at Bahia as you may have opportunities of communicating with against allowing themselves to be made use of by the slave-traders, who endeavour, by inspiring unfounded alarms, to defeat the action of Her Majesty's cruisers in the suppression of the Brazilian slave-trade."

Mr. Cowper, Consul at Pernambuco, who had reported to Her Majesty's government an attempt to land slaves in Brazil in 1855, wrote to Lord Palmerston, November 18, 1856, that he had been censured in the Liverpool press "for attacking one of our best customers." We have heard similar language lately.

It has been widely reported and generally believed that, since the reprisals, an English house was detected in one of the Brazilian Custom-houses in an attempt to pass a quantity of linen goods as cotton, in order to save the higher duty, and that the offence was condoned because the head of the house was a known "friend to Brazil." Even if the story should not be true, it yet explains the system.

I know, on the best authority, that the members of a deputation which came a few years ago from Manchester and Liverpool to press on Lord Palmerston the repeal of the "Aberdeen Act," went from their interview with the Premier to a luncheon in Cavendish Square at the Brazilian Minister's. My informant is a gentleman of high position and character, personally acquainted with some of the deputation.

The *Anti-Slavery Reporter*, edited by Mr. L. A. Chamerozow, the Secretary of the British and Foreign Anti-Slavery Society, is at this moment a zealous supporter of Brazil, credulously adopting every Brazilian statement. Mr. Newdegate lately mentioned in the House of Commons the notorious fact that seven high Brazilian Judges had been removed for corruption. Mr. Chamerozow says thereupon, "This is an error; the Judges, having completed their term of service, were placed in course upon the retired list." Whoever has made Mr. Chamerozow believe this has grossly imposed upon him.

I have referred in a previous chapter to the address to the Emperor of Brazil, got up by Mr. Chamerozow and the Anti-Slavery Committee, conveying sentiments about the "Aberdeen Act" very different from those of Her Majesty's government. In 1854, May 9th, Lord Campbell proposed to make such addresses to foreign Sovereigns misdemeanours, and said, in support of his motion, what is entirely to the point now, that persons or societies so acting "might thwart unconsciously the measures of their own government, they might lay themselves open to mystification and cajolery on the part of those with whom they interfered, and they might be made the tools of foreign powers in spreading in this country doctrines and opinions unfavourable to the government which then existed." Lord Brougham supported the motion, and also made some very pertinent remarks:—

"It was only when persons proposed to represent persons or bodies of persons in this country, and went as their representatives to a foreign power, that they came under the provisions of the bill. . . . He was one of those who would rather see representations on so delicate and exciting a matter as religion in the hands of the government than in the hands of individuals. In dealing with matters so exciting and delicate as those involving religious feeling, he thought it much more expedient to let them pass through the regular and constitutional channel."

Slavery is a subject hardly less delicate and exciting than religion for international discussion. I suppose it is the same Mr. Chamerozow who has lately been foiled by the Foreign-office and the Liverpool African Association in an attempt to purchase, with two others, from Pepple, King of the Bonny, exclusive rights of navigation and trading in the Bonny river.*

* Slave-trade Correspondence, Class B, presented 1864. (Africa, Bight of Biafra.) The members of the Society of Friends object to the use of armed force, even for the suppression of slave-trade. This is one thing, but it is another to be the eager advocate of a government which upholds slavery. In the *Anti-Slavery Reporter* of July 1st, notice is taken of a statement of mine in a despatch to Lord Russell, February 26, 1863, that "there is no sign of effort or preparation for the abolition of slavery," and the Editor says, "We are in a position to affirm that Mr. Christie is in error, and hope in our next to furnish authentic information on this point." Four monthly numbers have since appeared, without any of this hoped-for authentic information. Obviously, there might be a new state of things by July, 1864, which would not prove me to have been in error in February, 1863. But I am not aware of anything having been done to the last moment in Brazil towards the extinction of slavery. I have exposed, in Chapter VI., the misstatements of Senhors Andrada and Almeida Portugal; the former, Secretary of the late Brazilian Legation, addressing a deputation of the British and Foreign Anti-Slavery Society; the latter, strangely enough, an orator at the last annual meeting of the Society. Since that chapter was printed, a painful trial, reported in the morning newspapers of November 12th, has completed the exposure of the Chevalier de Almeida Portugal, who attended the Annual Meeting of the British and Foreign Anti-Slavery Society, as a friend of Christianity, and the "esteemed friend" of Mr. Chamerozow, to urge an agitation for the repeal of the "Aberdeen Act." See the report of the meeting in the *Anti-Slavery Reporter* of June 1, 1864.

## CHAPTER XII.

### BRITISH CLAIMS ON BRAZIL.

LAIMS CONVENTION OF JUNE 2, 1858—BRITISH CLAIMS—BRAZILIAN CLAIMS AGAINST FINAL JUDGMENTS OF SLAVE-TRADE MIXED COMMISSIONS AND AGAINST ABERDEEN ACT—SUSPENSION OF PROCEEDINGS OF THE COMMISSION—MY REMONSTRANCES AGAINST SUSPENSION—LAPSE OF COMMISSION—MY NOTE OF SEPTEMBER 11, 1860, NOT ANSWERED TILL NOVEMBER 1861—THE BRAZILIAN REPLY EXAMINED—MY NOTES OF APRIL 14, 1862, NOT ANSWERED BEFORE THE SUSPENSION OF DIPLOMATIC RELATIONS—LORD RUSSELL'S COMPLAINT THEREOF, JUNE 6, 1863.

PRESSING representations made by Mr. Scarlett to the Brazilian government in 1857, under Lord Clarendon's instructions, on the subject of an accumulation of claims of British subjects, many of them of long standing, to none of which previous Secretaries of State and Ministers at Rio had been able to obtain the proper attention of the Brazilian government, led to the negotiation of a Convention for a Mixed Commission for the settlement of claims of the subjects of either government on the other. The Convention was signed on June 2, 1858. Lord Malmesbury succeeded Lord Clarendon as Foreign Secretary in February of that year, but I believe it is notorious that the Convention was virtually Lord Clarendon's, and not Lord Malmesbury's. The Commission, under this Convention, was for the settlement of all claims on both sides, "which may have been presented to either government for its interposition with the other, since the date of the declaration of independence of the Brazilian empire, and which yet remain unsettled, or are considered to be still unsettled by either of the two governments." One Commissioner was appointed on each side, and the two held their first sitting at Rio, on March 10, 1859. Fifty-one British, and one hundred and eight Brazilian, claims were sent in to the Commissioners. The total sum claimed by British subjects may be roughly stated at about 300,000*l.*, and the total of the Brazilian claims exceeded a million and a half sterling. Lists of claims had not been exchanged and agreed upon before the conclusion of the Convention. The British claims were of various sorts: claims arising out of losses during the rebellion of Pernambuco in 1824, of Pará in 1835, of Bahia in 1837, and of Alagoas in 1844; claims to a large amount for overcharged customs-duties during the existence of the Treaty of Commerce of 1827, which was denounced by Brazil in 1844, and in which it was stipulated that the import duties on English goods should not exceed 15 per ent.; claims for other undue exactions of Custom-house authorities; claims arising out of non-fulfilment of contracts of the Brazilian government; claims for illegal fines and imprisonments, &c.* The Brazilian claims had origin almost exclusively in captures by British cruisers of Brazilian vessels suspected of carrying on the slave-trade.

It was only when the Commission had met in March, 1859, and the Brazilian claims had been sent in, that Her Majesty's government became aware of their nature, and

* A list of the British claims sent in to the Commission is printed in the Appendix.

that a very large portion of the Brazilian claims sent in were claims impugning decisions of the Mixed Commission Courts, which sat till 1845, under the Slave-trade Convention of 1826, and claims impugning the British act of Parliament of 1845, so well known under the name of the "Aberdeen Act."

As to the first of these two classes of claims, claims impugning the decisions of the Mixed Commission Courts, it had been expressly stated, both in the body of the Convention with Portugal of 1817 and in the regulations appended to it, all adopted in the Convention with Brazil of 1826, that the Mixed Commissions were to "judge without appeal." How, then, could it be conceived that the Brazilian government would think of appealing from the judgment of the Slave-Trade Mixed Commission Courts, declared by treaty to be "without appeal," to the new Mixed Claims Commission?

The two Commissioners at first agreed that such claims could not be entertained by them. Such a claim was rejected by them on June 7, 1859, in these words: "As to this vessel, the 'Santo Antonio Victorioso,' it was condemned by the Mixed Commission of Sierra Leone, May 21, 1840, and therefore this Commission cannot take cognisance of the case, since it was finally judged." *

But this decision did not please the Brazilian government; they were at hand to influence their Commissioner, who soon after informed his British colleague that he

* All the documents quoted and details given on this subject of claims have been made known in the Annual Reports of the Brazilian Ministers for Foreign Affairs; and the extracts which I have given are translated from the Portuguese. No correspondence on this subject has been yet laid before the English Parliament.

had changed his opinion as to the inadmissibility of such claims, and he unfortunately persuaded the British Commissioner to change his also; and accordingly a decision was come to in the case of a vessel called the "Principe de Guiné," on January 24, 1860, in which the two Commissioners, rejecting the claim on its merits, affirmed indirectly their right to review judgments of the old Slave-trade Mixed Commissions.

In the meantime Her Majesty's government had consulted the law-advisers of the Crown as to the Brazilian claims for capture or detention of vessels suspected of being slavers; and on February 21, 1860, acting by order of Lord Russell, I instructed the British Commissioner not to deal with such claims until he received further instructions. The British Commissioner having informed his Brazilian colleague of this instruction, the latter, with the approval of the Brazilian government, declined to continue work, and the sittings of the Commission were suspended on February 28, 1860.

The Convention under which the Commission was appointed contained the two following provisions:—

"The Commissioners shall be bound, under this Convention, to hold for the consideration of the claims at least eight sittings in each month, from the date of their first sitting until the completion of their labours.

"The Commissioners shall be bound to examine and decide upon every claim within two years from the day of their first meeting, unless, on account of some unforeseen and unavoidable suspension of the sittings, the two governments may mutually agree to extend the time."

I begged and entreated the Brazilian Minister for

Foreign Affairs to instruct the Brazilian Commissioner to return to the Commission, and so act until the receipt of the further instructions from Lord Russell as to effect a formal compliance with the requirements of the Convention. On March 20, 1860, I thus wrote to Senhor Sinimbú:—

"I have been informed by Mr. Morgan, the British Commissioner, that his Brazilian colleague has insisted on a suspension of the labours of the Commission, and that, while Mr. Morgan continues to present himself at the office on the usual days of meeting, Senhor Tolentino has constantly failed to appear since the 1st instant. I will simply note at present that the suspension was not absolutely necessary, and it cannot be maintained that it is unavoidable. My object in addressing this note to your Excellency is to make known the difficulties which may result from the actual proceeding of the Commissioners, and to urge your Excellency to do what is still possible to prevent disagreeable embarrassments. By the third article of the Convention the Commissioners are obliged to meet for considering claims at least eight times in each month. There is yet time for Senhor Tolentino to return to the Commission and hold eight meetings with his colleague before the end of the present month; and it is my duty to declare to your Excellency, with respectful frankness, that, if eight meetings do not take place during the present month, the provisions of the Convention will not be complied with, and the blame will not be with the British government, or the British Minister, or the British Commissioner."

Three days after I addressed a second earnest remonstrance to Senhor Sinimbú:—

"Senhor Tolentino insisted on the suspension of the labours of the Commission in consequence of Mr. Morgan's having informed him that Her Majesty's government were consulting the usual law advisers of the Crown on questions connected with the Brazilian claims, arising out of capture or detention of vessels suspected of carrying on the illegal trade in Africans, and that he had been ordered to abstain from dealing with any of these claims until he received further instructions. Your Excellency will observe that this is not an absolute prohibition to deal with such claims, but simply an order to abstain from dealing with them for a short time, until the arrival of further instructions, which are in preparation.

"I regret the necessity of this short suspension of work on Mr. Morgan's part as regards claims connected with the African slave-trade; but your Excellency will not fail to consider that the government of Brazil has the advantage of being near its Commissioner, and can at any moment give him advice and instructions, while the distance of the British Commissioner from his government necessarily causes difficulty when he asks for instructions, or has to receive them. Your Excellency must not, therefore, be surprised at the short and unexpected delay in sending instructions on questions somewhat intricate and of the highest importance.

"In these circumstances, I hope that the Imperial government will not consider it its duty to oppose the examination of some of the claims which have been presented to the Commission. And if any unjust advantage for the British claimants is feared, the Brazilian Commissioner might be instructed to confine himself for the present to the preliminary discussions of the claims, adjourning the sentences until Mr. Morgan shall have received the expected instructions."

All in vain. The Brazilian government insisted on the suspension, and the Commission never met again. On the 11th of September, 1860, I addressed a note to the Brazilian Minister, informing him of the resolutions of Her Majesty's government as advised by the law-officers of the

Crown. No answer had been given to this note on March 10, 1861, when two years from the first sitting of the Commissioners had expired. No agreement had been made between the two governments for an extension of the term of the Commission, and on August 12, 1861, the Brazilian government were informed that the government of Her Majesty considered that the Commission had, under the terms of the Convention, come to an end.

Thirteen claims in all had been decided by the Commission before its suspension at the end of February, 1860; five British, of which two were rejected; and eight Brazilian, of which five were rejected. Two of the Brazilian claims had been rejected because it was proved that the English government had long ago paid them; these were not connected with capture of slave-trade vessels. The three Brazilian claims in which compensation was awarded to the claimants were claims arising out of captures which had not been adjudicated by a Mixed Commission Court.

The total sum awarded in these three Brazilian cases was nearly 16,000*l.* The sums awarded in the three British cases favourably decided amounted to nearly 9,000*l.*

No answer was given to my note of September 11, 1860, until November, 1861, fourteen months after, when it was replied to in London, in somewhat irregular fashion, by Senhor Moreira to Lord Russell.

In my note the Brazilian government had been informed that Her Majesty's government could not consent to the review by the Claims Commission of the judgments, declared by treaty "without appeal," of the Slave-trade Mixed Commissions, or of proceedings under the "Aberdeen Act." They were reminded that Her Majesty's government had refused requests of the Brazilian government to refer judgments of the Mixed Commissions to the arbitration of a third power, and that the "Aberdeen Act" and the measures taken under it had been forced on the British government by the notorious continuance of the African slave-trade, and "the refusal of the Brazilian government, when called upon, to execute the obligations of the treaty of 1826." The note went on to say:—

"The Brazilian government knew well that none of the claims which were in discussion between the two governments, and which determined the proposal of a Mixed Commission, were connected with the slave-trade, and in the negotiation which ended with the Convention for the settlement of claims, no claims arising out of the slave-trade were mentioned or even alluded to.

"In view of what has been said, Her Majesty's government cannot consider the Brazilian government justified in pretending now to consider as unsettled claims, claims which the British government have invariably regarded as settled, and into whose merits it has for that reason always refused to enter.

"The Brazilian government rests, it appears, on the words of the 1st article of the Convention of 1858, which authorized the reference to the Mixed Commission of claims which were considered as still unsettled by either of the two governments; but the expression 'unsettled' employed in the Convention cannot have a meaning different from its ordinary meaning, or from that which was not only given to it by Her Majesty's government, but which Her Majesty's government even officially declared that it gave to it. The expression 'unsettled' must be understood between the contracting parties with reference to the negotiations which determined the conclusion of the Convention, and to the declared object of the Convention, and Her Majesty's government cannot consent to the admission, under such a pretext, of claims excluded during the whole course of the preceding communications between the two governments, and whose admission would entirely change the character of the Commission."

The note of September 11, 1860, concluded with the following declaration and proposal :—

"I am instructed to declare to your Excellency that, if the government of the Emperor will furnish that of Her Majesty with a list of claims, excluding those to which Her Majesty's government is irrevocably opposed, they will willingly consider of a new Convention based on an agreement for the examination of the claims of British and Brazilian subjects.

"But if the government of the Emperor does not think proper to agree in the exclusion of the disputed claims, Her Majesty's government is sorry to say that it has no alternative but to let the Commission expire.

"If Her Majesty's government shall be obliged to take this course, and to enter into special discussions with the Brazilian government as to the different claims of British subjects, which could more easily be decided by the Mixed Commission if its labours were not interrupted, it will do so with the deepest regret. But, whatever may be the inconveniences which will result, Her Majesty's government can in no case admit a pretension which would involve a departure from the policy long since adopted by Great Britain."

I have already said that the Brazilian government took fourteen months to answer this note. When the reply came, the Commission had ceased to exist already eight months before. The reply was long and curious.

It is difficult to imagine, in a serious State paper, which it had taken fourteen months to compose, such blunders and misstatements as are to be found in the memorandum sent in by Senhor Moreira to Lord Russell on November 20, 1861. This memorandum was replied to by me at Rio, under Lord Russell's instructions, on April 14, 1862.

The memorandum states that when the Commission suspended its sittings five English claims and four Brazilian had been decided. Five English is correct, but there had been eight Brazilian claims decided. Of four Brazilian claims thus ignored by Senhor Moreira, one was the rejected "Santo Antonio Victorioso" claim, in deciding which the Commissioners declared that they could not entertain a claim already finally judged by the Mixed Commission of Sierra Leone; and two rejected claims, not connected with the slave-trade, which had been previously paid by the English government. It was not convenient in this memorandum to mention the unpalatable first decision of the Commissioners on the finality of the judgments of the Slave-Trade Mixed Commissions, or to mention any Brazilian claims not connected with slave-trade.

Senhor Moreira stated indeed in his memorandum that all the Brazilian claims sent in to the Commission related to the slave-trade, and belonged to the two classes of claims objected to by the English government. The fact is, that there were in all nearly forty Brazilian claims which did not come within the two categories objected to by Her Majesty's government. It has been represented in this country, in accordance with Senhor Moreira's most incorrect statement, that the course taken by the English government excluded all Brazilian claims.

Senhor Moreira put a very curious interpretation on the word "appeal," from which Her Majesty's government contend that the judgments of the Slave-trade Mixed

Commissions are, according to treaty, exempt. He says that the appeal forbidden by the Treaty was—

"The ordinary appeal of captors or claimants to the same tribunal or another. An appeal of such ordinary character a government never employs, and especially appealing from a Judge appointed by itself, as would be the case of the Mixed Commissions. But the two governments, denying this appeal to the captured and captors, could not intend to renounce the right of reciprocally requiring reparation for wrongs inflicted on their subjects."

To this I replied:—

"Senhor Moreira says that the appeal which is not permitted is the ordinary appeal of captors or claimants from the decision of this tribunal to itself or to another. This is unquestionably a singular interpretation. The appeal from a tribunal to 'the same tribunal' would be a proceeding rather extraordinary than ordinary, and the treaties which created the Mixed Commissions did not create or mention any other tribunal, which, if these words did not exist, could serve as tribunal of appeal. If it is not an appeal to the governments which is forbidden, these words of prohibition would have no meaning at all. But not only was appeal to the governments for the revision of the judgments of the Mixed Commissions expressly forbidden: still further, the twelfth article of the regulations of the Commissions, annexed to the Convention of 1817, limited and defined the action of the governments. 'When the parties interested shall imagine they have cause to complain of any evident injustice on the part of the Mixed Commissions, they may represent it to their respective governments, who reserve to themselves the right of mutual correspondence for removing, when they think fit, the individuals who may compose these commissions.' That is, no revision of judgments by the governments, but the power of removal of unjust judges."

Senhor Moreira made a great point of acquiescence by Mr. Scarlett, the British negotiator of the Convention of 1858, in the Brazilian claims after they had been sent in to the Commission; and he stated that "Mr. Scarlett continued to reside at Rio during the first months of the sittings of the Commission, and was always fully informed by the British Commissioner of its discussions and labours, as well as of the nature of the claims sent in on both sides. . . . . If the claims which it is now sought to exclude were not the same as were contemplated in the whole of the negotiation which he himself conducted; if they were not within the letter and spirit of the Convention made by him, surely Mr. Scarlett would have immediately repelled them, and the British Commissioner would have immediately obeyed his instructions." To this it was easy to reply, that Mr. Scarlett, having signed the Convention on June 2, 1858, left Rio, never to return, before the end of that month, and nine months before the first sitting of the Commission.

Senhor Moreira stated that the discussions of the Commissioners ended "in admitting for consideration claims based on the injustice of the sentences given by the Mixed Commissions of Sierra Leone and Rio Janeiro," but took care to make no allusion whatever to the opposite decision of the Commissioners, registered in their minutes, in the case of the "Santo Antonio Victorioso."

I thus commented on a passage of Senhor Moreira's memorandum, in which he adduced—it is difficult to see with what object—a number of synonyms of the word "unsettled:"—

"Senhor Moreira endeavours to justify the opinion of the Brazilian government that the claims in question are 'unsettled' by mentioning some synonyms of this word. The phrase 'unsettled,' he says, taken in its proper and natural sense, corresponds in both languages to any of these others,—'not adjusted,' 'not regulated,' 'not decided.' It is not easy to see how these synonyms help the argument; the question in dispute between the two governments being one to be decided by good sense and not by dictionaries. Her Majesty's government will admit that the phrase 'unsettled' might be replaced by any of these others,—'not adjusted,' 'not regulated,' 'not decided;' but, even so, it may confidently ask what on earth can be considered settled, adjusted, regulated, or decided, if it is not that which has been decided, regulated, adjusted, settled by a tribunal without appeal?"

My note of April 14, 1862, concluded as follows:—

"Her Majesty's government now desire me to declare that they have before them claims of British subjects against Brazil, entitled to support, which they cannot permit to remain unredressed. But, desiring to avoid extreme measures, Her Majesty's government are ready to conclude with the government of Brazil a Convention for the establishment of a Mixed Commission, with the object of examining and deciding these claims, and other admissible claims of the same nature which Brazil may have to present against Great Britain. But Her Majesty's government, at the same time, peremptorily and finally declare that they cannot consent to refer to the Commission or admit for discussion any Brazilian claim connected with the African slave-trade decided by the Mixed Commissions, and subsequently by the British Vice-Admiralty Courts, or arising out of the execution of a

British act of Parliament, and that the new Convention must be so made as to exclude all these cases. For this end it will be absolutely necessary above all, and before the conclusion of any Convention between the two governments, that complete lists of the claims to be referred to the Commission should be prepared by each government to be submitted to the other, and that in case of a Convention being concluded, the lists, if accepted, should be incorporated in the Convention and made part of it. Her Majesty's government hope that the government of the Emperor, deliberating on the proposal now made, will favour them with an answer less tardy than that which was given to my note of September 11, 1860."

On the same day, April 14, 1862, I addressed a second note to the Brazilian government, proposing an arrangement for present payment of the awards made by the expired Claims Commission to some few British and Brazilian claimants.

When diplomatic relations were suspended in the summer of 1863, more than twelve months after these proposals had been made by the English government, no answer had been received from the government of Brazil to either of the two notes of April 14, 1862. All that the Marquis of Abrantes, Minister for Foreign Affairs, announced in May, 1863, in his Annual Report to the Legislature, was: "The Imperial government, before taking a definitive deliberation, thought proper to ask the opinion of the Council of State on these important subjects, to which it will in proper time give the due solution." It is to be inferred from this that the Council of State had not then given its opinion on the proposals conveyed in my notes, then thirteen months old.

Lord Russell referred to this in the despatch of June 6,

1863, in which, after Senhor Moreira had left England, he ordered our Legation to come away from Rio de Janeiro :—

"Her Majesty's government, under these circumstances, are fully justified in complaining that up to this time they are still left without a reply to the proposals conveyed in Mr. Christie's note of April 14, 1862, and that no steps appear to have been taken for the just settlement of various British claims, some of them of long standing, and of very considerable amount. Her Majesty's government, therefore, hope that the government of Brazil will, in its future intercourse with Great Britain, through whatever channel that intercourse may be carried on, act with that courtesy which is usual between governments; and also that the Brazilian government will without further delay frankly enter into the communication of their views as to the means by which a settlement of the long-pending claims may best be arrived at."

Diplomatic relations, broken off by the Brazilian government in June, 1863, have continued suspended till now, and it does not appear that Lord Russell's hint of another channel of communication has been taken, that any answer has even yet been made to the proposals of Her Majesty's government of April, 1862, or that any step has been taken in Brazil for the settlement of British claims. It will, I think, be admitted that a government which suspends diplomatic relations with another should not profit by that suspension of its own making for postponement of a settlement of the pecuniary claims of individuals.

## CHAPTER XIII.

### BRITISH CLAIMS ON BRAZIL.

### SIR HUGH CAIRNS AND MR. SEYMOUR FITZGERALD.

SIR HUGH CAIRNS'S STATEMENT, JULY 16, 1863—MR. FITZGERALD'S, MARCH 6, 1863—MR. FITZGERALD'S MISTAKES ABOUT GUATEMALA, MR. ELLIOT'S SPECIAL MISSION OF 1859 TO NAPLES, AND PARAGUAY—HIS IGNORANCE OF THE EMANCIPADO QUESTION—LORD JOHN MANNERS AND SIR JOHN PAKINGTON.

I HAVE, I trust, shown in the preceding chapter that the difficulties which have occurred about the settlement of British claims on Brazil are not the fault of the British government.

A Commission is created to settle miscellaneous ordinary claims on both governments "which yet remain unsettled or are considered to be still unsettled by either of the two governments;" this Commission had been proposed by the British government, whose subjects have claims on Brazil to the extent of about 300,000*l*., and the Brazilian government say not one word about slave-trade claims till the Convention has been signed and the Commission appointed, then swamp it with Brazilian claims, amounting to a million and a half, against judgments "without appeal" of the Slave-trade Mixed Commission Courts and against judgments and proceedings under the "Aberdeen Act," professing that they consider these claims still unsettled. When the British government, amazed at such a proceeding, consult their legal advisers and tell the British Commissioner not to deal with any slave-trade claims until he is further instructed, the Brazilian Commissioner strikes work, and suspends the Commission. The British government, some months after, communuicate their views to the government of Brazil, and the latter permit the Commission to expire, six months after receiving this communication, without making any answer to it. No answer is made for fourteen months. The British government then make a second communication, in April, 1862, proposing a new Commission on certain conditions, and asking for an early answer. When diplomatic relations are suspended fourteen months after, there has been no answer from the Brazilian government, and there is no answer yet, and no attempt yet to settle the claims, two years and a half after the last English proposals of April, 1862.

Sir Hugh Cairns, to whose honourable private relations with some of the claimants I have already referred, said in the House of Commons, on the occasion of Mr. Osborne's motion, of the English government, that it was "on account of the bad terms on which they were with the Brazilian government that they had utterly failed in obtaining a satisfactory adjustment." Is this true and just?

Last year, on the occasion of Mr. Seymour Fitzgerald's motion about Brazil, July 16, 1863, Sir Hugh Cairns treated this subject of the claims, and made many mistakes. He said:

"The Commission sat in Rio, under the inspection and with the consent of Mr. Scarlett, our Minister there, for a whole year. [Mr. Scarlett left Rio nine months before the Commission began to sit.] On the 23d of March, 1860, however, Mr. Scarlett informed the Commission that he had received a despatch from home requiring him to suspend its further sitting. [On February 21st, 1860, not Mr. Scarlett, but I, informed the British Commissioner that he was not to deal with any slave-trade claims till he received further instructions; on the 28th of February the Commission was suspended; and on the 20th and 23d of March I remonstrated strongly against the suspension.] And what, let me ask, was the cause of this instruction being issued? The government of this country said, 'You are taking in as Brazilian claims some of those which have reference to the decisions of the Mixed Commissions under the Convention of 1826, and the decisions of the Vice-Admiralty Courts, under the Aberdeen Act.' It is, I believe, perfectly well known that not only did the Brazilian government make these claims, but that there were no others. [There were others.] Is it, then, to be argued, in spite of the words I have read, that the Brazilians entered into the Convention merely to decide British claims? [There is no need at all to argue this.] Mr. Scarlett, at all events, on the 23d of March, suspended the sittings of the Commission [No, he did not,] notwithstanding that there was time to have gone on deciding on the claims. I therefore say it was broken up, and I wish the House to consider the importance of this fact with reference to our position."

If Sir Hugh Cairns was correctly reported on this occasion, a greater tissue of blunders never came from the mouth of a great advocate and orator. With unaffected respect for him I say, that he was either very badly instructed on that occasion, or that he gave too little attention to his brief.

Mr. Seymour Fitzgerald, who was Under-secretary for

Foreign Affairs for nearly a year and a half in 1858–9, and who has assumed the position of champion and protector of Brazil in the House of Commons, made this extraordinary statement on March 6, 1863:—

"Within a recent period Her Majesty's government had acted towards the Brazilian government in a manner which they would not have dared to follow towards any other government on the face of the globe. He alluded to their conduct in regard to the Mixed Commission at Rio. We established a few cases against the Brazilian government before the Mixed Commission, and when that government succeeded, by the unanimous decision of the Commissioners on both sides, in establishing some few cases against us, Her Majesty's government stopped all further proceedings, tore up the Convention, and refused to have anything more to do with it."

Allowing for some inaccuracy in this report, is it possible that anything like this should have been said by one who has been Under-secretary for Foreign Affairs, and must be conscious of additional responsibility for any words of his on a question with a foreign government? A greater misstatement was surely never made by a member of Opposition who has had the responsibilities of office.

I hope that Mr. Fitzgerald will believe that I write of him with a feeling of regard derived from former intercourse, and belief in his good dispositions. I have watched his proceedings with special interest, and retain the hope that his frequent inaccuracies come only from eagerness and carelessness, and that his manifest pugnacity is not settled factiousness. Let me give a few instances of the *curiosa infelicitas* of his statements and accusations.

On May 16, 1862, he made an elaborate attack on Lord Russell for his hasty ratification of a treaty with

Guatemala of 1859, by which the British government assumed the liability of the expense of making a road; and he was told in reply by Mr. Layard, that the order for ratification had been given by Lord Malmesbury before he left office, after taking the advice of Sir Edward Lytton, then Secretary of the Colonies; and Mr. Fitzgerald was then Lord Malmesbury's Under-secretary.

On June 29, 1863, Mr. Fitzgerald is reported to have reproached the present government with the employment, on a special mission to Naples, in 1859, of Mr. Elliot, the present Minister at Turin. He was sent on that special mission by Lord Malmesbury, a few days before he left office; and Mr. Fitzgerald was then Lord Malmesbury's Under-secretary.

In his speech on Brazil, on July 16, 1863, Mr. Fitzgerald made a contrast between our quarrel with Brazil of that year and a Convention with Paraguay made shortly before. But Mr. Fitzgerald omitted to say that the Convention with Paraguay of 1862 was the adjustment of a quarrel which had originated in orders given by Lord Malmesbury in 1859, just as he was leaving office, for the protection of an injured British subject. And Mr. Fitzgerald was then Lord Malmesbury's Under-secretary. Three years after, the quarrel was closed, when Lord Russell and Mr. Layard were in the Foreign Office.

Mr. Fitzgerald's ignorance of the whole question of the *emancipados* in Brazil, and of a document on this subject which had been printed by Parliament both last year and this, is fresh in our recollection. That ignorance did not restrain him from entering the lists with Lord Palmerston, and even after some days' reflection he ventured to reproach the Prime Minister for having accused him of ignorance. It is clear that a member of Parliament who has been Under-secretary for Foreign Affairs, and puts himself forward to attack her Majesty's government about Brazil, should have made the question of the *emancipados*, described in Blue-books annually presented to Parliament, his study. What might be an excuse for another member of Parliament, that he had not seen the Blue-books, could be no excuse for him. However, on the occasion of Mr. Osborne's motion, July 18th, Mr. Fitzgerald made some statements, which rather remind one of the words of "A Friend to both Countries" than prove a study of the Blue-books of which he speaks :—

"He had a number of statements, not derived from Brazilian agents, but from the Blue-books, which showed the Brazilian government, in regard to the *emancipados*, had the greatest difficulties to contend with. The territory of Brazil was immense, the plantations were separated by vast distances from each other, and the *emancipados* having been located in old times on the plantations, there was much difficulty in getting an account of them. It was evident, however, that the Brazilian government were making every effort in their power to get the negroes set free. In 1861, Mr. Christie mentioned that in one district letters of emancipation were being granted to the blacks in large numbers, and added, 'This I know to be true.' Also in the very last year the Brazilian government had been exerting themselves in the most praiseworthy manner in reference to the *emancipados*, and had set free a great many employed in the government-establishments."

Why, this is the "Friend to both Countries" over again! The statement attributed to me is not quite accurate. It is a reference to a despatch of mine, March 23, 1861, in which I forwarded to Lord Russell a note from Senhor Sinimbú, and said, "Senhor Sinimbú states in this note that the Minister of Justice has lately been granting letters of emancipation to these blacks in greater numbers, which is true." In the twelve months ending April 30, 1861, 110 free Africans were emancipated; a larger number than before, but not a very large one.

Lord John Manners and Sir John Pakington came to Mr. Fitzgerald's aid, when, on July 12th, Lord Palmerston called him to account for his ignorance in terms which Mr. Fitzgerald's friends appear to have thought harsh. I know well the chivalrous nature of Lord John Manners, by whom I have long been honoured with friendship. He has never been specially called upon to study Brazilian questions; *non omnia possumus omnes.* I feel sure that, if he should carefully examine the question of the *emancipados,* he will not think that Lord Palmerston's language about the conduct of the Brazilian government towards them was at all too strong. Circumstances also have enabled me in former years to judge for myself that Sir John Pakington is a fair man and a lover of truth. He knows something of the Brazilian government, having given special attention to the question of the Brazilian slave-trade. There was a time indeed when he seemed disposed to think Lord Palmerston rather too confiding in Brazilian promises. On July 14, 1851, he referred to an announcement in the Queen's speech of measures of the Brazilian government, and reminded Lord Palmerston that it was not the first time Brazilian announcements had ended in nothing. And in a debate which took place on a motion of Mr. Hutt's, in July, 1858, when Sir John

Pakington was First Lord of the Admiralty, he expressed himself frankly and forcibly as to the share which compulsion from England had had in the suppression of Brazilian slave-trade.

Mr. Fitzgerald has taken so prominent a part in the defence of Brazil against Lord Palmerston and the present government, that I hope to be excused for this digression. I trust that he will not be above reconsidering his hasty, incorrect accusations. He should eschew Brazilian agents. He should himself make a thorough examination of the Blue-books. I hope that what I have said will not offend him. He has talents and character which justify his high aspirations, and which, if joined with industry, some carefulness in statement, and a determination not to slip into factiousness, should ensure the success of his honourable ambition.

# CHAPTER XIV.

## BRAZIL, BUENOS AIRES, AND MONTE VIDEO.

TREATY OF 1828 FOR INDEPENDENCE OF MONTE VIDEO BY ENGLISH MEDIATION — DISPARAGEMENT OF BUENOS AIRES BY BRAZILIAN WRITERS—M. CHARLES REYBAUD—"QUARTERLY REVIEW" OF OCTOBER, 1860—PRESENT DISPUTE BETWEEN BRAZIL AND MONTE VIDEO—"THE BRAZILIAN AGENT'S" MISREPRESENTATIONS AND INCONSISTENCIES—HIS LONDON CORRESPONDENCE IN THE "JORNAL DO COMMERCIO"—BRAZILIAN REPRISALS IN MONTE VIDEO, AND ENGLISH REPRISALS AT RIO—THE RIO GRANDENSES AND THEIR MILITIA—PLUNDER OF THE WRECK OF THE "PRINCE OF WALES," AND MURDER OF THE CREW.

THE establishment of the independence of Brazil was soon followed by a war with the Argentine Republic, of which Buenos Aires is the capital, for the possession of the tract of territory lying north of the River Plate and east of the River Uruguay, which now forms the independent Republic of Monte Video, also known by the names of the Republic of the Uruguay, Oriental Republic, or *Banda Oriental.* This war, which lasted three years, and brought nothing but debt and disaster to Brazil, was terminated in 1828, through the mediation of England, by a treaty which established the independence of Monte Video, and bound both Brazil and the Argentine Republic to defend its independence and integrity.

There has since been frequently great jealousy of Brazilian interference in the affairs of Monte Video, and suspicion, perhaps unfounded, of Brazilian designs on its independence. It has been, on the other hand, the habit of Brazilian writers and agents to accuse Buenos Aires of intrigues at Monte Video, and to disparage Buenos Aires and its rulers for the exaltation of Brazil. Such is the tone which has been constantly adopted in France by M. Charles Reybaud, of the French press, who was notoriously in connexion with the Brazilian Legation in Paris. Such was the tone of the article on Brazil, which I have already alluded to, in the *Quarterly Review* of October, 1860, written by a person who had evidently never been in Brazil, and had got up the subject from books, many of them written under Brazilian influence, and with even some aid from the Brazilian Legation in London. The article is full of mistakes; its remarks on the relations of Brazil with the Argentine Republic furnish some notable instances of deception. The Reviewer says in this article :—

"The attitude of the Argentine Confederation towards Brazil, under the presidency of Urquiza, was one of hostility, and an incipient war between the two States was stopped by the mediation of England and France. It was the avowed policy of this unscrupulous man to form a combination of Spanish-American States against Brazil, and to wrest from it a considerable portion of its territory."

I was Her Majesty's Minister to the Argentine Republic during the greater part of the term of General Urquiza's presidency, and at the particular period referred to. The whole of this passage is misstatement. There was no "incipient war," no "mediation of England and France," no such policy on the part of General Urquiza. The Reviewer was misled by unscrupulous Brazilian writers.

In the month of April of this year the Brazilian government sent a special Envoy to Monte Video to demand redress for grievances complained of by the bordering Brazilian province of Rio Grande do Sul, with a threat of force if redress were not peaceably given. Monte Video was at the time distracted by civil war; and the Brazilian Envoy found the government which he was sent to treat with and threaten, imperilled and besieged by a rival General at the gates of the city. The Argentine Minister for Foreign Affairs, Senhor Elizalde, went to Monte Video from Buenos Aires, accompanied by Mr. Thornton, our Minister to the Argentine Republic, to endeavour to bring about peace between the contending parties in Monte Video. Their object was to tranquillize Monte Video.

Senhor Saraiva, the Brazilian special Envoy, was there, waiting and hoping to get his redress. The government could not do business with him while there was a formidable enemy besieging the capital. He joined Messrs. Elizalde and Thornton in their endeavours to bring the contending parties to terms. They acted together, and failed. After the failure of the negotiations for peace between the Monte Videan government and the rebel General, the Brazilian government, at the end of July, announced its intention of sending an army into Monte Videan territory to make reprisals. War between Brazil and Monte Video has since begun.

There appeared in the *Daily News* of August 26, a letter from the "Brazilian agent" under the signature of "A Friend to both Countries," volunteering an account of the demands and intentions of the Brazilian government, and of the negotiations which had been proceeding at Monte Video. Writing for the glorification of Brazil, he took care to omit all mention of Senhor Elizalde, the Argentine Minister, in the negotiations at Monte Video. Another reason for this omission will appear presently.

The "Friend to both Countries" discoursed as follows:—

"Meanwhile it is pleasant and agreeable to witness, in spite of the absence of political relations between their governments, English diplomacy in the Plate co-operating with Brazilian diplomacy in its efforts to bring about a pacification of the Oriental State, and thus frankly recognising the deep interest which Brazil, as a frontier and riparian State, has in the tranquillity of the Platine republics. This recognition by England is a great improvement on the former policy of the Foreign Office on some similar occasions . . . . It is satisfactory to observe that the English government, feeling the deep interest Brazil has in Uruguayan tranquillity, and recognising the duty of the Emperor to afford protection to so important a province as Rio Grande do Sul, should have directed or sanctioned Mr. Thornton's co-operation with Senhor Saraiva at Monte Video. In these combined efforts and common policy we have an illustration of what really cordial relations and sincere friendship between the governments of those two Ministers would unite to effect and would accomplish on a larger scale on this side of South America."

My comment on all this is as follows.

Mr. Thornton's expedition to Monte Video with Senhor Elizalde, the Argentine Minister, to try to restore peace to Monte Video, was not caused by recognition of Brazilian interest in the tranquillity of Monte Video, or of the Emperor's duty to protect his subjects, both of which are, of course, undeniable. They went to make peace in the River Plate. There can be nothing in the suspension of diplomatic relations between England and Brazil to prevent an English and a Brazilian Minister from acting together as pacificators of Monte Video, if the contending parties wish them both to act. The English Foreign Office has never denied and never could deny the interest of Brazil, "as a frontier and riparian state, in the tranquillity of the Platine republics." England has sometimes found it difficult to induce Brazil to act with her; sometimes, as in the case of the joint English and French Mission of 1852 for opening the navigation of the confluents of the Plate, she has received obstruction from Brazil when she had asked and hoped for co-operation. In this instance the joint efforts of the English, Argentine, and Brazilian Ministers have failed. So that, I fear, much encouragement is not gained from this example for joint action between England and Brazil on a larger scale. The fact is, that Brazilian influence is not great in the River Plate, and England generally can do almost as well without Brazilian aid. Brazil has lately been for a long time on bad terms both with Monte Video and Buenos Aires. She withdrew her Ministers from both in 1860; and diplomatic relations with both were only lately resumed. When in 1860 England and France invited and obtained the co-operation of Brazil in an effort to mediate between Buenos Aires and the other Argentine provinces, General Urquiza, as the head of the latter, positively refused to treat with the Brazilian mediator, and the mediation proceeded without Brazil.

The "Friend to both Countries" proceeded to relate

how the English Minister joined the Brazilian representative in his attempt at a pacification, before insisting on satisfaction for the injuries suffered by Brazilians. "It was in this attempt the English Minister joined him." Why not say that the Brazilian Minister joined the English and Argentine Ministers in their attempt? Then we are told that the Brazilian and English Ministers' suggestions having been rejected (poor Senhor Elizalde still always ignored!) "they left for Buenos Aires, where Senhor Saraiva received a popular ovation and the thanks of President Mitre and his government." These honours to Senhor Saraiva at Buenos Aires, of which I know nothing, and which rest on the authority of the "Brazilian agent," are important; important, of course, as contributing to display the Brazilian Minister as the prominent hero in this unsuccessful mediation, in which Mr. Thornton's part is represented as altogether secondary to Brazil, and Senhor Elizalde's is suppressed; but even more important for a reason which concerns the *Daily News,* because they tend to prove that Buenos Aires is not guilty of that criminal desire to make discord at Monte Video for her own aggrandizement and for the injury of Brazil, of which she had been accused by a writer in its leading columns on May 21st.

Senhor Saraiva received for his efforts to make peace at Monte Video a popular ovation at Buenos Aires, and the thanks of President Mitre and his government. Did he?

Yet, when the news arrived in May of the despatch of Senhor Saraiva to Monte Video to demand redress, a writer rushed into the columns of the *Daily News* to explain how it was all the fault of Buenos Aires. I reproduce a part of this article :—

"A sentence or two in addition to the letter of our intelligent Rio correspondent will suffice to explain the state of things in the Republic of Uruguay. Some months ago new political troubles broke out in that State, the independence and prosperity of which so unfortunately continues to be regarded with dislike, if not in the Argentine Confederation generally, at all events in its leading province of Buenos Aires. Brazil has respected and supported its independence, while Buenos Aires has repeatedly attempted to reduce it, under one form or other, to dependence. Whenever these attempts have been made, the lawless propensities of the frontier herdsmen of the Banda Oriental have broken forth, ravaging the property of the Brazilians of the Province of Rio Grande, both in and out of that Province. As it was when Rosas tyrannized over Buenos Aires and attempted the subjection of Monte Video, so is it now. . . . So long as outside that capital there are insurgents stimulated from the opposite side of the river [*i.e.* from Buenos Aires] seeking the overthrow of its present government, it may be too weak to enforce obedience to its policy on the frontiers."

But the glorification of Senhor Saraiva at Buenos Aires, which the "Brazilian agent" could not refrain from relating, proves that Buenos Aires is not so wicked. A further and more important proof he took care to suppress, the action of the Argentine Minister with Mr. Thornton to effect peace.

The course which the Editor of the *Daily News* honourably took of publishing my letters convinced me that he would sincerely regret, and would wish to repair, any injustice done by him to Buenos Aires in this matter.

The condemnation of Buenos Aires in his paper of May 21st had perhaps been circulated further, and produced a greater effect, than he dreamt of.

The London paid correspondent of the Rio *Jornal do Commercio* wrote from London to Rio on May 23d, two days after the appearance of the leading article :—

> "The explanation given in the English journals of the Brazilian naval expedition to Monte Video is considered amply sufficient. No one here doubts that the new disturbances in the Oriental Republic are the result of the intrigues of Buenos Aires, and a renewal of those ancient designs which we flattered ourselves had been done for for ever when the tyranny of Rosas fell. But it is seen that the Spanish hatreds of the Plata are inextinguishable, and it is also seen that, when they break out on the northern bank of that river, they are always accompanied by violence against the property and persons of Brazilians in the Banda Oriental."

I think I am safe in saying that Buenos Aires was not so universally and unhesitatingly condemned by British opinion as might have been inferred from the letter in the Rio *Jornal do Commercio.*

It may be taken for granted that the materials for the leading article of the *Daily News* of May 21st were supplied by the individual who, two days after, reported to the Rio *Jornal do Commercio* the convincing effect of his efforts, and who again, on August 26th, under the name of "A Friend to both Countries," complacently related the gratitude of the Buenos Airean government to the Brazilian Envoy for his efforts to make peace at Monte Video—the gratitude of that Buenos Airean government which on May 21st he had stigmatized as intriguing at

Monte Video to make discord and mischief for Brazil. I do not think I could furnish a more striking instance of the constant operations of the "Brazilian agent," who, to the detriment of both countries, to which he styles himself "a friend," misinforms the English public about Brazil, and then misrepresents to the Brazilian public his own handiwork in English newspapers as English public opinion,—who writes one thing anonymously one day, and another day under some other form or signature or in some other journal writes the very opposite, as it may suit his purpose at the moment.

He proceeded to state in the same letter that the Brazilian army would probably "cross the frontier and levy reprisals." The Brazilian President of the Council had stated this in the Brazilian Senate on July 23d, and added (I quote from the *Jornal do Commercio* of July 24th) that "the Imperial government only purposes to use the right of reprisals, which is not war properly so called, and that it will only accept war in case of its being indispensable."

This is very like what I wrote to the Marquis of Abrantes, December 30, 1862:—

"I need not tell your Excellency that reprisals are a well-understood and acknowledged mode among nations of obtaining justice otherwise denied, and that they do not constitute an act of war. The measures which will be taken by Admiral Warren are within the bounds of a state of peace. It rests with the government of the Emperor to remain within these bounds, or to transgress them."

The Brazilian army was likely to cross the frontier and levy reprisals in Monte Video. Senhor Carvalho Moreira was instructed to protest, and did protest, against the English reprisals within the territorial waters of Brazil as a violation of public right and of Brazilian sovereignty.

The "Friend to both Countries" added that "the wealthy and courageous graziers and proprietors of the Rio Grande do Sul are resolved to protect themselves, and to avenge their own wrongs, if the Emperor fail in performing that duty;" and that these "wealthy and courageous" borderers "have by law a large provincial militia of their own, especially organised for frontier defence."

Among these "wealthy and courageous" provincials are the wreckers and receivers of plunder, their aiders, abettors, and accomplices, who had to do with the wreck of the "Prince of Wales" on the coast of Rio Grande do Sul. It is recorded in a report of the Municipal Judge of Rio Grande (Senhor Garcez) to the Chief of Police (Senhor Callado):—

"The cargo of the barque was all plundered. Mariano Pinto and Manuel Rodrigues, who fled into the Oriental State, were not the only ones who robbed; it is known that many of the inhabitants, perhaps the wealthiest of the place, are devoted to this industry, but against these no proofs appear; there are no witnesses who will depose against them."

"That large provincial militia of their own, especially organised for frontier defence," was unable, not only to prevent the crimes of robbery and murder in the case of the "Prince of Wales," but even to bring one single criminal to conviction. I say, the crimes of robbery and murder, for Lord Russell said in his place in the House of Lords, July 11, 1863:—

"I must say my belief is that these men were murdered, and this, I am sure, is the prevalent opinion where the wreck took place."

And Lord Palmerston said in his place in the House of Commons, May 7, 1863: —

"Though we have no positive evidence on the subject, we have reason to believe that the crews landed on the beach, and, though carrying arms for the protection of themselves and their property, were overpowered by the people of the district, who with lassos dragged them from their shelter, and then murdered them in a barbarous and inhuman manner."

The "Brazilian agent" is, of course, of a different opinion; but, though he is the self-asserted heir of the policy of Canning, whom he brands as a blunderer, Lord Palmerston is the Prime Minister, and Lord Russell the Foreign Secretary, of the English nation.

## CHAPTER XV.

### THE REPRISALS IN BRAZIL.

THE PORTUGUESE MEDIATION—THE "BRAZILIAN AGENT" CHARGES ME WITH INDISCRETION—LORD PALMERSTON'S AND LORD RUSSELL'S CONTRARY OPINIONS—ARTICLE IN "QUARTERLY REVIEW" ON FOREIGN POLICY, APRIL, 1864—ITS MISREPRESENTATIONS ON THE BRAZILIAN QUESTION—LORD ROBERT CECIL.

IT had been my intention to conclude my letters to the Editor of the *Daily News* by telling, consecutively and completely, the story of the reprisals in Brazil; but the mail which arrived from Rio in the middle of September brought the account of a speech made in the Brazilian Senate on August 17th, by the Minister of Foreign Affairs, saying that "it was possible that the Portuguese mediation might continue," and that the Brazilian government "was waiting the result of the kindness of the Portuguese government as to the terms which might induce them to renew diplomatic relations with England." As it was to be inferred from these words that the Portuguese mediation was still pending, I determined to abstain from telling the story of what that mediation was concerned with. I had been in the belief, since Mr. Osborne gave notice of a motion for next session for the repeal of the "Aberdeen Act," until the coming on of which the "Friend to both Countries" was very anxious to postpone all discussion about Brazil, that those in this country knowing the feelings and watching the interests of the Brazilian government, regarded the mediation as at an end. I had not, therefore, been surprised at the rumour which followed the arrival of a previous mail from Brazil, that the terms recommended by the Portuguese government had been rejected by the Brazilian cabinet. It now, however, appeared that the Brazilian Minister for Foreign Affairs had publicly stated that the mediation was still pending.

My letters began with a reply to statements in the leading columns of the *Daily News* on the question of the free Africans or *emancipados*. A "Friend to both Countries" came forward to answer me; and on his provocations I proceeded from the first subject to several others, "Slavery in Brazil," "Commercial Relations," and "British Claims." None of these bore directly on the matter which has been the subject of mediation by the King of Portugal.

I had been led to propose to treat the subject of the reprisals by a statement in one of the letters of the "Friend to both Countries," that, if I had used the powers given me to accept an arbitration in the disputes about the "Prince of Wales" and the officers of the "Forte," "discreetly and prudently, the reprisals would never have been made, and the rupture would have been avoided."

Though I abstain from treating the subject in full, I shall record the opposite opinions of Lord Palmerston and Lord Russell, which may with most of my readers overbear the judgment, unsupported by proof, of an anonymous "Brazilian agent."

Lord Palmerston said in the House of Commons, May 8, 1863 :—

"Mr. Christie acted with great judgment, and with all the forbearance which is compatible with a proper and faithful performance of the orders which he had received."

Lord Russell is reported to have said in the House of Lords, June 19, 1863, in answer to Lord Malmesbury :—

"Mr. Christie acted in entire conformity with the instructions which I gave him. He argued the question with great temper and ability, and it was not until I instructed him to make a positive demand for reparation that that demand was made. Mr. Christie was not told to make an offer of arbitration, because I did not think that it lay with Her Majesty's government to make it. If we had made such an offer, the Brazilian government might have said, in its evasive way, 'This shows that you are not confident of your case,' and they would have tried some further delays."

And if this is not enough, Lord Russell has, in a private communication to me, used words which I have his permission to publish, that I "obeyed his instructions with fidelity and ability, and in a conciliatory manner."

While abstaining from the full narration which I had intended of the story of the reprisals, I will briefly allude to the version of the story which lately appeared in the *Quarterly Review* (Article, "Our Foreign Policy," April, 1864.) The Reviewer's narrative, deliberately composed and skilfully put together, may come to be regarded as a *locus classicus* on the subject. The Reviewer avoids the imputations against me made by Lord Malmesbury and the "Brazilian agent," and fairly describes me as acting in fulfilment of orders. But he is most unjust to the British government. Take his account of the state of the facts as to the plunder of the wreck of the "Prince of Wales," and the suspected murders of the crew :—

"Chiefly, it appears, on account of the evil reputation which attached to this population, the English Consul on the spot persuaded himself that this wrecked English vessel had been plundered and the crew murdered. The evidence on which he relied was not in itself very convincing. There were some indications of plunder. A Bible and some empty packing-cases were found in the house of the chief landed proprietor in the district. It was said that they were picked up on the beach, but of course it was possible that they might have been stolen from the wreck. Some chests, uninjured by the sea, were also found upon the beach. The crew were lost, and only four bodies were recovered. An inquest was held upon them, and the verdict returned was that they had been drowned; but of course it was possible that the verdict was false, and that the sailors might have been murdered. It was said that some other bodies had been seen, but when the Consul came down, only these four were to be found. The reason given was that the sand, which drifts in large masses upon that flat coast, had buried them so that it was impossible to discover them again. This might have been true. On the other hand, it might, of course, have been a falsehood, designed to conceal the fact that they had been made away with. This was the whole of what could be called evidence on the subject. There was, besides, a surmise on the part of the Admiral at Rio, who never came down to the spot at all, but merely decided on the reports of the Consul, that the fact that a certain boat was discovered in a certain position was an evidence that the crew, or some of them, had contrived to reach the shore in safety. But beyond these vague indications there was not a particle of evidence. None of the cargo of the vessel was found, which, as she was laden with iron and soda, and was wrecked at a considerable distance from the land, was not on the whole surprising."

I will only deal now with a few of these, almost all, wonderful statements.

"*Some indications of plunder!*" Every Brazilian authority admitted a wholesale pillage. The Municipal Judge, who accompanied the Consul, reported that he found on the shore "many empty crates of crockery, many barrels, chests, and cases, with evident signs of having been violently broken open and their contents pillaged;" and he added that it was evident that the cargo "had been entirely robbed by the residents of the neighbourhood." Mr. Vereker, the Consul, says he counted ninety-six crates on the beach, to say nothing of barrels, tin cases, and others. The Chief of Police described it to the President of the Province, June 27, 1861, as "a frightful pillage" (espantoso pilhagem).

"*The verdict returned was that they had been drowned!*" "*It was said that some other bodies had been seen, but when the Consul came down only these four were to be found!*" The Municipal Judge reported, like Mr. Vereker, that ten bodies had been found, and those of the captain, his wife, and a girl distinguished. The Inspector of the district and others gave evidence to this effect in official inquiries afterwards held. When Mr. Vereker went down he could not get to see any of the bodies or burial-places. At the inquest held on June 24th, seventeen days after the wreck, on four only of the ten bodies, the doctor who examined them did not say that they had all been drowned. He said of two of the four bodies that drowning was the "probable" cause of death, and that he saw no external sign of violence. In the other two cases he said he could give no opinion at all, the bodies were in so bad a state. It was seventeen days after the wreck, which was on the 7th. The Sub-delegate of Police had arrived on the spot, according to his own account, on the 12th, but he made no attempt to see the bodies then found or hold an inquest.

As to the story of the disappearance of six bodies said to have been buried through the shifting of the sands, few will dispute Admiral Warren's remark, or, if the word is preferred, "surmise:"—

"Even admitting that the winds and waves had drifted the sand over the graves, they could not have obliterated from the memory of those who buried them the place of their interment. It is also to be remarked that nothing whatever has been produced that was found on the bodies; and it is most improbable that they would have left the ship without some of their valuables about their persons."

How the writer came to know that the vessel was laden with iron and soda I cannot imagine. Mr. Vereker reported it "a general cargo." The Municipal Judge saw many empty crockery crates and barrels. The President of the Province says that the cargo consisted of coal, barrels of beer, crockery, &c. Mr. Vereker also speaks of merchandise, crockery, and coal, also tin cases of threads, handkerchiefs, and fringes.

Is there need to proceed? One might reasonably hope, in an organ of such high character as the *Quarterly*

*Review,* to find an international question, involving protection of British life and British commerce, calmly and carefully treated. The writer has not had, for an article written after a twelvemonth's interval, the excuse of haste or excitement, which might have served him for a speech made in the House of Commons in March, 1863, when the subject was new and thought promising for party polemics. Lord Russell is accused in this article of having fulminated his demands in the two cases of the "Prince of Wales" and the "Forte" only two days after he had received, on October 6, 1862, the full details of the latter question. The commonest care would have informed the writer that what Lord Russell received on October 6th was a communication from the Admiralty containing nothing but duplicates of what had reached him from me on the 22d of September, and that he had already received the main part of the story on the 2d of September, and was waiting for the supplement. The sharp and clever pen of the writer of this article is known, and his treatment of the Brazilian question much resembles the speech made on Mr. Bramley-Moore's luckless motion of March 6, 1863, by Lord Robert Cecil. The treatment in this article of the question of the officers of the "Forte" is not less unhappy than that of the question of the "Prince of Wales." It is not pleasing to see an Englishman of distinguished position, writing in a distinguished Review, discrediting the declarations of three English naval officers and gentlemen, one of them a chaplain, on the single opposing authority of a mulatto sentry, one of the lowest of the low, and taking pleasure in retailing the calumny—for calumny it is—circulated for obvious reasons, that the chaplain and two midshipmen were intoxicated. I have not the honour of knowing Lord Robert Cecil; but I have long known the Editor of the *Quarterly Review*, and I know him incapable of giving currency to what he might reasonably suspect to be incorrect. There are misstatements in this article on the Brazilian question which could not have been expected from a writer, however eager his temperament, of great ability and not less industry, having political responsibilities and of high political mark, and, moreover, of a noble, ancient, and historic lineage, which should have filled his blood with patriotism and gentleness.

The story of the questions of the "Prince of Wales" and the officers of the "Forte," and of the reprisals, yet remains to be told.

# APPENDIX.

## I.

*Extracts from "Correspondence with British Ministers and Agents in Foreign Countries and with Foreign Ministers in England, relating to the Slave-trade. Class B." Presented to Parliament.*

THE following despatches have been selected from an immense mass to illustrate some of the questions treated in the preceding Chapters; and they throw light on the great difficulties which have always attended English Ministers with the Brazilian government, and furnish examples of tone and language certainly not less severe than any to be found in recent correspondence, whether as to the questions which led to the reprisals or as to the question of the Free Africans. A succinct and consecutive account of Sir James Hudson's Mission in Brazil may be read in an article in the *Victoria Magazine* for May, entitled "Sir James Hudson in Brazil."

### No. I.

*Mr. Hudson to Viscount Palmerston.* (*Extract.*)

[GENERAL CORRUPTION OF CUSTOM-HOUSE OFFICERS AND LOSS OF REVENUE ASCRIBED TO THE SLAVE-TRADE—EFFECTS OF SLAVERY.]

Rio de Janeiro, *August 5th*, 1848.

Senhor Ferraz,* on the 21st ultimo, when debating the peculations which have recently taken place in some of the Custom-houses of this country, took occasion to point out how fertile in

* President of the Council, and Minister of Finance, 1859-61.

expedients and in trickery the trade in slaves had rendered some of the Custom-house officers of Macahé and of Rio de Janeiro.

Under the customs-laws of Brazil, goods re-exported pay a duty of 5 per cent. only to the State. The slave-importers, therefore, take up goods for re-exportation and ship them as though for the Coast, despatch their vessels from Rio de Janeiro to Macahé and other outports, there to complete their slave equipment, and at the same time, by connivance with the Custom-house officers, land the goods which they shipped at Rio, which are then smuggled up the country, and escape the duties of from 30 to 50 per cent. with which they ought to have been charged.

Senhor Ferraz, in commenting upon these facts, declared that in his opinion this vicious state of things sprang from the traffic in Africans, which demoralized and corrupted everything.

The law against the importation of slaves may be an obstacle, but the profit made is so enormous, and the pay of Brazilian customs-officers so small, that resistance to bribery has gradually become the exception, and one general system of corruption has tainted almost all. But this is not the worst part of the corrupt arts practised by the slave dealers; the unhappy officer, who is first tempted and then sold to these worst enemies of Brazil, falls with less scruple into the meshes of the net set for him by the smuggler, and thus the revenue, which is ample, if collected, is sapped and insufficient for the wants of the State.

It was discovered only last month that there was a defalcation in the customs-revenues of Pernambuco to the amount of 40,000*l.* sterling, and that in one department the officers had quietly pocketed the duties, and had kept no accounts at all. It is calculated at Rio de Janeiro that the public customs revenue is defrauded to the enormous amount of one-third of the receipts.

Senhor José de Assis, in a remarkable speech delivered in the Chamber of Deputies on the 22d ultimo, declared that this system of corruption may clearly be traced to the demoralization consequent upon the importation of slaves, hardening the heart, deadening the moral sensibilities, and laying the foundations of the splendid superstructure of vice, which the slave-importers have quickly raised upon them.

Senhor Goes,* on the 28th ultimo, said, in the Chamber of Deputies, that he had remarked an assertion in the Report presented by the Minister of Justice to the Chambers, that vigorous measures would continue to be employed against the traffic in slaves; but it appeared to him that this was the stereotyped expression of every Minister, and was limited entirely to the Report.

It has been admitted by public men of every shade of political opinion, that the importation of slaves produces laxity of conduct, corruption and demoralization amongst the public officers of Brazil, and particularly in that class who are employed to guard the interests of and to collect the public revenue. They feel too that an imported slave may prove an enemy, and never can be a friend.

It has long been admitted that the existence of slavery is a curse to Brazil; but when to that curse is added the still greater of thousands of barbarians annually imported and introduced into the very heart of society, where they become domestic servants and nurses in Brazilian families, impressing, unknown to or unremarked by the Brazilians, their very features upon society in this country, which is gradually and visibly retrograding and becoming more deeply tinged with the blood of the most worthless offcasts of the most worthless family of the human race; where the African is so notoriously sunk even in his own low scale, that the Creole negro spurns him as his dog, and, slave as he is himself, despises and maltreats his brother bondsman; it must infallibly result from such a state of things that this wretched class of beings carry with them into the very heart's core of Brazil depraved manners and conduct, and a disregard of all moral obligations.

* Senhor Zacarias de Goese Vasconcellos, the late President of the Council, and Minister of Justice.

## No. II.

### *Mr. Hudson to Viscount Palmerston. (Extract.)*

[PROJECT OF LAW FOR REPEAL OF BRAZILIAN LAW AGAINST SLAVE-TRADE—CONDUCT OF BRAZILIAN MINISTRY CONTRARY TO FORMER DECLARATIONS — INJURIOUS BEARING OF PROPOSED MEASURE ON AFRICANS ILLEGALLY IN SLAVERY.]

Rio de Janeiro, *October 15th,* 1848.

I had the honour to report to your Lordship in my despatch of the 12th ultimo, that the Brazilian Chamber of Deputies were discussing the project of a law the object of which was to repeal the Brazilian law against slave-trade, of November 7, 1831. The twelve first articles of that project have passed the Chamber of Deputies with certain amendments, a report of which I have the honour to enclose herewith; but when Article XIII. came on for discussion, the Chamber determined to discuss it in secret session. It was so discussed, and on the 26th ultimo Senhor Carvalho Moreira,* a Deputy for Sergipe, moved as an amendment that its further discussion should be postponed until next year, and this amendment being put to the vote was carried by thirty-two votes to twenty-nine.

I cannot congratulate your Lordship upon this determination of the Brazilian Chamber of Deputies. The measure, with all its hideous features of oppression levelled against an inoffensive, unresisting, unprotected mass of human beings, still hangs suspended, and may become law at an early period of next session.

That Brazilian government which has recently retired from office used every effort to force the Bill through the Chamber. They were met with a determined resistance from a small body of members who, more alive to the honour of their country and to its public engagements with Great Britain, stoutly maintained the position that the Convention against the slave-trade con-

* Late Brazilian Minister in London.

cluded by Great Britain with Brazil in 1826, is perpetual in the obligations which it imposes on this empire. This point was contested by the Minister of Foreign Affairs, Bernardo de Souza Franco,* who declared that he considered the project of law as in no wise militating against or as affecting those obligations, but on the contrary, as the project is directed against slave-trade, it is therefore in entire accordance with the stipulations of the Treaty of 1826.

That Minister is now fallen; but before his fall he never replied to the notes which I addressed to him upon this subject, and I know that he used his best endeavours to push the project through the Chamber of Deputies.

Your Lordship will remember that in a despatch which I had the honour to address to you on the 5th of August, I related the expressions used by Senhor Bernardo de Souza Franco, when declaring, in his place in the Chamber of Deputies, his determination and that of his colleagues to put a stop to the introduction of slaves into Brazil, and to substitute the labour of African slaves by that of white men, who were to be systematically introduced into Brazil under legislative enactment. These declarations were followed up by the seizure of a small depôt of slaves near Rio, and by the presentation to the Senate of a Bill to encourage the immigration of white colonists.

For a short time the public of this capital believed that the Brazilian cabinet were sincerely bent upon suppressing slave-trade.

The Colonization Bill was however no sooner presented than it was abandoned; and it was soon discovered that the slave depôts in and near Rio, where they abound, were not molested; that slave-ships fitted out in this and other Brazilian ports with the same impunity as heretofore; that at no period has the slave-trade been more active than at present at Rio, Bahia, Macahé, and Santos; and that at no time were slaves landed with less risk of interference on the part of Brazilian authorities.

* Now a Senator and Member of the Council of State, very recently appointed President of the Province of Rio de Janeiro.

When this state of things is contrasted with the declarations of the late Cabinet and of Members of the Legislature, with the abandonment of the Colonization Bill, and with the presentation to and discussion by the Chamber of Deputies, of the Project of Law No. 133, and with the earnestness with which the late government attempted to pass that Bill through the House; I imagine that your Lordship will agree with me in thinking that the unhappy, unresisting African, the object of all this bitter persecution, cannot trust to the friendship of Brazilian Cabinets.

Certainly at no period of the history of Brazil, and perhaps at no period of the world's history, has a more deliberate attempt been made by a government civilized and Christian, to reduce vast numbers of men to the condition of brute beasts; because this project of law, by substituting the legal presumption of slavery for that of freedom (which is the basis of the Law of November 7, 1831,) by repealing that law, and by enacting that no action can lie under its provisions, deliberately puts all slaves brought into Brazil since 1831 beyond the pale of the law. The legal presumption of freedom being destroyed, is it to be supposed that an African, kidnapped at Congo, can send to Congo for proof that he once was a free man?

As in duty bound, I reported to your Lordship the declarations of the late Brazilian Cabinet against slave-trade; the same sense of duty now obliges me to declare that it was time only that was wanting when the discussion of this project of law was adjourned till next session. The Budget and many other necessary measures were not voted, and members were anxious to return to their homes.

The animus of the project is evident; it is an attempt to escape from the obligations which Brazil has contracted with Great Britain; and it visits, in a Brazilian sense, upon the head of the unoffending African the sins of Lord Aberdeen's Bill of 1845.

## No. III.

### *Mr. Hudson to Viscount Palmerston.* (*Extract.*)

[THE BRAZILIAN GOVERNMENT COULD EASILY SUPPRESS THE SLAVE-TRADE IF IT CHOSE—EXECUTION OF ITS LAWS WANTED.]

Rio de Janeiro, *February 20th*, 1850.

A few simple measures of police on the part of the Brazilian government, would most effectually check and stop the Brazilian slave-trade. It is absurd to say that the Brazilian government cannot suppress slave-trade when we see them suppress a rebellion which had great ramifications and great popular support in one of the wealthiest and strongest provinces of this empire.

It is ridiculous to maintain that the Brazilian slave-trade, which is confined almost exclusively to 300 miles of the Brazilian coast, north and south of the Brazilian capital, and the extreme limits of which do not exceed one day's sail from Rio de Janeiro, cannot be greatly checked, if not entirely suppressed, by a proper exercise of the Imperial authority, and by due vigilance on the part of the Imperial magistracy and police.

But no Brazilian administration has hitherto adopted any efficient measure whatever for the suppression of the Brazilian slave-trade.

It is true, that no Brazilian government can check slave-trade so long as they permit their minor authorities to receive with impunity a bounty upon every slave imported ; it is equally true that no Brazilian government can suppress slave-trade so long as slave-ships are permitted to be armed, manned, fitted, and despatched to the coast of Africa for slaves, in broad day, and with the cognizance and permission of the Brazilian authorities, not only in the out-ports, but under the eye of the Imperial government, in the harbour of the capital of the empire.

As long, therefore, as this notorious and public assistance and connivance of the Brazilian authorities is tolerated by the Brazilian government, it is absurd to suppose that the planting of colonies of Europeans in Brazil can have any other effect than to foster and encourage slave-trade.

The excuse of the Brazilian government for this open violation of the law of Brazil, and of the Convention which subsists between Great Britain and Brazil for the suppression of the slave-trade, is, that the existing Brazilian laws for the trial of the offence of slave-trading are insufficient ; and his Excellency recommends the adoption of such legislative measures as will overcome existing difficulties, and enable the Brazilian government to fulfil the obligations which Brazil contracted with Great Britain in the Convention of November 23, 1826.

It is not so much new laws for the suppression of slave-trade which Brazil requires, as the due execution of those which exist.*

## No. IV.

### *Mr. Hudson to Viscount Palmerston.* (*Extract.*)

[MORAL AND ECONOMICAL EFFECTS OF SLAVE-TRADE AND SLAVERY—OPEN CONNIVANCE IN SLAVE-TRADE—NATIONAL DIGNITY.]

Rio de Janeiro, *February 20th*, 1850.

Your Lordship will receive by this packet a despatch enclosing a Report which the Minister of the Empire has presented to the Brazilian chambers, and upon which I have had the honour to offer some remarks to your Lordship.

It will be seen from the Report how the connivance of Brazilian authorities in the importation of slaves, contrary to the

* A Brazilian writer has lately said : "It was said that there was an innate inward predilection for slave-labour, so strong that it was utterly beyond the strength and power of any Brazilian government to put an end to the traffic. *Nevertheless, when the government wished the traffic to cease, it ceased.* I do not now inquire what were the causes which led to this suppression. I record the fact, and no one can deny it, that the African slave-trade ceased, when the government of our country wished that it should cease."—*O Brazil e os Brazileiros*, por Antonio Augusto da Costa Aguiar. Santos, 1862.

treaty stipulations of Brazil, to Brazilian public law, and to every principle of justice and humanity, has at last produced its fruits in a settled contempt for international engagements, a disregard for their own law, and a great lack of private morality.

Brazil having fostered the importation and sale of barbarians, is astonished to find her native population of the interior almost as barbarous as those of the wilds of Africa.

Her government sends physicians to districts where the people are decimated by small-pox, with instructions as to their cure and treatment; the physicians are treated as assassins and their remedies as poisons.

Her government establishes schools of primary instruction in a population of 5,500,000 souls, and the Minister reports that 35,608 persons are receiving instruction in them.

Brazil possesses a most fertile soil, yet her agricultural staples are reduced to two, and her agricultural implements to one, the hoe.

In the face of these evidences of the effects of slave-trade, and in spite of the most direct and flagrant violation of the solemn treaty-engagements of the Crown of Brazil respecting that traffic, the harbour of the Brazilian capital is open to ships, which with perfect impunity, and under the very eye of the government, fit out, go for, and return from the coast of Africa with slaves, as your Lordship will perceive from the enclosed returns. And yet, in the note which I have received from Senhor Paulino,* his Excellency persists in considering that the "national dignity" is wounded by the capture and destruction of such a floating shambles as the *Santa Cruz.*

It is to be lamented that his Excellency's sense of the national honour of his country is not as keen as it is respecting her "national dignity," a "dignity" which is attempted to be maintained at the expense of her honour, the deterioration of her interests, and the gradual but certain degradation of her people.

* Now Viscount Uruguay, Senator and Councillor of State.

## No. V.

### *Viscount Palmerston to Mr. Hudson.*

[CONTINUED VIOLATION BY THE BRAZILIAN GOVERNMENT OF ITS TREATY-ENGAGEMENTS, AND MODERATION OF THE ENGLISH GOVERNMENT.]

Foreign Office, *April* 13*th*, 1850.

Sir,—I have received your despatch of the 20th of February last and its enclosures, upon the subject of the seizure of the Brazilian slave-vessel *Santa Cruz*, by Commander Schomberg, of Her Majesty's ship *Cormorant*, on the 5th of January last, to the southward of the port of Rio de Janeiro.

I have to instruct you to present a note to the Brazilian Minister for Foreign Affairs, saying, that Her Majesty's government have received copies of the correspondence which has passed on this subject between the Brazilian government and yourself, and that they entirely approve the note which you addressed to Senhor Paulino on the 19th of February last; and that you are further instructed to request the Brazilian government calmly and seriously to consider the extreme nature of the rights which Great Britain has acquired against Brazil by the deliberate, systematic, and long-continued violation by the government of Brazil, of the treaty-engagements between the Crown of Brazil and the Crown of Great Britain; and you will say, that Her Majesty's government feel satisfied that the Brazilian government will, upon reflection, do justice to the great moderation and forbearance which the British government has hitherto displayed, by availing itself of those rights only in so limited a degree. But you will add, that Her Majesty's government hope and trust that the government of Brazil will henceforward, by a full, faithful, and efficient execution of its treaty-engagements, relieve Her Majesty's government from the necessity of proceedings, which, however much they may be justified and rendered necessary by the conduct pursued up to the present time by the government of Brazil, are nevertheless very painful to Her Majesty's government.

I am, &c.
(Signed) PALMERSTON.

## No. VI.

*Viscount Palmerston to Mr Hudson.* (*Extract.*)

[CANNOT TRUST TO BRAZILIAN PROMISES—FORCE ONLY WILL MAKE THEM SUPPRESS THE SLAVE-TRADE—DOUBTS THE POLICY OF THE PARTIAL SUSPENSION OF THE ORDER FOR CAPTURES OF SLAVERS IN BRAZILIAN PORTS AND WATERS WHICH MR. HUDSON HAD AGREED TO.]

Foreign Office, *October* 15*th*, 1850.

I have received and laid before the Queen your despatch of the 27th of July last, on the subject of the steps adopted by the Brazilian government in consequence of the recent proceedings taken by Her Majesty's cruisers on the coast of Brazil against slave-trade, and reporting the circumstances under which you had recommended Admiral Reynolds to suspend a portion of the General Order which he had issued with respect to the seizure of slave-vessels within Brazilian waters and ports.

In reply, I have to state to you, that I cannot doubt that you, who are on the spot, and who arrived at your opinion by personal observation, have formed a correct judgment as to the sincerity of the declarations made by the Brazilian government, that it is their intention really to put down the slave-trade; and you were therefore probably right in asking Admiral Reynolds to modify for a time the course of his proceedings against slave-trade on the coast of Brazil.

But I must confess that nothing which has passed conveys to my mind any other impression than that the Brazilian government felt that Brazil is powerless to resist the pressure of Great Britain; that they saw clearly that this pressure must, if continued, fully accomplish its purpose of putting down slave-trade, and that they were endeavouring, by every device they could think of, to obtain the greatest amount of diminution of that pressure, with the smallest amount of real concession on the part of Brazil. Senhor Paulino has been profuse in declarations and promises, but such things have never been wanting on the part of any Brazilian Minister; he has proposed, and the Brazilian government has probably passed, a Law, which, in its last modified shape, is certainly an useful addition to the Law of 1831. But the example of the Law of 1831 is sufficient to show that in Brazil the existence of a law is one thing, and its practical enforcement another, and a very different one. Therefore, until Her Majesty's government shall see that the two Laws, the one that of 1831, and the other that which has recently been passed, are actively and effectually, and without favour or partiality, carried into execution, Her Majesty's government cannot sanction the further continuance of any modification or suspension of any part of the orders under which Admiral Reynolds is acting.

Moreover, the reasons given by Senhor Paulino for asking for a modification and suspension of those orders do not appear to be sufficient or satisfactory. It is certainly true, as he says, that the capturing of slavers within the Brazilian waters by foreign cruisers is derogatory to the dignity of Brazil, but that which has already happened shows that this proceeding, instead of forming, as he represents it, an obstacle to concession on the part of the Brazilian government and parliament, has been, in fact, the means by which now at last, for the first time after nearly twenty years of ineffectual endeavours at persuasion, the government and parliament of Brazil have been brought to take any steps against slave-trade; and the early success, which so far has attended the employment of these means, can certainly afford no reason for prematurely abandoning them. With regard to the danger of collision which Senhor Paulino apprehends, if slavers should be captured under the guns of a Brazilian fort, there would be an obvious, and a most proper and effectual mode of avoiding such collision; and that would be, that the Brazilian government should give the most imperative orders to all officers in command of forts, not upon any account whatever to fire upon a British ship of war employed in capturing slavers; and such orders you will request the Brazilian government to give. There can be no justification for such firing upon a British ship of war, inasmuch as a British ship of war, in capturing a slaver under the guns of a Brazilian fort, is only doing that which by treaty and by law the commander of the fort ought himself to have done. The British naval officer should, however, in such a case, always communicate with the commanding officer of the fort in the first instance in order to obtain, if possible, his cooperation.

The plain fact is, that nothing can be effected with the Brazilian government on this matter, except by compulsion. Arguments and reason have long been used in vain. If a mere sense of duty and a regard for the engagements of treaties could have swayed the conduct of the Brazilian government, the Brazilian slave-trade would many years ago have entirely ceased. But it is manifest that the slave-traders have been able to exert over the Brazilian government, either by corruption or by intimidation, an influence which has overridden all sense of right and wrong, and all regard for legal and international obligations.

That influence can be overcome only by some counteracting pressure, and it seems clear that the proceedings lately adopted by the Admiral in concert with yourself, have produced precisely the sort of pressure which is calculated to counterbalance and overcome the influence of the slave-traders.

Her Majesty's government are glad that Admiral Reynolds did not consent to suspend making captures in the waters of Brazil generally, because it is quite clear from what has happened, that it is in the waters and harbours of Brazil that captures of slavers can best and with the greatest certainty be made; and if we were to agree to abstain from making captures within the three-mile limit, the efficiency of our squadron would be most essentially impaired.

## No. VII.

### *Mr. Hudson to Viscount Palmerston.*

[MR. HUDSON REVOKES THE SUSPENSION OF THE ORDER FOR CAPTURING SLAVERS IN BRAZILIAN PORTS AND RIVERS, WHICH HE HAD AGREED TO ON PROMISES FROM THE BRAZILIAN MINISTER, AND THE PRUDENCE OF WHICH LORD PALMERSTON HAD DOUBTED—HE ACCUSES THE BRAZILIAN MINISTRY OF BREACH OF FAITH.]

Rio de Janeiro, *January* 11*th*, 1851.

My Lord,—With reference to your Lordship's despatch of the 15th of October, stating the circumstances under which I should not be justified in continuing the temporary suspension of the execution of a portion ot the orders, with regard to the suppression of slave-trade, of the Rear-Admiral Commanding-in-chief on this station, I have the honour to transmit herewith to your Lordship the copy of a note which I have addressed to Senhor Paulino, the Brazilian Minister for Foreign Affairs, acquainting him that that temporary suspension is at an end, and stating my reasons for adopting this line of conduct.

I have, &c.

(Signed) JAMES HUDSON.

## Enclosure.

### *Mr. Hudson to Senhor Paulino de Souza.*

Rio de Janeiro, *January* 11*th*, 1851.

Excellent Sir,—When the Brazilian parliament passed, and His Imperial Majesty Don Pedro sanctioned the law against slave-trade of the 4th of September last, the civil and military authorities of the Queen in this country had good right to expect that the Brazilian government, who held office in order to carry out the Imperial will and the Imperial law, would have put that law and the law of 7th November, 1831, effectively in operation against the traffickers in human flesh.

When, on the 13th of July, your Excellency told me that you were prepared to put the navigation of your country under a foreign flag, if slave-ships were seized by Her Majesty's vessels in Brazilian waters, in accordance with the stipulations of a treaty; when I told your Excellency, that on condition of your putting your own laws in execution against slave-dealers without favour or partiality, I would incur the heavy responsibility of recommending the suspension of the orders to seize those slavers in your ports and waters; and when afterwards I reduced that agreement to writing, it was understood by your Excellency and by myself, that the Imperial will and the Imperial law should have fair play and due force; that there should be no compromising with the dealers in human flesh; that the slave-trade, that curse to Brazil and disgrace to our age, should be put down in Brazil by Brazilian power, that was to say, by your Excellency and by your colleagues, the guardians of the honour of this nation, and the practical expounders and enforcers of its laws.

I now ask your Excellency which of us has kept and which has failed to observe that agreement.

This is a serious matter: it is not a mere question of pressure upon a small knot of pirates and kidnappers, who by some mysterious agency are permitted to make Brazil their head-quarters; but as to whether the servants of the Crown of Great Britain and Brazil respectively have done their duty.

As the question, therefore, immediately at issue relates to the grounds on which I consented to take upon myself the responsibility of suspending the orders in question, it is but just that we should examine the engagement into which I entered with your Excellency.

The laws of this Empire, and the Treaty between Great Britain and Brazil for the suppression of slave-trade, bound your Excellency, in any case, to suppress slave-trade; but in addition to those motives for action in that matter, there was the engagement above referred to.

It was understood then, on the 13th of last July:—

1st. That your Excellency would present to the Brazilian parliament such a law as would enable the Imperial government to bring to justice vessels and persons engaged in slave-trade.

2dly. That the penalties, in order to prevent the equipment of ships for slave-trade, should be increased, and heavier bond required from ships engaged in African voyages.

3rdly. That measures should be adopted to prevent coasting-vessels carrying from port to port articles destined for the equipment of slave-vessels, and that bond should be entered into by them for the lawful performance of their voyages, and the legal use of such suspicious articles as they might carry.

4thly. That the slave-trade should be put down whenever the Imperial government was armed with the powers which your Excellency intended to demand of the Brazilian parliament.

These were the leading features of the pact into which I entered with your Excellency just six months ago; which was followed by your Excellency's speeches in the Chamber of Deputies and Senate: by the passing of the Law of the 4th of September; and by those assurances respecting the suppression of slave-trade, which, by your Excellency's desire, I have conveyed to my government.

I have now to consider and to point out where your Excellency has failed to comply with your own laws, and with the spirit and intent of our mutual compact, and with the Treaty of 1826.

1st. It was agreed, that all ships fitting for slave-trade in Brazilian ports and waters should be seized by the public authorities of Brazil.

It has been my duty since entering with your Excellency into the compact in question of the 13th of July, more than once publicly to call your Excellency's attention to the number of slave-vessels arriving at and departing from Bahia, and to the permission notoriously given to them to pursue their illegal traffic.

Seven vessels are at this moment fitting, or fitted for slave-trade, in Bahia, and they are only waiting the withdrawal of one of Her Majesty's ships now stationed there, to depart on their illegal voyages.

Twelve barracoons where Africans are publicly kept for sale exist in full activity in and near Bahia. No attempt is made by the public authorities to close them, to restore the Africans in them to that freedom to which they are entitled by law, and to prosecute their owners for this gross and flagrant violation ot the Imperial laws and international obligations.

One vessel, it is true, has been condemned at Bahia for attempting to break the Navigation Law, and Municipal Law of the empire, and the port regulations of Bahia. Her attempt was too gross a violation of those laws and rules, her cargo and fittings too palpably intended for slave-trade, for her to escape attention and punishment.

But why are not the other slave-ships and their owners subjected to a similar process?

Your Excellency is aware that on the 6th instant a large vessel, the *Indigena*, left this port, and was seized outside the harbour. She had her slave-deck laid, and her leaguers, bulkheads, gratings, and hatches, were such as are only used by slavers. No attempt was made to examine her by the authorities in this harbour, or to inquire into the nature of the fittings she had on board.

2dly. It was understood that all Africans landed in Brazil after the pact between your Excellency and myself, should be seized by the public authorities.

Your Excellency, indeed, has sent an Agent to Liberia to inquire whether that State will consent to receive Africans who have been illegally imported into Brazil, on condition, as I understood from your Excellency yesterday, that Liberia shall consent to pay the expenses of the passage of those Africans; a condition which, considering the resources of Liberia, and the date of her birth as an independent State, is, I imagine, an utter impossibility.

But is your Excellency aware that upwards of 5,000 African slaves have been landed in this and the adjoining provinces since your Excellency entered into the arrangement of the 13th of July; and that the Imperial authorities have seized but twenty-three of them, although the military force sent to seize those Africans was occasionally within three-quarters of a league of large bodies of them; as was notoriously the case at the Fazenda of Graça of Manguinhos, which is described by the Chief of Police of this Province in his public report, as being destined for nothing but the reception of illegally imported Africans; and at the Fazenda of Conceição, belonging to Breves, which is situated but three-quarters of a league from the Sacco of Mangaratiba, where the police force disembarked, which was destined to capture the Africans of the *Idelmunda* and *Carne Secca*.

Your Excelleney has doubtless heard the report that, although Graça is denounced by the Chief of Police of this Province as a violator of the Imperial laws, no process at law has been, or is to be commenced against him. The same immunity is accorded to Breves.

To these must be added the proprietors, shippers, and dealers connected with the cargoes of the *Astro, Sagaz,* and *Julia, Catão, Idelmunda, Tres Amigos,* and *Eleanor,* who are all perfectly well known. Your Excellency informed me yesterday that the Imperial government had determined to send a Sardinian baker, named Pareto, out of this country, on account of his being a foreigner notoriously engaged in slave-trade. But the owners of the slave-ships I have named to your Excellency are also all foreigners, all equally guilty as this wretched baker, and all equally subject to the action of Brazilian laws. Nevertheless, I do not hear of any attempt being made by the Imperial government to punish them.

Your Excellency cannot surely consent that men like Valencio and Frugoni, notorious slave-dealers, both of whom are suspected of having been engaged in the murder of Her Majesty's subjects, and one of whom is strongly suspected of having fired on Her Majesty's flag at Paranaguá, shall continue at large in Brazil.

That corrupt magistrate, Maya, of Guarapari, has never, to my knowledge, received the slightest censure or punishment for his proceedings in permitting the notorious slaver *Feiticeira* to fit out for slave-trade, or for having fired on the boats of Her Majesty's steam-sloop *Harpy*, after he had passed his word of honour that the *Feiticeira* should be delivered to the Imperial government, and her owners indicted for a breach of the laws of his country.

5thly. It was understood and agreed by your Excellency and by myself, that barracoons or depôts for the sale of Africans should be closed by the proper authorities. Your Excellency can scarcely be ignorant that depôts for this purpose exist at

Cape Frio.
Armação.
Rio de San João.
Rio das Ostras.
Macahé.
Campos.
Manguinho.
Piume.
Marambaia.
Mangaratiba.
Dois Rios.
Mambucaba.
Fazenda do Alegrete.
Itabatinga.
Sombrio, and
Perrequé.

6thly. It was agreed that proper precautions should be taken to prevent the employment of coasting vessels in slave-trade.

The recent trial of the *Amelia* at Pernambuco is proof of the extent to which this practice is carried; and recent reports show that no hindrance to the custom is attempted, especially from Bahia along the coasts of Alagoas and Pernambuco.

I am not aware that the agreement into which your Excellency entered with myself, namely, that coasting-vessels should give bond in money for the lawful employment of those suspicious cargoes which they so frequently carry, has ever been fulfilled.

Finally. It is clear that whilst these things continue, your

Excellency cannot lay claim to any share in the suppression of the slave-trade.

That trade continues; interrupted, it is true, by that pressure upon the slave-dealers which produced a temporary check; but the pressure removed, we see a relapse to the former apathetic indifference to the provisions of laws and the stipulations of treaties produce a corresponding reaction on the part of the slave-dealers.

Your Excellency, on a review of the proceedings of Her Majesty's authorities in this country, will find that in no instance have they departed from the letter and the spirit of the compact into which I entered with your Excellency on the 13th of July.

The Rear-Admiral and myself, in endeavouring to consult the desire of the Imperial Cabinet, agreed to incur a heavy amount of responsibility. But as we see that our conduct on that occasion is either not appreciated or is misconstrued, as we have failed in our endeavours to induce the government of the Emperor of their own accord to act up to their own laws, the will of their Sovereign, and the obligations of their treaties, we have no other course left open to us, consistently with our public duty, than to resume that conduct which we hoped the action of the Imperial Cabinet would have rendered unnecessary; and it remains to me, therefore, but to state to your Excellency, that the provisional suspension of the orders to seize slave-ships in accordance with the spirit and letter of the Treaty of 1826 is at an end.

I avail, &c.

(Signed) JAMES HUDSON.

## No. VIII.

### *Viscount Palmerston to Mr. Hudson.*

[REPLY TO REFUSAL BY THE BRAZILIAN GOVERNMENT TO APPOINT A MIXED COMMISSION TO EXAMINE AND FREE SLAVES HELD IN ILLEGAL SLAVERY—RIGHT OF HER MAJESTY'S GOVERNMENT TO DEMAND THE FREEDOM OF SLAVES ILLEGALLY IMPORTED.]

Foreign Office, *July 5th*, 1851.

Sir,—I have received and laid before the Queen your despatch of the 12th of May last, inclosing a copy and translation of a note dated the 26th of April last, which you received from M. Paulino de Souza, in reply to the note which, in compliance with the instructions contained in my despatch of the 8th of November, 1850, you addressed to him on the 18th of February last, proposing to the Brazilian government the establishment of a Mixed Commission at Rio de Janeiro, which should be empowered to investigate the cases of negroes suspected of being illegally held in slavery in Brazil, and to declare whether such negroes are or are not free.

I observe that Senhor Paulino, in his reply to your note, merely states that the Brazilian government, in common with those of all other independent nations, execute their own laws in their own country, and will cause them to be executed by means of their own tribunals and authorities; that they cannot, therefore, allow the creation of a Commission wherein foreign Judges shall have votes and exercise jurisdiction within the empire; and that the creation of such a Commission being the principal object of the proposed Convention, it cannot be admitted; and I perceive that Senhor Paulino has accordingly declined to enter into any examination or discussion of the Convention which you submitted to him upon this matter, and that he has sent back to you the draft which you proposed to him.

I have now to instruct you to say to Senhor Paulino in reply, that the functions which Her Majesty's government wish to see performed by the Mixed Commission which they have proposed to the Brazilian government, would consist, not in trying and sentencing Brazilian subjects for a breach of the Brazilian laws against slave-trade, but simply in determining whether negroes who might be brought before such a Commission were entitled to be free, as having been introduced into Brazil in violation of a Convention by which Brazil bound herself and remains bound to Great Britain to prevent the introduction of slaves into the Brazilian empire.

The fact of an immense number of slaves having been introduced into Brazil after the conclusion of, and in violation of, the stipulations of that Convention, is not disputed by the government of Brazil; and the right of Her Majesty's government to claim that such slaves shall be restored to freedom is equally undeniable.

It is moreover to be observed, that the Convention which Her Majesty's government have proposed to Brazil for establishing a tribunal competent to investigate the cases of such persons, would not establish any new principle. On the contrary, it would merely give a new operation to a principle which was admitted by Brazil in the Convention of 1826, and was acted upon and in force in Brazil from 1831 to 1845.

It is evident that the functions of such a Mixed Commission as Her Majesty's government now propose, in affirming and decreeing the inherent freedom of a negro on Brazilian territory, would be perfectly analogous with the functions of the Commission which from 1831 to 1845 possessed and exercised the right of affirming and decreeing the inherent freedom of a negro found on board a Brazilian ship, which by international law is considered as Brazilian territory.

The negroes whose freedom was decreed by that Mixed Commission between 1831 and 1845 were actually in Brazilian territory when their cases were adjudged by that Commission; and if a Mixed British and Brazilian Commission sitting at Rio de Janeiro has been acknowledged to be competent, without violating any international principle, to sit in judgment upon a negro who was at the time in Brazil, and to declare such a negro to be a free man, and by such declaration to deprive his pretended owner of all right or title to him, what essential difference could it make in point of principle, whether such negro was brought illegally into Brazil a month before, or had been brought thither several years before; or whether he was landed in Brazil by the boats of a cruiser employed in suppressing the slave-trade, or by the boats of a vessel engaged in carrying on that traffic?

If indeed there is any essential difference in point of principle between these cases, that difference consists in this, that the negro who has been landed, many months or several years before, by the boats of a slave-ship, and who has since his landing been subject to the miseries of illegal slavery, has endured a heavier wrong than the negro who has been recently landed by the boats of a cruiser from a captured slave-ship; and such a man is therefore more urgently entitled to that remedy and protection which the sentence of the Mixed Court would afford him.

I am, &c.

(Signed) PALMERSTON.

## No. IX.

### *Mr. Southern to the Earl of Malmesbury.*

[CASE OF A "FREE AFRICAN" WHO HAD SERVED SIXTEEN YEARS IN THE MILITARY ARSENAL WITHOUT ANY REMUNERATION.]

Rio de Janeiro, *December 13th*, 1852.

My Lord,—With reference to my despatch of the 14th of July, and previous despatches from this Legation, on the subject of the improperly-called "emancipated" Africans, I have the honour to enclose to your Lordship a copy of a note recommending to Senhor Paulino's protection one of these unfortunate individuals, who applied to me to intercede in obtaining his freedom, having now been in slavery sixteen years, or six longer than the term of his apprenticeship.

I have, &c.,

Henry Southern.

Enclosure.

*Mr. Southern to Senhor Paulino de Souza.*

Rio de Janeiro, *December 10th*, 1862.

Sir,—I beg to recommend to your Excellency's protection the bearer of this note, the emancipated African, Romão, who has now served in the Military Arsenal sixteen years—six years beyond the time prescribed by law, and without having received any recompense for the period which he has passed in slavery since the expiration of the time when he was entitled to be set free.

I feel the utmost confidence, that in placing this poor man in the hands of your Excellency, I am taking the surest step for procuring him ample justice, and at the same time I am calling to your Excellency's memory the condition of so many hundreds of unfortunate creatures placed in the same circumstances as this individual.

I avail, &c.,

Henry Southern.

## No. X.

*Mr. Consul Cowper to the Earl of Malmesbury.* (*Extract.*)

[COASTING TRAFFIC IN SLAVES—ITS CRUELTIES—TREATMENT OF SLAVES IN BRAZIL.]

Pernambuco, *May 6th*, 1852.

There is one point still open for the exercise of the humane and friendly influence of your Lordship with this government, the continued exercise of which would render the cessation of the African slave-trade incomplete. I allude to the coasting traffic in slaves, which obtains so universally here. It is attended with all the horrors of its prototype; the same forced transportation from country, for from Pará to Rio Grande do Sul is as distant and in all respects as great a banishment as from the coast of Africa to Brazil, without even the poor excuse of ameliorating the condition of the negro, made use of by the Africo-Brazilian slavers; the same disruption of natural ties of parent, child, brother, or sister,—the same eternal separation from these and from friends; indeed, my Lord, most painful scenes are witnessed here at the departure of almost every steamer, and it could scarcely be termed an improper interference of Her Majesty's government to use its friendly offices with this, with a view of putting a stop to this heartless traffic; and it would test the sincerity of its anti-slavery professions.

I enclose to your Lordship a table published by the department of police, showing the number of these unfortunates for whom passports had been granted during nine months. You will perceive that the Secretary of Police has not deemed it necessary to refuse them for African blacks, although his government has declared the importation of Africans to be piracy ever since 1831, and consequently few, if any, African slaves should exist, nor has he thought it improper to publish the fact. Your Lordship will also observe that helpless infancy fails to excite the humanity of the slave-trader: forty-one children under ten years of age were banished, and three sucking babes without their mothers.

The general treatment of slaves may almost be as well imagined as described. Under a system so unnatural and so irresponsible, it depends entirely upon the character of the master, for the very limited protection afforded to the slave by law is neutralized by the abject dependence of his position; he is for all practical purposes in no better position than an animal in Great Britain, who is there also protected by law; for he dare as little make use of the faculty of speech in complaint as the other is capable of doing so: the latter has one advantage, that he finds human beings to sympathize with and speak for him, but the slave never does. I have so often described the atrocities to which these persons are subject, that I need not repeat them; but they may be conceived when I re-state that I was an eye-witness to an unfortunate slave cutting his throat at a dinner-table at which I was a guest; and that invitations were issued in this Province by the proprietor of an estate to witness the boiling alive of a slave, in the cauldron of his estate. Urban slaves are less dependent, and consequently less worked and better clothed than rural ones, who are not uncommonly worked for twenty hours out of the twenty-four, including a period termed on the estates, "Riningu." Emancipation is very rarely practised.

## No. XI.

### *Mr. Howard to the Earl of Clarendon.*

[CONVERSATION WITH VISCOUNT PARANÁ ABOUT THE REPEAL OF THE "ABERDEEN ACT."]

Rio de Janeiro, *January 4th*, 1854.

My Lord,—At an interview which I had yesterday with Viscount Paraná, the President of the Council of Ministers, his Excellency introduced the subject of the British Act of Parliament of August, 1845, and of the right of search exercised by Great Britain over Brazilian merchant-vessels, and complained at great length of what he termed the injustice of the proceedings of the British government towards Brazil, saying that they constituted a luxury of oppression.

Viscount Paraná took up the string of his complaints from a distant epoch, and asserted that, even during the operation of the Convention of 1817, the British cruisers had made illegal captures, and the British government had refused to act upon awards given by the Mixed Commissions. He then commented severely upon the enactment of the Bill of 1845, previous, as he said, to the proposition of a new Convention in lieu of that which had expired, and upon the stringent measures taken in 1850 by Her Majesty's government within the territorial limits of the Empire, at a time when the Brazilian government were seriously occupied with the suppression of the slave-trade; and he contended that all the efforts of Her Majesty's government had proved inadequate for that object, and would have continued so, whilst the violence of the acts of the British cruisers had produced irritation in the public mind, and thus impeded the action of the Brazilian government, which was then sincerely desirous of putting an end to the traffic. The efforts, on the contrary, which the Brazilian government had made within the last few years had been crowned with the most complete success; and the slave-trade, which had previously flourished, notwithstanding our cruisers, was now extinguished. The Brazilian government were consequently authorized in expecting that Her Majesty's government, who must be convinced of their good faith, would renounce the exercise of rights not given to them by international law, and would repeal the Act of 1845, which, moreover, as an exceptional measure, ought to cease when the object for which it had been passed was attained.

Without entering into the particular questions that had arisen during the period when the Convention of 1817 was in force, I replied that the British government were not to blame for the cessation of that Convention, of which notice had been given by Brazil; that the Act of 1845, which had been reluctantly resorted to by the British government, was the necessary consequence of its termination without the conclusion of a new Treaty, and of the long course of violations by the Brazilian government of the perpetual obligations contracted by Brazil under the Treaty of 1826, violations which had continued to within a recent epoch; for it was notorious that the Brazilian government, if they had not directly encouraged the slave-trade, had countenanced it, and connived at it. It was, I said, the continued violation by Brazil, during a period of upwards of twenty y. the of the sacred duty she had undertaken to suppress the slave-trade, which had forced Her Majesty's government in 1850 to make a more extended use of the powers accruing to them from the Treaty of 1826, and under the Act of 1845. The effect of the adoption of the more stringent course in question had not been, as his Excellency maintained, to impede the action of the Brazilian government, but it had been, on the contrary, in the opinion of those persons who were most conversant with the subject, to give the necessary impulse to the Brazilian government; and, in support of my statement, I quoted the evidence of Senhor de Andrade, who, before a Committee of the House of Commons during last session of Parliament, had admitted that the activity of the British cruisers had precipitated the conduct of the Brazilian government.

The circumstance of the late endeavours of the Brazilian government towards the suppression of the slave-trade having met with success, only proved the justice of our former allegations that the Brazilian authorities could, if they had chosen it, have done much to put an end to it.

I further observed that Her Majesty's government had made frequent proposals to the Brazilian government for a new Treaty, which had been declined, and that as recently as last summer they had brought forward a fresh draft of Treaty, not differing materially from our Treaty with Portugal, and providing for a suspension during its operation of the exercise of the powers conferred upon the British government by the act of parliament of the 8th of August, 1845.

This draft of Treaty had likewise, I understood, been rejected by the Brazilian government, and, under the circumstances, I did not see how Her Majesty's government could consent to repeal the act of parliament in question, however ready they were to acknowledge the humane and honourable course now pursued by the Brazilian government; nor did I think it likely that they would be willing to abandon, in respect to Brazilian merchant-vessels, a right of search which they have exercised on the high seas in respect to Portuguese and Spanish vessels.

Although the slave-trade was checked at present, yet, as your Lordship had observed to me in a late despatch, the spirit of slave-trading still existed in Brazil; the conversion, I said, of the people of Brazil, from slave-trading principles, appeared to me to be too recent to be complete, and I felt persuaded the unassisted efforts of the Brazilian government would be insufficient to put down the traffic; and that, were the check placed upon it by our cruisers removed by the withdrawal of the latter, it would be revived in such a manner as to baffle the means at the disposal of the Brazilian government for its suppression. I therefore regretted that the Brazilian government should have thought proper to remonstrate, as they had done in the notes I had lately received, against the continued exercise of the right of search over Brazilian merchant-vessels by Her Majesty's cruisers; I said that matters had been going on satisfactorily, and I thought the Imperial government had better have left well alone.

Viscount Paraná rejoined by repeating the opinion he had expressed, in the former part of our conversation, relative to the Act of 1845, to the sufficiency of the means at the disposal of the Brazilian government to suppress the slave-trade, and inadequacy of those employed by Her Majesty's government; and remarked, with regard to the latter point, that were the Brazilian government even now to cease their repressive measures and remain with their arms folded, without, however, doing anything to favour the trade, we should see how incapable we should be of keeping it down; such a course, however, they would not pursue. He denied that the Brazilian government had ever countenanced the slave-trade; though he admitted that they had not, at one time, taken any active measures to suppress it. Public opinion, which was then in favour of the slave-trade, had prevented them from doing so. In 1848, however, a change of Administration took place. The opinion of the Council of

State was taken; the dissolution of the Chambers in 1849 prevented anything being done in that year; bnt in 1850 the government brought forward and carried through the Legislature their measures for the suppression of the slave-traffic, and since that period their efforts had been crowned with complete success. This brought his Excellency again to the revocation of the Act of 1845, as a concession which he considered the Brazilian government had a right to expect.

With regard to the draft of a new Treaty lately proposed by Her Majesty's government, the President of the Council stated that he did not reject it; that he would not say that it might not be adopted; but he would not sign that Treaty or any other, unless the Act of 1845 were previously repealed. Weak nations could not with honour make the same concession as more powerful countries, and it had now become a question of self-pride (*amour propre*) with Brazil that the Act in question should, in the first instance, be rescinded, and he, for his part, would never have the moral courage to propose to the Legislature the adoption of a Treaty whilst that Act remained in force. The Opposition might wish him perhaps to do so, but he would not give them that satisfaction. His Excellency further observed, that if Her Majesty's government were to satisfy the Brazilian government by repealing the law, and should no Treaty be concluded within, say, a couple of years, and the necessity of the law be shown, Her Majesty's government would certainly, considering the feeling existing in England respecting the slave-trade, find no difficulty in inducing Parliament to re-enact it, in the same manner as bills concerning Ireland had been allowed to expire, and had subsequently been re-introduced and put into force. In answer to an inquiry which I had addressed to his Excellency whether there was any truth in a rumour which had been mentioned to me, that there was a question of his proceeding to England on a mission connected with the subject which we were discussing, he replied that there was no foundation for it; that it was not the intention of the Brazilian government to propose any new Treaty; they were willing to let matters stand as they were, and as long as he was in office, whether with or without a Treaty, he would strain every nerve for the suppression of the slave-trade.

I need not trouble your Lordship with a detail of the further remarks I addressed to his Excellency, except to state that I said I did not see what harm the Act of 1845 did to Brazil; that I thought the "*amour propre*," to which he had alluded, was misplaced; and that, as to repealing the Act with the chance of being obliged to re-enact it, it was painful enough for Her Majesty's government to have been obliged to apply once to parliament for the powers it conferred upon them, and it would therefore, it appeared to me, be better to retain them than incur the risk of having to make a second application to parliament.

I think it right to state that at the commencement of our conversation Viscount Paraná said that he should speak to me without reserve, but that he of course did so only as an individual member of the government.

I have, &c.

(Signed) HENRY F. HOWARD.

## No. XII.

### *Mr. Howard to the Earl of Clarendon.*

[THE BRITISH CRUISERS AND RIGHT OF SEARCH NECESSARY TO AID THE BRAZILIAN AUTHORITIES IN MAINTAINING THE DISCONTINUANCE OF THE SLAVE-TRADE.]

Rio de Janeiro, *January 4th*, 1854.

My Lord,—With reference to the subject of my two preceding despatches, I beg to state that the opinion of the best-informed persons on slave matters with whom I have had an opportunity of conversing, concurs with the humble one which I have formed, that the presence of Her Majesty's cruisers on the coast of Brazil, and the possession by them of the right of searching

Brazilian merchant-vessels, although they may not have at present the opportunity of making captures, serves as a most wholesome check, not only upon the slave-dealers, but likewise upon the Brazilian authorities, and that were the powers under which they are now acting withdrawn, without the substitution of others equally efficient, the consequence would be the revival of the slave-trade.

I have, &c.

(Signed) HENRY F. HOWARD.

## No. XIII.

### *The Earl of Clarendon to the Chevalier de Macedo.*

[THE SLAVE-TRADE WOULD NOT HAVE BEEN SUPPRESSED IN BRAZIL BUT FOR THE PROCEEDINGS UNDER THE "ABERDEEN ACT"—THE BRAZILIAN GOVERNMENT CANNOT DISPENSE WITH THE AID OF THE BRITISH CRUISERS—ENCLOSES REPORT OF CONVERSATION OF MR. SOUTHERN WITH SENHOR PAULINO, ADDRESSED TO LORD MALMESBURY.]

Foreign Office, *July 6th*, 1854.

M. le Chevalier,—I have the honour to acknowledge the receipt of your letter of the 27th ultimo, referring to a debate which took place in the House of Commons on the previous day, respecting the Act of Parliament of 1845, relative to the Brazilian slave-trade, and complaining that in the course of that debate Lord John Russell and Viscount Palmerston attributed the late cessation of that traffic in Brazil to the operation of the Act in question.

I beg to observe to you in reply, that although the Brazilian government are entitled to full credit for the praiseworthy exertions which they have made since 1851, for the suppression of the African slave-trade, and although it would be much more agreeable to me to dwell exclusively upon what has been accomplished by Brazil in the last two years, and to pass over the painful records showing the course pursued during the previous twenty-six years in regard to the engagements which Brazil contracted towards Great Britain by the Treaty of the 23rd of November, 1826; yet I feel bound to express my sincere conviction that the existence of the Act of 1845, and more particularly its stringent enforcement in the year 1850, contributed materially to bring about the present improved state of affairs.

With regard to this point, I am able to appeal to the testimony of a distinguished Brazilian Minister, who took a prominent part in the discussions upon these latter transactions,—I mean Senhor Paulino de Souza, whose statement as to the salutary effect produced by the exertions of the British cruisers even in 1850 will be found in the accompanying report of a conversation which the late Mr. Southern had with his Excellency in 1852.

I have likewise to call your attention to the fact, that during the present year the Brazilian Minister for Foreign Affairs has informed Her Majesty's Minister at Rio de Janeiro, of three expected arrivals of African slaves on the coast of Brazil. These communications were of course made to Mr. Howard, in order that he might apply to the British Naval Commanders on the station to afford their co-operation in preventing these apprehended violations of Treaty and Brazilian law; and it appears to me that if Her Majesty's government were to propose to parliament to repeal the Act of 1845, they would incur a serious responsibility, and wantonly deprive themselves of the means of effectually assisting the Brazilian government with their support and countenance in counteracting the plots of the slave-dealers whose activity on the coast of Africa has of late been very much increased.

I am, &c.

(Signed) CLARENDON.

Enclosure.

*Mr. Southern to the Earl of Malmesbury.*

Rio de Janeiro, *May 10th,* 1852.

My Lord,—With reference to the statement which has been made by the Brazilian government, that the summary proceedings of the British cruisers had rather retarded than aided in the suppression of the slave-trade on this coast, I think it right to report to your Lordship that in a conversation I had lately with the Minister for Foreign Affairs, his Excellency stated to me that he and his colleagues had found it vain to argue with their countrymen—slave-holders, buyers, and sellers—on grounds of philanthropy or political economy; that the line of argument the Ministry had used and found most efficient was this:—"You see the number of years that the forces of the British government have been directed towards the suppression of the slave-trade; the treasures it has lavished on the means of intercepting that traffic. We ourselves know by experience that no consideration holds it back when there is a question of the slave-trade; and now that it appears resolved to put down the slave-trade, and is proceeding with more vigour than ever, can we suppose that it will draw back? And if this state of things continues, what can come of it but war? And if we go to war with England, what will become of the capitalists, agriculturists, and merchants of Brazil?"

His Excellency distinctly stated to me, that by such arguments as these, used in the very moment of the application of the strongest measures of the British cruisers against the Brazilian slave-traders, he and his colleagues had prevailed upon influential persons to support, or at least not to oppose, the Government in co-operating with the agents of Great Britain in their determined persecution of this inhuman commerce.

I have, &c.

(Signed) HENRY SOUTHERN.

## No. XIV.

### *Mr. Howard to the Earl of Clarendon.*

[DISADVANTAGES FOR ENGLISH RESIDENTS IN BRAZIL—CUSTOMS-TARIFF AND ADMINISTRATION OF INHERITANCES—GENERAL CONVICTION THAT THE SLAVE-TRADE WAS SUPPRESSED BY THE ACTION OF THE ENGLISH GOVERNMENT.]

Rio de Janeiro, *August* 10*th*, 1854.

My Lord,—Amongst the observations in the Chevalier de Macedo's note of the 27th of June last to your Lordship, on the subject of Viscount Palmerston's speech in the House of Commons on the question of the repeal of the Act of Parliament of 1845, a copy of which note, and of your Lordship's reply of the 6th of July, your Lordship has been so good as to forward to me in your despatch of the 8th of the same month, I remark that he takes credit to the Brazilian government for modifying their customs tariff in a manner favourable to the consumption of English goods, and for granting the demands of Her Majesty's government relative to the property of Englishmen dying intestate in Brazil.

Upon the first point, I beg leave to remark, that from the information which has been furnished to me by English merchants here, it appears, that since the expiration of our commercial Treaty with Brazil of 1827, when British goods became liable to a duty double that to which they were subjected under the Treaty, no essential modification of the Brazilian tariff profitable to British merchandise has taken place.

With regard to the second point, if the Chevalier de Macedo means to imply, as appears from his note, that the Brazilian government have yielded to the requests of Her Majesty's government on the question of inheritances, he is in strange ignorance of the real state of the case; and either cannot have received, or must have overlooked, the Report presented to the Legislature, on the 15th of May last, by the Minister for Foreign Affairs of his own country, in which Senhor Limpo de Abreo refers to the still unsatisfied demands of Her Majesty's government on the subject, and publishes some of the correspondence of Her Majesty's Legation here with the Brazilian Foreign Department. If the Chevalier de Macedo could be the means of settling this question as satisfactorily as he seems to think it has already been arranged, he would confer a great benefit upon Her Majesty's subjects residing in this country, as well as upon Her Majesty's servants, who, for the last nine years, have been labouring in vain to induce the Brazilian government to accede to the reasonable wishes of Her Majesty's subjects.

Your Lordship having completely refuted, in your reply, the arguments by which M. de Macedo has sought to disprove Viscount Palmerston's observations, attributing the cessation of the slave-trade in Brazil to the operation of the Act of 1845, and to its more stringent enforcement in 1850 and 1851, I will only take the liberty of remarking, that his Lordship's opinions, as confirmed by the expression of your Lordship's own views, are those of all the many foreign residents in this country with whom I have conversed on the subject, and that their accuracy is admitted by all the impartial Brazilians I have met. Moreover, I am confident that the greatest part of those Brazilians who think it patriotic publicly to deny their justice, are internally convinced of it.

I have, &c.
(Signed) HENRY F. HOWARD.

## No. XV.

### *Mr. Howard to the Earl of Clarendon.*

[PROJECT OF LAW FOR OBLIGING OWNERS OF SLAVES TO MAINTAIN THEM WHEN DISABLED BY AGE OR ILLNESS—COMMON PRACTICE OF FREEING SLAVES WHEN UNFIT FOR WORK.*]

Rio de Janeiro, *August 12th,* 1854.

My Lord,—I have the satisfaction of enclosing herewith translation of a project of law proposed yesterday in the Chamber

* See page 70. Sir William Ouseley makes the following statement bearing on this subject: "Cases not unfrequently occur of neglect and

of Deputies by Senhor Wanderley, the President of the Province of Bahia, and ordered to be taken into consideration, providing that the owners of slaves who shall grant freedom to such of them as may not be able to maintain themselves in consequence of old age or disease, shall not be exempted from the obligation of supporting them; and that slaves who beg for alms with the consent of their masters, shall *ipso facto* be considered as free.

The benevolent object of this motion on the part of Senhor Wanderley, in his quality of Deputy, is to remedy the abuses which, I am sorry to learn, are not unfrequent, of masters freeing their slaves when their services are no longer of any value, and thus turning them adrift destitute, as well as of masters sending out their slaves to beg for the profit of such masters.

I have, &c.

HENRY F. HOWARD.

## No. XVI.

*Mr. Howard to the Earl of Clarendon.*

[ADVERTISEMENTS IN NEWSPAPERS FOR SALE OF NEGROES ILLEGALLY SLAVES.]

Rio de Janeiro, *November 9th,* 1854.

My Lord,—I have the honour to inform your Lordship that I yesterday notified to the Brazilian Minister for Foreign Affairs

abandonment of slaves in old age, which, in effect, amount to virtual homicide. This is contrary to law, as a master is bound by its letter to maintain his slave in sickness or in health, and when incapable of labour from age or otherwise. But it need hardly be observed that, where laws are made and administered by slave-holders, their due execution for the interests of the slaves is frequently evaded, or utterly disregarded. On one occasion I recollect my European servants finding, in a shed near the entrance of grounds pertaining to my house, a decrepit old mulatress, in the last state of misery and hunger. On inquiry, it appeared that she had been driven from her owner's house, as having become burthensome and useless, and was forced to beg a subsistence; weakness and hunger induced her to seek a refuge near my house. She was too weak at first to be moved; and after having been fed and attended to for some days, died of debility and the effects of previous suffering." (Ouseley's "Notes on the Slave Trade, &c." 1850. p. 41.)

the approval conveyed to me in your Lordship's despatch of the 5th ultimo, of the notes which I had addressed to his Excellency on the 17th and 18th of July last respectively, relative to advertisements offering for sale African negroes, who, from the ages attributed to them, must have been introduced into Brazil since the year 1831.

I took the same opportunity of communicating to his Excellency your Lordship's approvals contained in your despatches of the 1st and 3rd of July, of my previous notices of the 5th and 10th of May, relative to the advertisement of the illegal sale of a young African negress; and to the baptism, in the first instance, as a slave of the daughter of a free negress.

I have, &c.

HENRY F. HOWARD.

## No. XVII.

*Mr. Howard to the Earl of Clarendon. (Extract.)*

[BRAZILIAN STATEMENT AS TO THE EXTINCTION OF SLAVE-TRADE—REMISSNESS OF BRAZILIAN GOVERNMENT ABOUT THE EMANCIPADOS.]

Rio de Janeiro, *May 28th*, 1855.

Viscount Abaeté proceeds to claim for Brazil the whole merit of the suppression of the slave-trade, saying that the reluctance on the part of Her Majesty's government to repeal the Act of 1845 is the more remarkable, as it is undeniable that the extinction of the trade in the empire is solely and exclusively the effect of the legislative measures decreed by the Chambers, and the means employed by the government.

Under the head of Emancipation of free Africans, Viscount Abaeté gives an account of the communications exchanged between Her Majesty's Legation and himself on that subject, and states that he considers the discussion to be terminated.

Whilst I am always willing to acknowledge the efforts which are made by the present Brazilian government for the suppression of the slave-trade, I regret to say that I observe much remissness on the part of the Imperial authorities in carrying out the partial measures of their own government for the actual setting at liberty of the so-called free Africans who have served private individuals during fourteen years; for, as your Lordship is aware, the Brazilian government withheld emancipation from those who are employed in the public establishments. The consequences are, frequent applications from free Africans to Her Majesty's Legation, and the necessity of the latter interfering in their behalf. The language that I hold is, that such interference is by no means agreeable to Her Majesty's Legation, and that I am surprised that the Brazilian government do not avoid the humiliation which it entails upon them by taking the matter vigorously into their own hands, and seeing that justice is really done to those unfortunate individuals in whose welfare they profess to interest themselves.

## No. XVIII.

*The Earl of Clarendon to Mr. Jerningham.*

CAUTION TO BRAZILIAN GOVERNMENT THAT IT MAY BE NECESSARY TO REVIVE CAPTURES IN BRAZILIAN WATERS.]

Foreign Office, *January 9th*, 1856.

Sir,—With reference to my despatch of the 29th ultimo, I have to direct, that if you should find the Brazilian government inactive with regard to the late landing of slaves at Serinhaem, and if it should appear that they are not disposed to discover, or to punish, when detected, the persons concerned in that affair, or in any other similar acts of slave-trading, you will state to the Brazilian government that, if they do not prosecute and punish the persons who have been engaged in these slave-trade transactions, the British government will be obliged again to put in force the provisions of the Act of Parliament of the year 1845, and while British cruisers will exercise on the coast, in the rivers, and in the harbours of Brazil, that watchfulness and activity which the agents and officers of the Brazilian government neglect to use, British Courts of Justice will pronounce those decrees of condemnation from which Brazilian Courts may be found to shrink.

I am, &c.

(Signed) CLARENDON.

## No. XIX.

*The Earl of Clarendon to Mr. Jerningham.* (*Extract.*)

[DISSATISFACTION WITH PROCEEDINGS OF THE BRAZILIAN AUTHORITIES IN THE CASE OF A LANDING OF SLAVES AT SERINHAEM.]

Foreign Office, *January 17th*, 1856.

I have received your despatch of the 14th ultimo, enclosing copies of a correspondence which has passed between you and the Brazilian Minister for Foreign Affairs, respecting the landing of Africans which was effected at Serinhaem in October last, and stating that the Brazilian government have now entered seriously into the investigation of that affair.

It would appear, however, by a despatch which I have received from Her Majesty's Consul at Pernambuco, dated the 19th ultimo, that the prosecution of the parties concerned in the landing in question is by no means carried on with vigour; and I have, therefore, to instruct you to impress upon the Brazilian Minister for Foreign Affairs the very serious nature of this case, in which the local authorities seem to be gravely implicated, and you will call upon the Brazilian government to use every effort to prevent the revival of the slave-trade, for which it is evident that preparations are making.

## No. XX.

### *Mr. Jerningham to the Earl of Clarendon.* (*Extract.*)

[TREATMENT OF EMANCIPADOS IN GOVERNMENT EMPLOYMENT.]

Rio de Janeiro, *April 9th,* 1856.

Your Lordship is no doubt aware that the *emancipados,* in consequence of the government Decree of the year 1853, are entitled to their certificates of perfect freedom after serving fourteen years in private families, being hired out by the government to them at a low rate. However, these free blacks must then present a petition in form to the Minister of Justice, who, usually, but not in some instances without a little urging on by Her Majesty's Legation, grants them their liberty.

But the Imperial government considers the time which the *emancipados* have served in their own employ as not giving these unfortunate people the same title to reap the benefit of the above Decree, which is evidently a manifest injustice, especially as the labour which is pressed upon them in government establishments, on public roads, in arsenals, and in barracks, is generally of a more arduous nature than that which the hired *emancipados* have to perform in the service of the nobility and gentry, who are not unfrequently good and easy masters.

In conclusion, I beg to state that it appears to me very desirable that Her Majesty's government should have the kindness to emit an opinion upon this point; for, in the eyes of justice and humanity, it would seem that the Imperial government, who are bound to re-export, at some time or other, those free blacks, or *emancipados,* as they are termed, to Africa, should not be allowed to consider them as their legal property, and keep them in a situation which presents them hardly a gleam, whether they give satisfaction by good behaviour or hard work, of ever recovering their liberty.

I am happy to say, however, that lately, but not without frequent messages, I have been able to obtain the freedom of a free African named Desiderio, of the Mina nation, who had been constantly in the government employ since the year 1835, having been seized by the Brazilian police at the *engenho* of Cabrito, in the Province of Bahia, shortly after being landed; and the other day he came to thank me for having procured him his certificate of freedom.

## No. XXI.

### *Mr. Jerningham to the Earl of Clarendon.* (*Extract.*)

[COASTING TRAFFIC IN SLAVES FROM THE NORTHERN PROVINCES—DANGERS OF THE WANT OF LABOUR IN THE NORTH.]

Rio de Janeiro, *September* 11*th*, 1856.

The number of Ladino blacks [blacks imported coastwise] which have been imported into Rio from the northern ports, makes me apprehensive either that something wrong has occurred somewhere, or that it will soon be the case; for, how can the northern Provinces, where negroes are most required, afford to supply the Rio and St. Paul's markets, when they themselves, decimated by cholera, stand more in need of that kind of labourers for sugar-plantations under a hotter sun than in those Provinces where coffee and Indian corn, &c., requiring infinitely less toil, are chiefly cultivated?

A Brazilian gentleman to whom I frankly communicated my suspicions, told me that he did not think at present Africans were imported into the northern Provinces, but that the planters there, poorer than those in the southern ones, were compelled by necessity and debts to sell their slaves, which were greedily bought up at Rio de Janeiro and St. Paul's, where they fetch at present enormous prices. He also assured me that later, if colonists were not imported into the southern Provinces in a sufficient quantity so as to force the black population up to the north, there would be great danger of the northern planters, for the sake of hands, embarking in contraband speculations.

One thing, however, is certain; the black population during the last year have suffered severely, and the prices paid here for Ladino slaves are enormous; those on the coast of Africa are excessively small. The people here have no great liking for Portuguese or Island-men; they prefer Creole blacks, and, if the truth were known, they would prefer Africans to Creoles. This, I am convinced, is the private feeling of most people, particularly those who are engaged in agriculture, whatever may be their ideas on the heinousness of slave-trade.

## No. XXII.

### *Mr. Scarlett to the Earl of Clarendon.* (*Extract.*)

[ACQUITTAL OF THOSE IMPLICATED IN THE SERINHAEM AFFAIR—THE MINISTER OF JUSTICE PROPOSES TO DISMISS THE JUDGES.]

Rio de Janeiro, *December* 11*th*, 1856.

I have received a despatch from Mr. Cowper at Pernambuco, informing me that the Court, called the "Relacao," which sat in judgment on all those persons who were accused before it of having a hand in the landing and theft of African slaves at Serinhaem, has absolved the parties so accused, including those who are known to be guilty, and those who are considered by Mr. Cowper as innocent of the charges which were made against them.

This iniquitous decision, according to Mr. Cowper, has been arrived at by an equal division of the votes of the six Judges who tried the case, the parties being then by law entitled to an acquittal on account of the doubt.

Against this decision the *Promotor Publico*, or Attorney-General of Pernambuco, appealed to the Superior Tribunal of Rio de Janeiro; but I am informed that the Brazilian law does not admit of any appeal under such circumstances, and those who were accused stand for ever absolved.

The Minister of Justice, however, Senhor Nabuco, in consideration of a strong opinion he entertains of the injustice of the decision, and of the bad effect it will have in setting at liberty those who are believed by the Brazilian government to be guilty, has determined to dismiss from their offices all the Judges who were engaged in the cause; and as this act is an arbitrary one, he means to appeal to the Chamber in the ensuing session for a justification of his own conduct.

## No. XXIII.

### *Mr. Scarlett to the Earl of Clarendon.* (*Extract.*)

[COASTING TRAFFIC IN SLAVES.]

Rio de Janeiro, *April 1st*, 1858.

On the receipt of a despatch from your Lordship, which I have already acknowledged, dated December 8, 1857, accompanying the copy of a communication from Mr. Consul Cowper at Pernambuco, exposing the abuses which have so often been, for some time, practised at the northern ports of Brazil by an extensive exportation of negroes to other ports, and to their removal by sale to parts of the Empire at a distance from the districts in which they were born and brought up; I immediately addressed to Viscount Maranguape a note on this subject, a copy of which I have the honour to enclose, founded upon your Lordship's instruction to me on that head, and on Mr. Cowper's statement.

## Enclosure.

### *Mr. Scarlett to Viscount Maranguape.*

Rio de Janeiro, January *8th*, 1858.

The Undersigned, &c. has been instructed by his Government to appeal, strongly, to the justice and humanity of the Imperial government on the subject of the coasting trade in Brazilian slaves, which has for some time been a disgrace to this country.

And, in order to show that this iniquitous trade exists, and continues,—the Undersigned regrets to add, with the permission of the Brazilian authorities,—the Undersigned has the honour to enclose an extract from the Pernambuco *Jornal do Commercio* of the 22d of September last, depicting some of the horrors connected with this traffic.

The state of the steamer *Imperatriz*, upon her arrival at Pernambuco from Maranham, referred to by this publication, is not a solitary instance, but one of weekly occurrence.

The Undersigned is unable to comprehend the reported policy of that Province in encouraging the free export of the slaves, and strictly prohibiting their import, one effect of which is unquestionably to make Maranham, according to the *Jornal*, the Coast of Africa of Brazil.

The Undersigned is convinced that the Province of Maranham, on account of its latitude and burning climate, is the least likely to obtain hereafter the aid of the white free labourers, instead of black slaves, and the consequent removal of the black Creole population will only render it the more impossible to fill up the vacancy thus created, by any other means than that of resorting to the still more iniquitous and illegal traffic in slaves from the Continent of Africa, which, in spite of the Government, the *fazendeiros* will be ultimately tempted to renew.

The Undersigned trusts that the Imperial government will, on reflection, take the same view of this question as that taken by the government of the Queen, and that it will not hesitate, when the Legislature meets, to propose a law prohibiting the export or removal of slaves from the Provinces in which they were born, and as a primary step, to interdict, at once, vessels subsidized by the government, carrying its mails, troops, &c. and commanded by officers of the Imperial Marine, like the *Imperatriz* and others, from carrying these unfortunate people to other Provinces for the purpose of being sold at a distance from their natural homes. The Undersigned, &c.

(Signed) P. CAMPBELL SCARLETT.

## No. XXIV.

### *Mr. Christie to Lord J. Russell.*

[ADMISSION BY LEADING BRAZILIAN STATESMEN IN 1860 THAT THE ENGLISH GOVERNMENT HAD JUSTIFICATION FOR ITS FORMER PROCEEDINGS, WHICH CAUSED THE SUPPRESSION OF THE SLAVE-TRADE.]

Rio de Janeiro, *August 27th,* 1860.

My Lord,—In some late discussions in the Senate on a project of law concerning nationality of children of foreigners born in Brazil, the opponents of which have accused the government of being influenced in promoting it by pressure from the French government, some allusions have been made to the measures taken by the Brazilian government in 1851 for the suppression of the slave-trade under pressure of the vigorous proceedings of British cruisers in Brazilian waters; and it is gratifying to see that Brazilian statesmen now avow in public, without contradiction, that England had previously just cause of complaint of the non-fulfilment of Treaty obligations.

The Viscount Uruguay (Senhor Paulino de Souza, who was Minister for Foreign Affairs in 1851), supported the Nationality Bill, and observed, in reply to the taunts of fear of the French government, that when in 1851 the Brazilian government demanded of the Legislature the framing of measures to suppress the slave-trade, they were reproached for acting under the pressure of a foreign government, and his answer was, that he asked for the means of fulfilling a national engagement contracted more than twenty years before. "And the consequence has been," added the speaker, "that instead of despising us, foreign nations have given us esteem and honour."

Senhor Vasconcellos, a speaker against the Nationality Bill, took up Viscount Uruguay's reference to England and slave-trade, with the remark that no comparison was to be made between the present case and the former difficulties with England about the slave-trade, because the complaints of England were just, and founded upon a Treaty.

No contradiction was offered to these remarks, and no further reference made to them.

I have, &c.

(Signed) W. D. CHRISTIE.

## No. XXV.

### *Mr. Christie to Lord J. Russell.* (*Extract.*)

[DIFFICULTY OF OBTAINING INFORMATION ABOUT THE FREE AFRICANS—WAGES DUE TO THEM.]

Rio de Janeiro, *December 20th*, 1860.

Since I addressed your Lordship in my despatch of the 17th of May, on the general question of the free blacks in Brazil, I have had frequent occasion to consider this question further, and your Lordship will have seen by my despatches relating to the Ypanema affair what difficulty there is in obtaining information from the Brazilian government about these blacks, and how long some of these employed at Ypanema have been in servitude. The free blacks of Ypanema, to whom my attention has been accidentally called, are only a few of some 5,000 or 6,000 detained in real captivity by the Brazilian government. The same difficulties which have met me in my endeavours to obtain information about them would attend any inquiries that I might institute about any other small detachment; and I feel that the only way of satisfactorily dealing with this question is to take it in the gross.

I cannot think, however, that the government of Brazil could refuse to furnish Her Majesty's government with a detailed list of all the free blacks who were handed over to them, explaining what has become of them, whether dead, emancipated, or still in service; and the emancipation of all who have served beyond the term of apprenticeship prescribed by the Brazilian laws might then be demanded by Her Majesty's government.

It was prescribed by Treaty that these blacks should be employed "as servants or free labourers," and the Brazilian government guaranteed their liberty. A very important question for them is wages. They have been either employed by the government in public establishments, or let out to private individuals.

Senhor Limpo de Abreo stated in his note to Mr. Howard, of the 3rd February, 1854, that the wages of the free blacks were designed by the government to meet the expenses of their re-exportation to Africa. Mr. Howard pointed out in reply (3rd March, 1854) that the Brazilian instructions of the 19th November, 1835, provide that "the produce of the hiring shall be applied either in aid of the expenses of the re-exportation of the Africans or for their benefit," and he suggested that, as re-exportation was abandoned, the Imperial government should apply the accumulated wages in some other way for the benefit of the blacks.

Mr. Howard in the same note mentioned the case of a free black who was permitted on his petition to leave Brazil, but received no wages, and was even required to pay for his passport.

On the 10th of December, 1852, Mr. Southern recommended to the Minister of Justice a free black who had served sixteen years in the Military Arsenal, and had received no wages.

It seems to me that Brazil may gain much by retaining these blacks as freemen in the country, instead of re-exporting them, as had been originally designed, and that the Brazilian government are in every way bound, on emancipating them, to pay over to them, for their benefit, a fair balance of reasonable wages.

## No. XXVI.

### *Mr. Christie to Earl Russell.*

[FREE AFRICANS TREATED AS SLAVES BY BRAZILIAN GOVERNMENT—CANNOT GET INFORMATION.]

Rio de Janeiro, *November* 12*th*, 1862.

My Lord,—In the last Annual Report of the Minister of Marine, there is a detailed account of the Brazilian naval establishment at Itapura, situated in the most remote part of the Province of St. Paul's, about the removal to which of free Africans I have been endeavouring in vain, for two years and more, to obtain information from the Brazilian government: I refer to my despatches of August 27 and December 17, 1860, and of January 24 and June 3, 1861, printed in the two last Blue Books. The report I have referred to mentions, that of free Africans and slaves, thus mixing them together, there are in all 131 in the establishment of Itapura. The coupling in this way of free Africans and slaves will help to show your Lordship how the free Africans are practically treated; and if no other motive existed, the inquiries which I have been making during the last two years should have led the Brazilian government to ascertain the number of free Africans in distinction from the slaves. But it seems as if the Brazilian government are determined not to give any of the desired information about the free Africans.

Itapura is considered a most unhealthy place, and its great unhealthiness has been the subject of much discussion in the last Session of the Legislature.

I have, &c.

(Signed) W. D. Christie.

## No. XXVII.

### *Mr. Christie to Earl Russell.*

[RENEWED APPLICATION FOR ANSWERS TO LONG UNANSWERED NOTES.]

Rio de Janeiro, *December 15th*, 1862.

My Lord,—I enclose a copy of a note which I have addressed to the Marquis of Abrantes, in obedience to your Lordship's instructions in your despatch of November 8, to remind him of my many notes, long unanswered, about the free blacks.

I have, &c.
(Signed) W. D. CHRISTIE.

### Enclosure.

### *Mr. Christie to the Marquis of Abrantes.*

Petropolis, *December 8th*, 1862.

M. le Marquis,—Her Majesty's government have desired me once more to remind you of my many notes long unanswered, from two years and a-half to a year and a-half old, of which I urgently reminded Senhor Taques in two notes addressed to him on the 17th of April, on the subject of the free blacks handed over to the Brazilian government by the Mixed Commission Court under the provisions of the Treaty of 1826.

Her Majesty's government desire me to say on this occasion that the Africans have all served more than the time prescribed by the Brazilian legislature for their apprenticeship, and are therefore incontestably entitled to their unrestricted freedom, and that, as they were emancipated under the conjoint auspices of the British and Brazilian governments, Her Majesty's government feel themselves in duty bound to see that faith is kept with them.

I avail, &c.
(Signed) W. D. CHRISTIE.

# APPENDIX.

## II.

## BRITISH CLAIMS ON BRAZIL.

(*From the Brazil and River Plate Mail of July* 21, 1864.)

The sums claimed amount to Rs. 2,057,754 089, or upwards of £225,000, exclusive of several claims for amounts not stated. Mr. Layard has given the gross total at £300,000, subject to deduction on examination. The annexed list is from the Appendix to the Annual Report of the Brazilian Minister for Foreign Affairs of 1860 :—

| | |
|---|---|
| Duncan, Hardman, and Co. : losses in revolution of Pernambuco of 1824 | Rs. 13,738 345 |
| Various English merchants of Pará : losses in the revolution of 1835 | 694,262 767 |
| Marcos Lima, of Pará : losses in the revolution of 1835 | 25,000 000 |
| Various English merchants of Bahia : losses in rebellion of 1837 | 99,282 143 |
| S. Samuel : disappearance of gunpowder deposited with the Government of Bahia in 1837 | sum not stated. |
| Thomas Tobin : for powder robbed by the rebels at Bahia in 1837 | sum not stated. |
| The English Vice-Consul in Maceio, James Burnett: losses in the revolution of Alagoas in 1844 | 24,354 869 |
| Miller and Findlater : losses in the rebellion of Bahia | 85,454 401 |
| The owners of the vessel *Perseverance* : loss of ship and cargo by collision of vessel of Brazilian Government | 50,263 255 |
| George F. Dickson and Co. : capture of brigantine *Felix* by a Brazilian vessel of war | 60,078 012 |
| Donald Campbell and G. F. Dickson : supplement to last claim | sum not stated. |
| The owners of the brigantine *Clio* and cargo : for the capture by rebels at Salinas and plunder of the cargo, and assassinations of the captain and crew | sum not stated. |
| Owners of the *Clio:* supplement to the last claim | sum not stated. |
| The officers of the frigates *Raleigh* and *Inconstant:* for wine and beer sold by order of the Custom-house authorities | 871 709 |

| | |
|---|---|
| The owners of the brigantine *Constantine*: for detention, with cargo on board; by order of Custom-house, giving preference to French vessels . . . . . . . . . . | Rs. 1,551 644 |
| Persons interested in various English vessels: for abstraction of objects indispensable for navigation of the vessels | sum not stated. |
| The Government of Her Majesty: for duties levied by Rio Custom-house for medicines, provisions, &c., sent from England for the English squadron . . . . . | 50,183 114 |
| W. Petty and Co., of Rio de Janeiro: for restitution of a payment made to Custom-house . . . . . . . . | 2,012 813 |
| The English creditors of the late Don Antonio Uzet, of Pelotas: claim against the distribution of the property by the Judge of Orphans . . . . . . . . . . | 9,500 000 |
| The English creditors of the bankrupt house of Thomas Dutton and Co., of Bahia: for embargo placed by Provincial Government on all the property of the bankrupt house on account of a disputed privileged claim of the public Treasury . . . . . . . . . . | 50,183 111 |
| James Lang, of London: for non-fulfilment by the Imperial Government of a contract made with its official agent in London . . . . . . . . . . . | sum not stated. |
| John George Young: for difference of value in the securities with which the Government paid his claim under judicial sentence . . . . . . . . . . . . | 116,248 315 |
| Hesketh, Wilson, and Co., of Maranham: for the value of 232 barrels of flour thrown into the sea by the authorities . . . . . . . . . . . . . . . . . | 3,248 000 |
| Widow of General Brown: for arrears of pay of her deceased husband . . . . . . . . . . . . . . | sum not stated. |
| Richard Rogers, of Parahyba do Norte: for value of vessel of his destroyed . . . . . . . . . . . . . | 6,163 755 |
| James Crabtree and Co., of Pernambuco: on account of fine imposed by the Pernambuco Custom-house on the captain of the ship *Indian* . . . . . . . . . | 5,350 800 |
| Thomas Barber: freight of brig *Laura* . . . . . . . | 21,155 552 |
| Georgina Pascoe Younghusband: a grant of land promised to her grandfather, Barreto, by King John VI. . . | no sum. |
| Johnson, Bielby, and Co., of Bahia: for value of some spars sold to the naval arsenal . . . . . . . . . | 45,904 880 |
| James Crabtree and Co., of Pernambuco: for excess of duties charged on two cargoes . . . . . . . . . | 4,475 641 |
| Sdler, Fenton, and Co.: for excess of duties paid in the Custom-house of Maranham . . . . . . . . . . | 16,091 709 |
| Joahn Currell and Sons: similar overcharge at Pernambuco | 50,610 549 |
| James Bryson and Co. excess of duties at Rio de Janeiro | 6,312 576 |
| Various English merchants: excess of duties at Pernambuco | 42,051 346 |
| Heyworths, Crabtree, and Co.: excess of duties at Pernambuco . . . . . . . . . . . . . . . . . . . | 90,096 083 |
| William Moon and Co.: excess of duties at Rio de Janeiro | 280,476 390 |

| | |
|---|---|
| W. Ewart, Sen. and W. Ewart, Jun.: excess of duties | sums not stated. |
| Robert Horne: excess of duties | |
| Thomas Bradshaw do. | |
| Ferguson and Co. do. | |
| Francis Watson, English sailor: for unjust imprisonment and prevention of embarcation at Maranham | Rs. 300 000 |
| Charles Lucas, English pilot: for unjust imprisonment at Pernambuco | 1,200 000 |
| John Swan, civil engineer: for imprisonment at Estrella, on account of an accident on the Mauá Railway in 1857 | 1,500 000 |
| Edward Gibbon Swan and Charles Smallpage: for arbitrary imprisonment at Breves in the Province of Pará and the losses which resulted | 100,872 000 |
| Edward Hammond: illegal detention at the fort of Coimbra, province of Mattagrosso | |

The following British claims were settled by the Mixed Commission before it ceased to sit in March, 1860, and the amounts given are the sums awarded:

| | |
|---|---|
| Merchants of Monte Video | 24,267 061 |
| James Calder | claim rejected. |
| William Youle | 6,000 000 |
| Captain of brig *Pauline* | 2,143 200 |
| Proudfoot, Muir, and Moffat | claim rejected. |

Thus a total amount of Rs. 32,410 321, or about £8,850, was awarded by the Commission. This sum has not yet been paid. Mr. Christie proposed to the Brazilian government, by order of Earl Russell, on the 14th April, 1862, an agreement for payment of the awards made on both sides; but the proposal has not been replied to by the Brazilian government; and the same may be said of the proposal made by Mr. Christie on the same day for a new Commission for examination of British and Brazilian claims, lists to be previously exchanged. Earl Russell, in his despatch of 6th June, 1863, observed as follows:—"Her Majesty's government under these circumstances are fully justified in complaining that up to this time they are still left without a reply to the proposals conveyed in Mr. Christie's note of the 14th April, 1861, and that no steps appear to have been taken for the just settlement of various British claims, some of them of long standing, and of very considerable amount. Her Majesty's government, therefore, hope that the government of Brazil will, in its future intercourse with Great Britain, through whatever channel that intercourse is carried on, act with that courtesy which is usual between governments, and also that the Brazilian government will, without further delay, frankly enter into the communication of their views as to the means by which a settlement of the long-pending claims may best be arrived at."

THE END.

information can be obtained
Gtesting.com
e USA
050422
06B/271

9 783752 589184